Hot Water Sisters

Women Who Can,
Women Who Do,
Women Like You

CANDACE CADE

ARCHWAY
PUBLISHING

This is a work of fiction. All of the characters, names, incidents, organizations, and dialogue in this novel are either the products of the author's imagination or are used fictitiously.

Scripture taken from the New King James Version®. Copyright © 1982 by Thomas Nelson. Used by permission. All rights reserved.

Archway Publishing books may be ordered through booksellers or by contacting:

Archway Publishing
1663 Liberty Drive
Bloomington, IN 47403
www.archwaypublishing.com
1 (888) 242-5904

Because of the dynamic nature of the Internet, any web addresses or links contained in this book may have changed since publication and may no longer be valid. The views expressed in this work are solely those of the author and do not necessarily reflect the views of the publisher, and the publisher hereby disclaims any responsibility for them.

Any people depicted in stock imagery provided by Getty Images are models, and such images are being used for illustrative purposes only. Certain stock imagery © Getty Images.

ISBN: 978-1-4808-6372-9 (sc)
ISBN: 978-1-4808-6373-6 (hc)
ISBN: 978-1-4808-6371-2 (e)

Library of Congress Control Number: 2018946814

Print information available on the last page.

Archway Publishing rev. date: 7/30/2018

Eleanor Roosevelt once said, "Women are like Tea Bags… We don't know our Strength… Until we are in Hot Water."

These Women, in these stories, Discovered Strength that they never realized that they possessed.

You will too.

Contents

Forest Primeval

A TRUE LOVE STORY NEVER ENDS

I had been coming to *The Peaceful Forest Gods Resort* literally my whole life. However, I never understood why I always felt like I was being drawn back here. My parents met here when they were just young teenagers. Their own parents brought them to the resort for a family vacation. My Mom said it was love at first sight for both. This is where they spent their honeymoon and my Mom swears that I had been conceived here. Every year, we returned on my parents' wedding anniversary. When I was old enough to have a vote, I started asking them if we could come back here on spring and summer vacations as well. I never wanted to go to Disney World or the beach or other kid-friendly locations. I just wanted to return here... to the trees. I just wanted them to leave me alone, so I could disappear into the forest. Some irresistible force was pulling me out there.

My earliest memories of this resort are the ones where I kept trying to get away from my parents and out into the dense forest behind it. I could not have been more than five or six years old when I started trying to get to those trees. When we were at the pool, I tried to run into the forest. If we went to the tennis courts, I wandered out into the trees. I loved to hike, explore, and camp out because those things took us out into the forest. Even then, I tried to escape to be on my own out there. Someone was constantly calling me or dragging me back from the forest. Something else was constantly calling me and dragging me deeper into the lovely green darkness. When we left for home, I wept as if my heart would break.

I even dreamed about the forest. I drew pictures of it. I wrote stories about forests and trees. Nobody knew how deeply this place affected me. Somehow, I knew that they would never understand my obsession. However, I knew that I had to keep coming back here. Mom and Dad started to be concerned about me when I was around eleven or twelve years old. That was the first time that I managed to get away by myself. Apparently, I was alone in the forest for several hours. Strangely enough, I cannot remember what went on during that time. What I do remember is following a beautiful little deer deeper and deeper into the woods. When they found me, it was almost dark, and I was miles away from the resort. All the adults were terrified until the search party found me. I was not scared at all. I had felt safe and happy to be out there.

Both of my parents wept and clung to me as the police officials and resort employees interrogated me for hours. I remember how one officer rubbed my head and said, "Margarite, you could grow up to be a good Forest Ranger." That comment seemed to comfort my Mom, so I hung onto the idea and repeated it often. Truthfully, I did not intend to be a ranger, or even know what that meant, until I did some research when I got older. However, we went to a couple of Ranger Stations where I learned a lot about the history and topography of this area. We also joined the Scouts, and I began to learn survival skills and all about plants and animals. We had many classes about Indian Lore and everything you could ever want to know about Indians. I should have paid more attention to the Indian stuff. Indians, frontiersmen, and covered wagons did not interest me at all. I especially did not want to hear about the savagery and killing by the Indians. Nor did I want to know about the relentless eradication of all those Native American Indian tribes. It seemed that Indians were Taboo to me.

I loved learning about all the trees and plants and the other vegetation that forms the undergrowth of every woodland area. Everybody loved the wild animals and birds we saw out in their natural habitat. I can identify many birds and animals by their tracks and the sounds they make or the scat with which they mark their territory. Once, I smelled a rattlesnake den. The older woodsmen in the group were quite impressed with that. Snakes do not bother me. I have "Milked" rattlesnakes for a college professor to help him earn his doctorate. We both got extra credit for that project. My knowledge of most animals is quite impressive for a city girl.

I did *not* like to study bears. Bears bothered me when I was young. I did not like bears. They frightened me more than any other predator. Just thinking about a bear being in the area would make me so nervous that I could hardly think. They are at the top of the food chain. Bears can do whatever they want to do…whenever they want. They are intelligent and unpredictable. They are dangerous. I guess bears were Taboo to me, also. When my Dad realized what a problem I was having with them, he went and bought me several types of bear deterrents. One was an air horn to hang on my belt, plus several different kinds of spray that they do not like. He even ordered me a green flashlight that hurts their eyes. It was quite expensive. Dad gave it to me for my fifteenth birthday. Mom was shocked at the price and gave me a severe "talking-to" about taking care of it.

I never escaped into the trees again. My parents began to urge me to go other places for vacations. They wanted me to take friends along for company. All that talk frustrated me. I cried and promised whatever they wanted if they would just take me back to the Peaceful Forest Gods Resort. I only wanted to vacation there. When I was younger, I had often asked why we could not move out there. Of course, that only upset my family and made them more vigilant as I got older. They frequently asked me all kinds of psychological questions about why I wanted to be there all the time. I was too young to understand any of that. However, even very young kids know when to lie, when to cover up, and when to shut up.

Because of all the worry about my getting "lost in the forest," Dad started taking me to all kinds of extreme sport/survival events involving kayaks, guns, and everything else that you can imagine. Even though I thought that I was covering some things up well, my parents were still fearful of what would happen to me if I ever escaped into the trees again. Everyone thought that I had to be a real "Tomboy" because of all the outdoor activities that I was involved with. Nobody knew how I really felt about those things. I only tolerated them because I knew that I had to humor my Mom.

She thought that she was helping me prepare for my future Forest Ranger career.

By the time I was sixteen and could drive, I knew more about conquering the forces of nature than I knew about music, clothes, or school. I did not even have a steady boyfriend. I seldom dated and had only one close friend. She was really my Mom's pick as a friend. I was a loner. Most people did not know me because I was not interested in them or the things they did. I already knew that I was *different*. Mom could not handle those words, (*I'm different*), and I only said them to her once. Her fear and worry about my being *different* caused us all a great deal of stress. I tried even harder to please her by doing whatever she needed me to do. I just did not want to cause either one of my parents any more heartache. What a basket case I had become. I never told anyone about my obsession to go back to my *Forest World* and never return to the real world again. In fact, my own thoughts and dreams confused me. Sometimes, I was frightened because I could not remember the hours that I was alone in the forest. I know that my parents were worried about me, and that also caused me to have very High Anxiety. Most of all, I just wanted them to keep taking me back to my real world in the forest. That was where I felt like I really belonged. I guess I will never know how much pain I caused them. I can only go forward from here.

So, let me tell you about the *Forest Primeval.*

Those words come to me because of the old, old poem called *Evangeline, A Tale of Acadie, 1847,* written by Henry Wadsworth Longfellow. The Prologue starts with these words;

> *This is the forest primeval. The murmuring pines and*
> *the hemlocks, Bearded with moss, and in garments*
> *green...*

*This is the forest primeval; but where are the hearts
that beneath it leaped...*

Those words had a profound effect on me. I immediately identified with that poem and memorized large portions of it. I read and
re-read it for years. It is the story of a young girl that is searching
for her true love. It is an epic poem of great tragedy and loss. I tried
to get everyone I knew to read it. They all thought it was too de-
pressing and old fashioned for me. However, I love it because of the
setting and the constant references to the great forests of Acadie,
Evangeline's home. I felt like the forest was The True Home of My
Heart, too.

I also loved and memorized a lot of *The Song of Hiawatha*, which
was another epic poem written by Longfellow. My favorite part of
this work, "Hiawatha's Childhood," starts with this description of
Hiawatha's home;

Dark behind it rose the forest,
Rose the black and gloomy pine-trees,
Rose the firs with cones upon them...

Much of Hiawatha's story focuses on his natural outdoor environment. As you well know, that was my favorite subject.

When I was eighteen years old, in my senior year of high school,
my parents celebrated their twentieth wedding anniversary. They
planned to go to Hawaii for a week. I was to spend that week with
my Aunt Cindy, but I decided to go to The Peaceful Gods Forest
Resort instead. It took some real conniving and manipulation on my
part, but I finally got things arranged so that I could get away on
my own. I am ashamed of the lies that I told everyone. However, it
seemed to be necessary at that time. I was young, stupid, and desperate. When I say desperate, it seems strange, but I felt *absolutely
desperate* to get back to my Forest Home. My parents had spent my
whole life trying to keep me from doing exactly what I was getting
ready to do.

I drove the seven hours from my school to the Forest, arriving after midnight. I did not stay at The Peaceful Forest Gods Resort because all those people knew me too well. I made a reservation almost twenty miles away in a less expensive place that was famous with college partyers. It was still a Five Star Resort, so I felt it would be safe. They had individual little efficiency cabins with a small kitchenette, T V, and free WI FI. Most people would describe it as "Remote." I requested a place as close to the trees as possible. No one would know me or miss me over there. I had plenty of practice keeping people out of my life. After all, I was a loner that wanted to be left alone.

After I checked into my room, I opened the windows, so I could see, hear, and smell the forest. All the little night insects were singing. There was a breeze causing the trees to sway slightly, and a beautiful moon surrounded by millions of stars. It seemed to be such a perfect night that I decided to go ahead and walk outside for a few minutes. My intention was to stroll down by the picnic table and just sit there for a while. The night was alive with dancing fireflies. There was a graveled walking path leading into the distance. Nice benches were visible in the moonlight, so I wandered further into the beckoning woodlands.

I have no idea how it happened, but at some point, I stepped out of that five-star resort… into a ***Long-Ago Time.***

Stay with me. Even though you think I am crazy, now, please just hear me out. Just let me tell you what happened. I cannot begin to explain any of this. However, it is imperative that I talk it through. Please listen, even if you do not believe me.

After I started walking that night, I simply kept going. A force was pulling me away from this place, this world, this time. Crossing into the Long-Ago Time did not frighten me as much as you would think. It was like a pleasant dream or something. One second, I was just… gone. Gone from…Now. I was gone from…Today. I was suddenly *Back Then*. I was in the *Forest Primeval*. I was different, and the entire world around me was different, too.

I knew that I was no longer... I. I was no longer me. I was... Her.

We were together, inside my body. Her thoughts were in my brain. I was kneeling by a stream, looking at myself, her, us (?) in the water. She was a polar opposite of the real me. Her hair was long and dark. Her complexion was much paler than my own, and her big brown eyes stared into my own face. In the now, I was tall and tan, with big green eyes and fair hair that I kept pretty short and spiky. I thought she was beautiful, like a small woodland sprite, or a fairy, or something that I cannot define. She seemed like so much... more... than a regular girl like me.

In the distance, I heard a voice calling, "Kate! Katie! Where are you, girl? Kate, you better answer me!"

Instinctively, I whispered to myself, "Kate. I am Kate. I was Margarite, but now, I am here, and my name is Kate. My Mama is calling me home."

For some reason, I did not want to answer her, and I certainly did not want to go home. Of course, this was how I always felt in the *Now Time* also. I wanted to stay out here ... *Now, and Then.*

"Kate, you have chores to do this mornin'! Your Daddy will likely tan your hide if you do not come home right now! Kate... Katieeee! Honey, please answer me..."

Her voice was trailing off as if she was moving away from me and giving up on finding me or getting me to answer her. Part of my heart was sad for my Mom, (both then and now). However, part of my heart was feeling glad that she was going home. We would be fine out here. We belonged out here. Mama needed to go on back to the cabin where she belonged. She would be fine, too.

We sat still looking into the water for a few more minutes. Her eyes were not looking at her reflection at all. Kate was looking for something else in the water. We were waiting for someone/some-thing else to appear. Someone else was supposed to be here with us. In my brain, I knew that we were a little bit scared. We were also eagerly anticipating this arrival. There was a feeling of love here in

Kate's heart, but also great confusion. We were looking into the water but waiting for something/someone to come up behind us. Sharing my brain and heart with Kate felt weird, yet somehow, complete. Now I knew why I was always a loner. No one had ever made me feel whole, until now.

Kate completed me today.

Suddenly, our heart started pounding wildly, and I knew that whatever Kate was waiting for was very close now. We both felt his presence behind us. Kate continued to look into the water and wait for whatever was coming. She was longing for this presence to come closer. We love him. This is the first time in my life that I have felt love for anyone beside my own family. My mind knows that there is danger here, but I cannot wait for him to appear. We do not turn around. We just keep looking into the water, waiting.

When I hear the grass behind me crush under his weight, his face appears in the water. Kate's heart is beating wildly, and she wants to turn around to him, but she doesn't move. Our hands are trembling, and tears are filling our eyes. Never have I ever experienced such total joy/fear/love/confusion all in the same instant. Hot breath ruffles my spiky blonde hair. We cannot move for several long seconds.

In the clear spring water, I see a huge bear standing behind a beautiful little antelope.

You cannot imagine how my brain reacted to that vision. For a split second, I thought that I had gone Insane. Almost immediately, Kate's face re-appeared in that reflection, and now, a strong, handsome young Indian man was standing behind us. He placed both of his hands on my shoulders, and Kate whirls around into his arms. She clings to him and weeps tears of joy as his arms crush us to his chest. We stand as still as statues as he whispers Indian words of love to us. I whisper how much I love him. How long it has been since we touched each other! How much I have missed him. My thoughts and my speech are in turmoil. My Now time is becoming

the Long-Ago Time. I cannot tell if I am Now, or Kate is Now...
Time is all twisted up in my brain.

He gently turns my face up to his and looks deeply into my eyes,
Kate's eyes, and he sees into my heart. I can barely speak.

Words form in my brain and I finally say, "I know you. I remember you. *Avonaco.*"

His name, Avonaco, means *Mighty Bear*. I did know him. I knew
him as my love. I knew him as my own soul. He was the other half
of Kate. She is the other half of me.

His hands hold my face as he speaks, *"Choovino...* Kate, Nayeli,
Kate. I love you. Wikkimak, my wife, nuttah."

We look deep into each other's eyes.

I understand that Choovino is Kate's Indian name.

Choovino, the Young Antelope.

Kate is the Young Antelope, and he is the Mighty Bear.

But, wait...wait. Who am I?

Why am I here?

Where is here?

When is here?

Panic begins to fill my heart as I try to reason things out. Kate
is remembering (?) things in my brain to help me understand what
is happening. Not what is happening now, but what happened in
The Long-Ago Time. There is no rational way to explain all of
this. Believe me, I do realiz how impossible all of this is; but I can
only relay the truth to you as it was revealed to me through Kate's
memories. Please allow me to take you back there to show you how
things happened.

We, (Kate and I) are following three cows through the trees to
water. We have a long, pointed stick in our right hand, but we do not
have to use it. We love the cows, Star, Money, and Daisy, and they
love us. They are eager to please us, and we never poke them with
that stick. Many times we have climbed onto their backs and ridden
them like other people ride horses. Star and Daisy both have those

corresponding white shaped marks on their dark reddish-brown foreheads. Money is named that because Papa had to spend so much of it on her. She is the best milk cow that we have ever had. As a matter fact, she is the best in the whole county. She has become famous around here for her milk, butter, cheese, and her sweet disposition. She is invaluable to us, and it is my job to care for her and the others. I mean, Kate takes care of the farm animals. Her memories and thoughts have become mine now. Kate works hard for many hours every day. She is strong and brave, and I am proud of her.

Kate's memories show us following the three cows down to the stream for water. They move slowly because they are grazing in the grass as we make our way down the hill. I love being out here. I love getting away from the farm and my mama's constant attention. I have heard people say that she "Dotes" on me too much. I think that is true. See, Mama could not have any other children. She got pregnant a couple of times, but she was never able to carry a baby more than a couple of months. That hurt her and my papa badly. She was beautiful and smart, and very feminine. Papa was handsome, strong, and hard- working. They were both ashamed that they could not have any more babies. Our lives were difficult, and they needed other strong, young backs to help work the farm. They need my help.

Ever since I turned thirteen, six months ago, Papa has encouraged me to pick a nice hard-working boy to marry. He wants me to be friendly to *Stefan Anderson*, whose family lives on the right side of our property. He plans for me to marry him and build our home right between our parents' houses so we can both still work on both of their farms. That is the way things are done out here in this Long-Ago Time…But I do not really like Stefan in that way. I am too young to understand what all that is about. Mama says she will start teaching me how to breed babies soon. Papa says for her to do it now, since I know all about the cows and pigs and other farm animals. This whole idea frightens me…

Kate is showing me another memory, now. I am deep in the

darkness of the forest looking for Sassafras plants that Mama wants for her Tea. She makes the best medicinal Teas of anyone in this area. Mama knows what kind of Tea to brew for every ailment. She can make poultices for healing wounds. She even stitches people up if they come and ask her to. She has birthed many babies. Many folks think of her as a Medicine Woman. That is an Indian term for Healer. I have learned a lot about doctoring from Mama. She helps with animals, too. Sometimes, I ask her questions, and she is so pleased that I am interested in following in her footsteps. Papa and Mama love me and want what is best for me. I love them deeply, too. I try to please them in every way I can.

While I am bending low to look for the roots, I see thick, dark red blood on the grass in front of me. This is fresh blood, and I know that this means that someone or something very close to where I am kneeling is hurt badly. I search the surrounding area for some human or animal footprints. Both become dangerous when wounded. Papa has taught me a lot about animals. I respect and fear them. Even the small ones like possums and coons can tear you up if they are sick or hurt. In my heart, I know this is human blood. Someone is lying in pain nearby. My natural instinct is to run and get Mama. But maybe I should see how I can help right now.

"Hello… I can help you. My Mama is a Healer, and she has taught me how to stop your bleeding. I can help you… Hello? Are you there? Can you speak or make a sound to let me know where you are? I can help you…"

I was looking all around as I called out to the wounded person. There was much more blood now, which caused me concern and alarm.

"Mister, I can help you if you will just let me see your wound… You can trust me. Even if I cannot stop your bleeding, I can run get Mama. She is a true Healer. Mister? Can you hear me?"

I tried to make my voice kind and compelling. There was way too much blood, now. This person could die from this amount of blood loss. Something in my heart told me to hurry and find the victim. The bloody trail was leading to the stream. Which was very good news. Maybe the cold water would help the blood to clot. I found the footprints at the water's edge. It was obvious that the person was wearing moccasins… like an Indian. Fear gripped my heart as I considered what to do next. I knew that there were Indians in the forest, but I never saw, or heard them. Everyone told horrible stories of Indian massacres in this area. We thought those days were over. I now prayed that those days were truly over. If there was a seriously wounded Indian nearby, I could be in grave danger right now. I could be scalped, killed, or even worse. What should I do now?

At that very moment, I heard a low moan from somewhere right across the water. It sounded as if that could be his last gasping breath. Without thinking anymore, I started wading into the stream to see if I could help this wounded man. It never occurred to me that it could be a woman. No Indian woman would dare to get this far from her tribe. When I reached the far bank, I started calling to him again.

"Hello? Can I help you? Please, I only want to help…" He had fallen into a crevice caused by countless floodwaters circling around the base of a huge cypress tree. It took all my strength to half drag him onto flat ground where I could doctor him.

Just as I thought, he had some terrible wounds on his right leg and other minor ones on his left. He was very badly hurt and had lost too much blood. His breathing was shallow and labored. His chest barely rose as he struggled to draw in some air. Mama had told me that blood carries the oxygen into our bodies, and when someone cannot breathe, we can blow air into their mouth to give them some oxygen. She had even breathed life into animals before. I knelt beside this Indian and gently blew some air into his mouth by covering his lips with mine. I counted to four and did it again… then again. He would need me to do this for several minutes before I could begin cleaning and binding his legs. Then I would continue to do it until he was able to draw oxygen into his lungs by himself. Thank God he was so close to the clean, fast- running, shallow water. I pulled his shattered legs into that cold water and tore away as much of the bloody, tattered buckskin as I could.

Then, I saw how terribly he had been hurt.

My heart grieved when I finally began to clean his gashes. I pulled some healing roots from my skirt pocket and began to crush them in my hands. Sometimes we had to make do with what we had on hand. There was no way for me to make Tea right now. Nevertheless, I crushed the leaves and roots with a little water to make a thick lumpy paste, which I thinned down with some more water. I used my bonnet to contain as much of the soupy mixture as I could. Every now and then, I would breathe life into his mouth. When I had worked the roots and leaves into a good poultice, I pulled his legs out of the stream and started packing his wounds. The cold water had probably numbed his pain some. He was looking better and breathing easier. However, I needed to poke, prod, and push the healing poultice into his torn flesh right away. He groaned weakly, and I worked very quickly. I had to roll him over so that the backs of his legs could be doctored, too. I was horrified to see the severity of the wounds. What in the world could have caused so much deep tearing in a human body? Periodically, I touched his lips with a drop or two of water. He was too weak to swallow more than a drop or two at a time. Mama had warned me about too much or too little moisture when a person was unconscious.

After I gave him more "Breath of Life," as Mama called it, I scooped up several handfuls of moss from the stream. I laid this over the deepest wounds first, then the less severe ones. After that, I covered both of his legs with mud. Mama had taught me how the plants would heal and stop bleeding. The moss would draw out all poison and swelling, and the mud would protect the wounds. In addition, when you did this, no bugs could get into the wounds and cause bad infections. It would be dark in just a short while. Suddenly, I felt exhausted and scared. I was a long way from my home, and

I had no light or food… What was I to do now? I knew that Star, Money, and Daisy would have started for home by now. They were smart animals and well trained. Papa would come for me as soon as they showed up without me. I prayed that would be soon.

I looked worriedly at the man lying beside me. He was young and… beautiful. He was truly beautiful. I know you are not supposed to say a man is beautiful, but there was no better description for him. He had Raven black hair and golden/ bronze skin, with dark eyelashes and perfectly formed facial bones. Beautiful. Earlier, I had noticed how strong and muscular his young body was. He truly seemed to be beautiful and perfect in every way. He was breathing better but not deep restful breaths that would draw in the life-giving oxygen that he needed to heal. I bent and placed my lips on his and breathed into his mouth several times.

I remembered how my friend Mary Elizabeth told me to close my eyes when a boy kisses me. When I asked Mama, she had agreed.

"Kate, if you really like a boy, your eyes will close by themselves. If you do not care much for him, and he is kissing you, you will want to close them. Sometimes, it is best to close your eyes and think about something else."

As I breathed into his mouth, I felt my eyes closing by themselves. For a split second, I imagined that he was kissing me. In fact, his lips seemed to soften and open a little under my own. That felt so nice. I breathed more air into his mouth, and he seemed to receive it.

When I opened my eyes, he was looking at me! I bet I jumped a mile when I saw that. What in the world would he do? What should I do? Embarrassment and confusion flooded my whole brain. I am sure that my face was as red as a beet.

I scuttled backwards away from him as I mumbled something about sorry and not really kissing him.

How childish and foolish I was. His eyes never left mine, even though I tried to look away from him. Darkness was slowly creeping upon us and I was afraid of what could happen to us in the dark. I stood up and said that I really needed to be home long before now. As I was smoothing my clothes and babbling about finding my way home, he spoke a few words to me. He was looking at me as if he was trying to remember who I was.

He said, "Choohowee? Choovino?"

Of course, I could not understand his language, but those two words seemed to be very important to him because he repeated them several times. He motioned for me to come closer. Whatever he said to me, his voice was soothing to my spirit.

He seemed to be saying, "Just calm down, Kate. It is too late for you to start walking home now. Just calm down. Don't worry; you are safe here. I will take care of you."

He reminded me of my Papa when he spoke to a troubled horse or a wounded dog. That made me feel better.

He was about halfway sitting up, but I could tell that he was in bad pain. He looked down at his legs, then back to my face. Clearly, he wanted to know if I had doctored him. I made a sort of shrugging motion with my hands as I nodded my head. Then I sort of played like I was pushing him to lie back down. He had gone a little pale as pain filled his eyes.

"You are very badly hurt. It will take time for your wounds to heal. You must rest. Do not move around right now. I'll get you some water." Again, I said, "Water. Drink water."

He seemed to be startled as I moved past him toward the stream. Again, he asked, "Choohowee? Choovino?..."

I told him that everything was OK as I motioned toward the stream and said, "Water" again. I made a drinking motion with my hands, and he seemed to relax some. As he lay back down, I knelt and scooped water into my hands. He would not get very much water this way, but I did not want him to get strangled. As I held my cupped hands to his lips, he looked intently into my eyes. I could not look away from him. He seemed to be communicating directly with my heart. I had never felt such a strong connection with another human being. I had no idea what was going on between us. For some reason, we seemed to belong together. I know how crazy all of this sounds, but it is all true. Kate's recollection was flawless. She was helping me to accept these memories as my own.

After the last few water drops fell onto his lips, I wiped his forehead with the back of my left hand, and I laid the palm of my right hand along his jawline. Beautiful. He raised his left hand and placed it over mine on his face. He murmured, "Choohowee? Choovino?" I will never forget how important those words were to him. They seemed to resonate in my spirit, also. All I wanted was for him to be OK.

I loved him instantly.

His arm relaxed as he fell asleep. I am sure that he was weak from blood loss. There was no doubt that he had been through a terrible ordeal and he needed to rest and recuperate. I was exhausted, too. It seemed only natural for me to lie down by his side. I could not get home safely at this hour, so I may as well try to sleep myself. In the morning, my parents would find me, and we would have to deal with their anger and accusations. They would be devastated by my choice to stay here tonight. I would not be able to explain myself to them. They would not understand. I could not understand any of this either. Exhaustion dragged me down into sleep.

The next thing I knew, dawn was breaking, while my parents screamed my name nearby. My patient was gone. No doubt that he feared what my Papa would do to him if he found us sleeping together out here. I was heartbroken to think that I would never see him again.

"Mama! Papa! I'm here. I'm safe. Mama, I'm OK."

My voice has hoarse from lying on the ground all night. In a minute, both of my parents were hugging me and sobbing.

Mama held me at arm's length and asked me, "Where are you hurt, Katie? Where is the bear? Where did he hurt you, Katie?"

My Papa was searching the nearby forest intently. "Where is the bear Kate? Where did he go? Where are you hurt?"

These questions came from Papa, as he circled around Mama and me on high alert. He never turned his back to the Forest Primeval. I was very confused as I asked them what bear they were talking about. Mama had been feeling all my bones as she looked for wounds on my body.

"I'm not hurt, Mama. I never saw a bear. Why do you keep asking me about a bear? What bear?"

I guess Mama was satisfied that I was OK, because she once again pulled me close and sobbed hysterically. I kept telling her that I was OK, but Papa continued to stand ready to kill something with his long 45-70 rifle. That gun can kill a bear from a long distance. It was the most powerful gun a man could buy.

"Mama, please, please stop crying and tell me what is happening. How did you find me?"

Papa turned to face me, looked into my eyes, and said, "We followed the blood trail and the bear's footprints from our barn. Those two things led us right to you. Katie girl, I thought you were dead."

His voice broke as he began to weep openly. He bent closer to me and kissed the top of my head. When he put his hand on the back of my neck, I felt his fingers trembling.

"I'm OK, Papa. I really am OK. Please don't cry. I can't stand to see you cry."

He nodded several times and wiped his eyes on his sleeve. He looked me up and down and said, "I just don't understand where all that blood came from. I pictured you torn limb from limb. Those bear paws were huge. No human being could survive an attack from an animal that size. I just knew that you were dead, Katie."

Papa's words chilled me to my bones as I finally realized what must have happened… The bear had found us and killed My Indian while I slept. Maybe he had died, as I lay right beside him? Maybe he was dead when the bear got here? Surely, I would have heard him if he had cried out in agony? What in the name of The Dear Lord God had happened here last night? I could not imagine how horrible it must have been for him to be torn to pieces after he had already been so badly hurt. I cried as my heart broke within me. I tried to speak.

"Mama, there was an Indian…I doctored him just like you taught me. He was so badly hurt. I wanted to save his life, Mama…"

My words trailed off as I sobbed. Both of my parents looked at me intently with a hundred questions in their eyes. I could not speak as my Papa told Mama that it must have been that the Indian had been creeping around our house until he saw the bear. The bear had attacked him before I found him. Then the bear had come back for his prey later. Mama started pulling me to my feet as she muttered thanks to God for sparing my life. Now, we all wanted to get as far away from this area as we could…as fast as we could. What if the bear came back? We rushed toward the safety of our home.

Papa went first with his big gun ready, but he continually circled around us looking for any danger that might be lurking in those trees. He would protect us with his own life if anything came to hurt us. My heart ached as we fled through the forest. How could my first love be totally gone? Dead? Even though I did not even know his name, I knew that I loved him completely. How cruel to have only seen him for those few moments while I was trying to save his life. If only we could have met under better circumstances. If only he could have worked with Papa and won his respect. If only…if only everything had been different. I would never forget how it felt to have his lips on mine. I would always see his eyes as he looked deeply into my soul. I would never forget his voice soothing me to sleep. I would never forget how it felt to have his hand covering mine. I loved him, and I always would. Kate's memories were so powerful that I was sobbing and shaking. I rubbed my hands along my arms trying to comfort myself. I could not stop her thoughts and emotions from ruling inside my/our brain.

My parents were moving as quickly and cautiously as they could. When we got closer to home, some of our panic subsided. Mama and Papa were constantly looking for the huge bear. I was constantly looking for traces that My Indian was still alive. Again and again, I questioned what had really happened last night. What strange things occurred while I slept? How could a bear covered in blood lead my parents to me...and then completely disappear from the face of the earth? All these things seemed to be impossible, Yet I had personally experienced everything, myself. I knew all of it had really taken place...or I was totally insane. I did not feel insane. He was real. I know he was real. At first, I asked my parents if they were sure that the Indian was not hiding somewhere along the trail...Maybe he had been able to climb up into a tree when the bear came back? I did not think that he would have left me there alone. I believe that he would have died trying to save me from the bear. Could it be that some of his own people found him and carried him to safety? I prayed that was the truth. I could not believe that he was dead and that I would never see him again.

It occurred to me that I should not tell anyone what had happened out there. It would be best for all of us to remain quiet about that night. Evidently, Papa was worried about those same things because later that afternoon he told Mama and me not ever to mention those events to anyone, ever. We all agreed that we could not explain what took place out there. Papa looked at me and said they would just "Watch and wait." I guess he meant they would watch me and wait to see if I went insane again? Or, wait to see if they lost their minds? Maybe he meant to watch for the bear? None of us was sure what he meant, but we all knew that we could never discuss that night with anyone, ever.

After that day, I/Kate was constantly feeling drawn back to the Forest Primeval. You would think that fear would have made me hate and avoid the forest. Nothing could have been further from the truth. I was compelled to go out there all the time. Of course, I never let either of my parents know how much I wanted to go back to where they had found me that day. I felt like I had to go and find My Indian. This truth would have killed my parents. They were both still very skittish and nervous about my being hurt. It was important to stay away from anything that could upset them again. When Papa tried to talk to me about Stefan, I would cry and tell him that I felt like God wanted me to stay… pure. He was often confused and angry when I spoke of God. I knew that he was not equipped to deal with anything spiritual, so that was my excuse for celibacy. Once, I told Mama that I should go to a convent somewhere. She was so horrified that I had to recant for fear that she would lose her mind. We were not even Roman Catholics.

After a few weeks, they began to think that it would be best for things to get back to normal. I had asked about Star and Money and Daisy many times. I told Papa that I wanted to care for the farm animals as I had always done. He needed my help and could not afford to hire anyone else. He suggested that Stefan could come work for him; and I wept uncontrollably until he said he would not ask him. I begged him to let me do my chores and stop making me stay indoors all the time. To my surprise, Mama told him that she thought I was right. We all needed to get back to normal as soon as possible. Mama said for Papa to let me take the cows down to the stream, feed the chickens, ride the horses, and do all the normal chores that I always did before. Papa paced and rubbed his chin nervously. He kept looking toward the trees, and Mama reminded him that there was no sign of any danger from bears or anything else. I guess he was ashamed to admit that he was afraid, because in a short while, he said that I could go outside if I kept Rebel with me all the time. Rebel was our watchdog that loved me completely. Rebel was fearless, and Papa had trained him to hunt and to herd sheep or goats. He was a wonderful working dog that was a big help to all of us.

I agreed to Papa's terms quickly. Rebel would protect me if he could. We were all still worried about the bear…but I had to get out of that house and look for My Indian. How I wished that I knew his name. It seemed foolish to think of him as "My Indian." However,

that was what I called him, in my own mind. Once, Mama asked
me about him, and when I told her what I had done, she was very
proud of me. I asked her if he could have survived that night. We
both knew that the second bear attack would have been fatal. Still,
in my heart, I could not believe that he was dead, not until I saw his
dead body with my own eyes.

That evening, I walked the three cows back down the trail to the
stream. Rebel had to go with Mama to a baby birthing several miles
away from us. We never knew how long she would be gone, and Papa
sent Rebel to protect her. I was glad. It was my first trip out here since…
that night. Everything looked beautiful to me. The trees and grass were
so fragrant and welcoming. Every birdsong cheered my heart. The rushing waters seemed to be whispering songs of hope and joy. It felt as if I
were going home, as if I belonged out there; out in the Forest Primeval.
My spirit was rising with each step I took. How wonderful to be en-
folded by the arms of those huge trees. When we reached the drinking
place, my three friends waded in and gulped thirstily. After a minute
or so, they all looked across the water to the clearing on the other side.
A beautiful young antelope stepped into a patch of sunlight and gazed
intently at us. She did not appear to be afraid of us at all. As I watched
the antelope, I felt compelled to touch her. I just had to feel her silky
fur. She did not run away from me. On the contrary, this beautiful little
deer appeared to be waiting for me…wanting me to get closer to her.

When I stepped onto the other bank of the stream, the little
antelope began to walk toward me. As I stretched out my hands with
my palms up and open, she walked right into my outstretched arms,
like a beloved friend. She nuzzled my neck and hair as I stroked her
neck and sides. The poor little thing was shivering, and her body felt
hot. I noticed that she seemed to be tired or weak. Nothing like this
had ever happened to me before. Wild animals flee from humans…
they do not come to us and allow us to pat them. What in the world
could be going on here today? Was this someone's pet? She began
to back away from me a little, making soft snuffling noises, and

tapping her little feet as she looked into my eyes. She would take a step or two, then look at my face and sort of nod her head toward the Forest Primeval. It was obvious that she wanted me/Kate to follow her. She slid her head under my hand as we began to walk into the trees. Somewhere, in a long-buried memory, I felt like I had done this before. I remember this little deer from long ago.

Within a very few minutes, I was hopelessly turned around and lost. That is a common dilemma in areas with big trees. People always think that they will just turn around and go right back out of the forest. However, once they are surrounded by all those tree trunks, they become disoriented because they all look the same. Sounds are muted by thick undergrowth, and the trees block most of the light. All those things cause confusion and panic. Sadly, many have gone into the forest, lost their way, and perished from exhaustion, exposure, thirst, and even starvation. None of those things bothered us in that Long-Ago Time. We belonged here. Kate's memory tells me again that we belong here, in this Forest Primeval, together.

My heart absolutely leaped into my throat when I realized that Kate was the Little Antelope!

What? How had Kate been transformed into this woodland creature? Kate was a beautiful young girl like me. Kate and I are one. I am she. She is me. She was not an antelope. I am not an antelope. Yet this animal was apparently nodding her little head at me, as if to say, "That's right, Margarite. Now you've got it right, Choohowee."

"Wait!" I almost screamed the word.

Inside my brain, I was running and screaming like a lunatic.

Perhaps I was insane after all.

Kate rubbed her head against my stomach and chest and snuffled to me again. I was a blink away from total hysteria, but she comforted me. She knelt at my feet, folded her legs, and lay down.

She looked up at me as if to say, "Relax, Choohowee. Everything is all right. Just rest, relax, and calm down. We are safe here. We belong here."

Tears were cascading down my cheeks, and my whole body was shivering with shock and fear. Still, she was peaceful as she welcomed me to lie down beside her. I collapsed and wept uncontrollably for a little while. There did not seem to be any explanation for what was happening to me. It must be that insanity had driven me into this world of confusion. My head was throbbing with every pounding heartbeat.

Kate laid her head on my arm and gazed up into my eyes. I saw that her eyes were very tired, and she was having a hard time breathing. Clearly, she was ill, maybe even dying. Why? Why had she come to find me? What strange force bound us together? Where was the young lady that had been speaking her memories into my brain? How could this transformation be possible? Suddenly, Kate's ears perked up and she stared intently into the Forest Primeval behind us. My human ears could not hear what hers had, but I knew something was coming. I felt something coming toward us. An eerie silence descended upon the forest as all the woodland creatures got very still and quiet. Birds and insects are like watch dogs. Except dogs bark, and small wildlife get silent. My hair was literally standing on end as the something got closer and closer to the little clearing where Kate and I were lying. I wanted to stand and run, but my legs were too shaky to support my weight. Instead, I drew the beautiful Little Antelope onto my lap and felt her trembling just like I was.

Heavy footfalls accompanied the appearance of a huge bear across the glen from us. I thought I would faint from the sheer terror that overwhelmed me. I could not even scream. No sounds came out of my mouth. I would die out here without even a whimper. Or maybe I was insane. Maybe my body was at home with Mama and Papa? Could all of this be caused by a brain sickness? This cannot be real! I must be insane. The bear had stopped as soon as he saw us. He was not growling or moving toward us. There was no sign that he intended to kill us. His eyes were fixed on me, and both of us were transfixed by his appearance. Poor Little Antelope was too weak to run also. She did not even struggle in my arms. She could only stare as the huge predator took one tentative step in our direction. If she were healthy, she would have been miles from here long before this. She would have smelled him when he was far away and escaped with her life. Why was she not trying to escape now? Why was she lying calmly on my lap? I wanted to protect her, but I did not have any way to do that.

As the bear took another cautious step toward us, instinct was screaming at me to run. Clutching Kate to my chest, I tried to scramble back into the trees to hide. She made a weak mewling sound as if she were in pain; then she began to flail weakly in my arms. Oh, no! Surely, I was not crushing what little life she had left in her! I could not put her down or the bear would eat her. Terrified, I shrank into a heap with my face close to hers. She kept looking at the bear, and tears began to spill out of her eyes. I felt her heart beating next to my own. It was filled with pain and longing. I felt the bear coming closer with every passing second. Kate and I would die here together today. Some bizarre fate had drawn us here for this very moment. We can feel his breath ruffle our hair. He will strike us with his huge paw and tear us apart with those cruel teeth. I try to pray that my death will be quick.

"God, please don't allow us to suffer. Please be merciful to us in death."

For the first time, the bear began to make guttural sounds deep in his chest. He sounded like he was in terrible pain. Is the bear wounded? Is that why he is being so cautious? A small ray of hope flutters in my spirit. There are many stories of strange experiences with bears in this area. Could it be possible for me to survive this encounter and even nurse the Little Antelope back to good health as well? My thoughts were pure chaos. Terror had addled my brain.

"Choovino… Kate, Nuttah, Nayeli wikkimak."

A man's voice began speaking tenderly to us. Instantly, I knew that it was My Indian's voice. I know his voice. I will never forget it.

He has come out of the Forest Primeval to save us from this terrible attack. When I whirled to face him, the certainty of my own insanity struck me like a lightning bolt.

Standing beside me, the bear is…changing.

The top half of a man is swirling out of the bottom of a bear.

He is becoming a human being!

Who would ever believe that anything like this could happen?

How can this be?

How can a bear change into a man?

As he "becomes human," the Indian reaches out and gently takes Kate from me. He is weeping as he kneels with her in his arms. His words of love are giving some strength to Kate. His tears are falling on her tiny body when the Young Antelope also begins to transform. Right in his arms, *she is becoming Kate again.* Can the folklore about "Shape Shifters" be true? Tales of people becoming animals are common in every society on earth. Those myths never die. Is it possible that these two are Shape Shifters? Unable to trust my eyes or my brain, I am frozen in this moment.

Kate is very weak as she speaks "Avonaco… Nuttah, My heart. I love you also. Nayeli. Avonaco, I do not wish to leave you, My Love. The Great Spirit, Mundoo Heamawikhio, calls me. He will receive me into his Peaceful Tuwa Wikkiup. All will be happiness, hantaywee, there. Ayelena, I wait for you."

His shoulders shake with sobs. "Kate, Choovino, Nayeli. I love you."

She raises her right hand and lays it along his jawline, and he covers it with his left.

I feel their deep love. I feel both of their hearts breaking. Kate's thoughts come to me again. She is terribly weak, and I know she is using all her strength to help me understand how we all got here. Her left hand reaches out to me, and I hold it gently as she speaks into my brain.

"We fell in love that first night when I found him wounded. He had been caught in a bear trap, but I saved his life, makawaze. I did not know that he was "Eluwilussit" a Holy Man. He has very strong medicine. We wanted to be husband and wife, wikkimak. Avonaco could not leave his tribe. He was to be the chief, hiamovi. I could not leave my family…I was all they had. We became wild creatures that could escape human bonds and meet in the forest. His great medicine has kept us safe for so many years. All our ancestors have crossed the river; yet, we still have life. Now this creature must go to Mundoo Heamawikhio, the Wise One Above. My time has come. My Spirit lives…but not this flesh. Avonaco can no longer save this body."

The realization of truth hit me and took my breath away. At last, I knew why I was here. Kate's spirit needed to continue. Her body would return to the earth, but her sweet, beautiful spirit would be lost in this Forest Primeval. She would be alone out here because her spirit could not cross the wide river in peace. Avonaco would grieve and lose his "Medicine."

"Margarite, Choohowee, you chose to come to us when you were a very young girl. We did not force you. You came into the forest, calling to us. We called you Choohowee, Young Turtledove, because you called to us… as a Turtledove calls to her mate. You told us that you belong here, in the Great Forest, with us. You did not want to leave us then. Will you stay with us now? We need your strength and youth. You can help him… He will give you happiness, hantaywee. You will be young, strong, and beautiful, huritt, for many generations. Please… Margarite…"

With her last bit of strength, she pulls his hand down to mine. Our fingers lace together instinctively. We need to hold onto someone. We are both losing a part of ourselves. I feel Kate's spirit slipping away from us.

"Take care of each other. Heal each other… Love… each…"

Kate is gone.

Avonaco breaks down completely as he utters a soul wrenching "Aiiee, Choovino…Kate, nuttah nayeli…I love you."

He buries his face in her neck and groans under the weight of an unbearable grief. It seems natural for me to reach out my hand and stroke his raven black hair. Beautiful. Huritt.

Kate's body shifts back into the little antelope as her spirit flies across the river to Mundoo Heamawikhio.

He welcomes His sweet child home, hinto, into his Peaceful Tuwa Wikkiup.

She waits for us there.

"Avonaco." As I speak his name for the first time, he slowly raises his tear- stained face to mine.

With my right hand, I wipe a tear away and lay my hand along his jawline. He covers it with his left hand. Questions are filling the space between us. My own tears roll down my cheeks as I speak the words that will form my future.

"Avonaco, nuttah, My Heart, Nayeli, I love you. Margarite, Choohowee, wikkimak, wife, family, hantaywee. Happiness, Avonaco?" He places his left hand along my jawline and wipes teardrops away with his thumb. I cover it with my own.

Choovino, Kate has disappeared, flying on a breath of love and light, leaving a small empty space between us. We stand, close together now, and join both hands in front of us.

"Margarite, Choohowee, huritt, beautiful wikkimak, wife, family. Hantaywee, happiness, Margarite? Happiness Choohowee?"

Yes, I will be happy here.

I belong here, this is home, hinto.

His hands are trembling slightly as he holds mine.

I take a tiny step into his arms and lean my head on his chest.

I feel the heartbeat of the *Mighty Bear*.

He lifts my face to his and searches deep into my soul with his ageless eyes.

My hands rise to stroke his long dark hair.

"Beautiful. Huritt."

Truth

SHE WAS NOT LOOKING FOR A KNIGHT
SHE WAS LOOKING FOR A SWORD...
ATTICUS

OK. I AM GOING TO WRITE THE TRUTH.
THE WHOLE TRUTH, AND
NOTHING BUT THE TRUTH.
SO HELP ME GOD.

Our family vacation was just perfect. We had fun every day. We enjoyed the countryside, and each other. It had been a long time coming. Family -- that is all that really matters. Our family had been through a lot. We had some serious problems. All families do. We were just like everyone else. We had the good, the bad, the ugly, and the indifferent. Just like everyone else does. In the final analysis, family is all you really have.

Really. When someone is dying, or even just sick... all that matters to them is the People that they love. You know what I'm talking about. People want to see their family, friends, and loved ones when they are in a crisis. Even if they are angry or hurt, or disappointed by their loved ones, it does not matter. Sometimes, it matters more. Sometimes, people will make peace, or restitution, or whatever it takes to see the ones that they have been estranged from for years. Money, cars, houses, and other physical possessions take second place to family. This vacation had a healing effect on all of us. We laughed, we cried, and we talked. Looking back on it now, I cannot believe how it all turned out.

I cannot believe that our vacation ended with Murder.

I said that I would write the truth. I will. It is going to be very, very hard for me. Nevertheless, I will write the truth about what happened. Maybe writing it all down will help me get on with my life. Maybe I can find some peace or justification for the whole thing.

Don't get me wrong.

I do not regret the murder.

As a matter of fact, I am thankful to God that I was able to do it.

I am so thankful that He helped me do what I had to do. Do you think that you could commit murder? Have you ever thought about that? Strangely enough, I had thought about it before. If we would all be truthful, before God, we would all say that we had thought about it.

All of us have seen the news reports, the movies, and the newspaper stories about the unthinkable. We have all had to face the horror and evil of the world that we live in. I'm talking about murder, torture, rape, and worst of all, someone hurting a child, my child, or your child. Some nameless, faceless, demonic force taking a child, and hurting that child...

Nothing in our lives could prepare us for that unbearable heartbreak.

Of course, we always choose to believe that none of those things could ever happen to us. None of the horrible evil that we know about could ever touch our lives. Our minds could not conceive of that kind of fear, pain, sorrow, or devastation in our own families. However, we know that other victims' families felt that way, too. We fear that even thinking about it could bring it down on us. I keep on saying "we" because I know that you feel the same way that I feel. All of us are basically the same. Basically.

OK. The whole truth. I promised, and I must get on with it. So, here goes.

I suggested horseback riding and a river rafting trip. Who wouldn't want to do those cool things? Me. I did not want to do either one of them. But after refusing to ride horses, I knew that I had to ride the rapids. Oh goody. I hate being wet. I hate the river. Well, not the river, itself. It's the smell, the mud, the moss, the wasps, and all that other stuff that I object to. Anyway, the grand kids were expecting me to ride the horses and the rapids with them.

So I got out of one of them, but the rapids were an unpleasant reality for me. Luckily, the water was not very high and consequently, not much white water was to be expected.

Thank God for that. I get motion sickness.

I settled in on the huge rubber (?) raft and asked God to help me get through this as quickly and dryly as possible. After the initial discomfort of wading through the water to get into the raft, I was pleasantly surprised to discover that I was liking the whole thing. I do enjoy being outside. I love the sun, and wind, and mountains, and beaches, and sunsets, and everything about the outdoors. I spend as much time as possible outside. I work outside in my garden and yard all the time. I go camping and many other "outdoorsy" things whenever I can. I am good at all that.

This raft trip was only one of many water/boat trips that I had been on. However, it was the first for my middle granddaughter, **Dawn**. She has not been involved with very many outdoor type activities. I was semi-afraid that she would not like it. That is a lot of money to spend for something that the kids do not like. I only suggested it because I had promised my husband that I would do it for years. I owed him a raft trip.

Sitting in the boat with my cold, wet feet, I really took time to study the scenery around us. It seemed that every tree, fence, meadow, cliff, deer, and bird that we saw was especially beautiful that day. With very little white water to threaten me, I had time to relax and enjoy my family and myself. An "other-worldly" quality seemed to settle over us after a short time. We all were just pleased to be there together in such a spectacular landscape.

I am not a very observant person. I have a dear, dear friend that says to me, "Do you know what it is that you're looking at?" Brother, when he says that, I just about croak because I know that I have missed something MAJOR. I always say something like, "You know that I'm clueless, so just tell me what it is that I'm looking at." He always does.

Thank God for people who see and understand what's going on.

That day on that river, I was suddenly aware that I was really seeing the world around me. Not just seeing it but also actually soaking it in. It was so spectacular. I was thinking how blessed I was just to be there with the people I love. This was a day to be treasured and remembered for years to come. I was hoping that my beautiful teen-age granddaughter was aware of how precious this time was. I hoped that she and the rest of the family were taking in this fabulous scenery as gratefully as I was. My eyes literally could not absorb enough of it.

I suddenly became aware that I was looking through the trees at a man's face.

It amazed me that I was seeing a person in this remote area. For a short minute or so, I was able to see him before he saw me. I can tell you for a fact that my whole life changed in that instant. It was not just his long, dark, unkempt hair that alarmed me. There was a palpable, physical foreboding in the air around me. A cold fear gripped my heart at the thought of what his presence could mean to us. There was no doubt that he meant to harm us in some way. I sensed that in my spirit.

In less than a fraction of a second, my world was completely and irrevocably altered.

As I tried to figure out what was happening I realized that his entire focus was on my granddaughter, Dawn. There was no mistaking the intensity of his gaze on her. Thank God that she was oblivious to his presence and my reaction to it. I wanted to scream, but I knew that would be a big mistake. I knew that I had to be quiet and controlled. I felt that I had to remain calm and keep silent about him. I think that I knew, even at that first minute, that I had to hide the truth about him from my family. I did not want the men and boys to try to do something about him. I did not want to appear to be hysterical or cryptic.

Most of all, I did not want to scare Dawn.

All of this went through my mind in a blinding flash of time. I just knew that I knew. I did not need any explanation. I knew that he was our worst nightmare. You know that we can feel those kinds of things. It's a kind of gift from God. This terrible knowledge was so overwhelming that it took my breath away. I was frightened out of my mind. The evil was there, in my life, as I had always feared. He must have felt my stare. When he turned his eyes on mine, there was no going back. I met his gaze and tried to discern the intention of his heart. As I feared, it was like looking into a black hole. In that split-second, I knew that he would try to destroy our lives. I had to stop him. It was up to me. No one else even knew that he existed.

He was my dreadful secret.

In the same flash of time, he was gone. I could no longer see him, but I still felt him. His dark shadow covered me from that moment on. You might ask how I could know this for a certainty, without any doubt. All I can tell you is that I knew. Moreover, that knowledge was too awful for me to bear. I knew that he watched us the whole day. He was there, on that riverside somewhere, watching. Watching Dawn.

My flesh was paralyzed with fear and loathing. But my spirit was screaming, "No! No! No! You Will Never Hurt Her! God as my witness, you will never hurt her." I cannot begin to tell you how I made it through that day. I remember them asking me if I was OK. Was I seasick? Was I mad? What's wrong? I could not behave in a normal way. I was too scared and heartsick to join in the family fun. Thank God that no one else knew the truth. It was imperative that they did not know the truth.

I could not protect all of them. I could not even protect Dawn or myself. How was I going to proceed? How in God's name was this Grandmother going to destroy this predator?

He was a predator. He was out looking for a victim. There were a couple of occasions in my life when I could have been a victim. I had chosen not to. I even told the local police officials that I was not a victim and that I would not be victimized. Someone would have to work hard to make me a victim, and they would not enjoy it. Bold talk. I was young.

Now I was older. I knew the truth about myself and the world around me. I knew nothing about the kind of darkness and obsession I had seen in his eyes that day. It was often displayed in movies. I did not watch those movies. Many, many books were written about creatures like him. I had no desire to read those books. I had spent my whole life in a nice, clean, healthy, upright, moral world. The few times I had to enter into the darkness, I knew that God was with me and would get me out.

Don't get me wrong, I am no angel. I have plenty of sins and failures, but I also believe in God and His goodness. He has seen me through every valley, every shadow, every heartache, and every death that I have ever had to endure. I know Him. I trust Him. He was my only hope then, and He is my only hope now. This is the truth.

That day on the river, I vacillated between faith and despair. I believed that God could do anything. However, I was pretty sure that I could not do much. Maybe I couldn't do anything at all. Telling my family about him was out of the question. I was not able to handle the possible repercussions of that. I would have to take this on by myself. They probably wouldn't even believe me. I could not handle the pain of rejection and derision if they did not believe me.

It was kind of like when someone knows that they have cancer… and will die.

Strangely enough, those people are frequently stronger than those around them are. Sometimes they act as if they believe they will be OK. They comfort their loved ones and help them get through the ordeal of dying. Even though they know the truth, they still try to help and protect the ones they love. It takes a certain kind of courage and strength to help others help you die. I felt like I had to help my family stay safe, but I did not know how.

My best and only real hope was the knowledge that to be forewarned is to be fore-armed. I knew, and I was going to arm myself against the day when he would strike. How? How would I prepare for the unthinkable? How could I defend against the unimaginable? In truth, I am just a grandmother who saw a man staring at her granddaughter on a raft trip. Who could help me get ready for an assault that could happen at any time?

There were some houses and cabins along the river. Some of them were clearly occupied. Others looked abandoned. There might be some kind of clue about his identity there, but I doubted it. Maybe that was too easy. That was just wishful thinking on my part. But, he had appeared to be at home there. He had a certain proprietary air about himself. He looked as if he belonged there. Like it was his river and we were trespassing there. Maybe he watched all the people who came down his river.

Maybe he was just waiting for the right girl.

It made me sick to think that maybe Dawn was not the first... or the last... NO! The LAST ONE was the last one. I would not consider any other alternative. Even though a feeling of inadequacy overwhelmed me, I was also enraged. In just those few hours of rafting, I made some life-changing decisions. I mean it when I say that. My life would never be the same. Neither would his. I would die trying to stop him. If I failed, I would want to be dead anyway.

He would have to kill me... to keep me from killing him.

Truthfully, just writing these words now scares me to death. I have never felt so scared and helpless before or since. At the same time, I had a certainty in my spirit that I would see this thing through to the end. So I came to all these frightening decisions in such a short period of time that it just seemed impossible. It could not be true. Yes. It was true. I told you that I was going to write the truth. I will.

I believe that The Truth will set us free.

OK. I finally got my mind to work enough to ask the guide some questions about the area and the people and the history of that stretch of river. Nothing of any value was revealed. I could not exactly ask about serial killers or anything like that. They were just general questions about the terrain and how remote and accessible the roads were. How long a walk to civilization? What roads passed near here? Did he ever see locals that did not want his tour going through their property? My husband and sons were interested in these facts and joined the conversation enough to make it seem more normal.

I wanted things to seem normal. I still felt that if I acted normal, I would feel better. It was normal for me to appear to need Dawn's help getting out of the boat and up the hill. It was normal for me to go into the woods when she needed to go whizz. I even tried to joke with her about how she was feeling on this trip. Was she happy? Was she "connecting" with nature? I needed to know how she really felt in her spirit. Did she feel him out there?

She and I are famous for our intuition.

We both have "feelings." All our friends are amazed at how often we discern things that can only be revealed by God. As young as she is, she is very spiritual. Many times, we have felt like something was not quite right with a certain person, place, or thing. She and I have discussed how other people are just totally clueless while our skins are crawling and our hair is standing on end. Surely she felt something that day. No. She did not say a word to me about any bad feelings or warnings. She revealed nothing that I could use to help me… to help her.

I picked up a heavy, volcanic-looking rock as soon as I could. I am a big rock collector. I have rocks from all over the United States. Therefore, carrying this rock with me did not appear to be insane. I would have used it to bash his skull in if I needed to. But, somehow, I knew that he would not try anything when all the guys were with her. The truth is that people like him are usually cowards that can only intimidate young girls and children. That makes them even more despicable.

I stuck close to Dawn and tried to make it seem as if I was the one who wanted her to help me. After all, I am old and overweight and not as sure of myself as I once was. She seemed to tolerate that OK for a while. However, I knew that she would get tired of me hovering over her very quickly. I could not afford to alienate her with any bizarre behavior. I could not tell her the truth about the predator either.

The situation had to be handled with extreme care, or I would not be able to keep her in my sights. This ordeal was just beginning. The day would soon fade to darkness and she would be in much more danger then. I was starting to feel frantic about leaving the river. I knew that he would follow us, and I simply could not bear that. Every minute of the coming days would be Hell for me. What if I were unable to interfere with his plans here? What if he followed us home? It seemed more and more likely that he would do that. Study her, stalk her, and strike when she felt relaxed and safe...I could not allow him to follow us or invade our home.

He must stay here forever.

If he had been abducting victims from here, the guide would have capitalized on the "spook factor" of that. Obviously, he acted on his deviant plans somewhere else. My thoughts were impossibly filled with plans of stopping him today. I mean right now. Today. Nothing was going to make me feel better until he was dead. I was not going to face the ordeal of a trial. Dawn would not be put through that. In fact, she did not ever need to know the truth about any of this.

I began to develop my plan.

We are a hunting family. Our parents and siblings all hunt. Our roots are in the country and outdoor activities. Finding and using a gun was not going to be a problem for me. We have many guns, and I own several pistols and rifles. Although I am a pretty good shot, I am not a hunter. I do not like to kill animals. You cannot imagine how much I am opposed to the idea of killing a living human being. However, ending his life was a certainty to me. It is astounding how quickly and completely I became convinced that all of this had to happen...and it must happen quickly.

My mind was whirling frantically as we all climbed out of the raft and got ready for the long van trip back to where our cars were parked.

We had guns in the cars. We would all be together, and I knew that this monster would not show himself now. How would I find him before he found Dawn alone? How could I possibly maintain any sense of normality while I knew he was out there, watching and waiting? Time was on his side. He knew this area. He might even be a native.

We lived in another state. Home seemed like it was worlds away from me right now. I refused to entertain the idea of his wicked presence invading our home. He could not follow us and contaminate our family's living space. None of us would ever be safe or happy again if he followed us home. Dear Lord, what am I going to do? How can I draw him out and still protect Dawn? I must force him to act now. I must be in control of things, not him. He will have to come and take her away from me... from us.

It will not be easy for him.

Nothing will be easy from now on. This is the hardest thing that I will ever have to face. If only I could tell the guys the truth. If only I didn't have to do this alone. But I know that I must act alone. I cannot control my husband or sons. I can barely control myself. But I must. Besides, if things go wrong, I cannot watch any of them be hurt. I just cannot bear to think of losing any of them. If someone has to be hurt, or killed, or go to jail, it will be me. I'm older, but I'm stronger in the old-fashioned way that only hard-working people get strong. It's a mental and a physical strength that most young people don't know or understand. I cannot reveal anything to any of them.

God forbid that the monster would put his hands on anyone that I love.

All the horror stories that I have ever heard about or read about keep jumping into my mind. I must focus on the here and now. I cannot allow myself to be distracted by the fear and anxiety that threatens to overwhelm me. Do not think about what might happen. Do not give in to my natural emotions. Rise above the negative and crippling thoughts of "What if?" I must act normal. I must be smart.

I must get to him before he can get to her.

Dawn and I share some genetic interests and similarities. All parents and grandparents can see parts of themselves in their family members. Both of us were born addicted to caffeine. She loves coffee as much as I do. We can drink it all morning and be ready for more by three or four in the afternoon. At home, she and her friends go to coffee bars to hang out. She actually drinks it while she's there. I realize that coffee may be the key to my success. I can send Dawn out for coffee this evening. I can follow her.

I can wait until he strikes, and then, I will strike him.

We plan to have dinner at the cabin tonight. I know that no one else will want coffee, so I won't make a whole pot. It's perfectly reasonable to assume that Dawn will want to run down to the coffee shop and get us a cup of gourmet coffee. I will follow her. That's it. This will work. It must work.

Riding back from the raft trip in the van, I keep on looking behind us, knowing that he is back there. He must follow us to find out which cars are ours. He must follow us to see where we are staying. He may know that I saw him, but he has no idea that I am planning to end him. He will never suspect that an old grandmother is plotting how she will trap and kill him. He probably thinks that I was unaware of what was in his mind when he was creeping around up there on the riverside. I cannot believe these things myself. It is inconceivable even for me, and I'm the one doing it. Truthfully, it is inconceivable.

He is following us.

Using the skills that I have learned while observing Burn Notice, NCIS, Blue Bloods, and all the other TV cops for over fifty years, I have spotted him. Just like on TV, he is staying well behind us. There is no mistaking that shaggy hair. He is driving a non-descript SUV, just like on TV. It's probably stolen. I expect that he will drive something different when he comes after Dawn. I will not look for a particular vehicle. I will only watch her. I will not let her out of my sight.

He will not know that I know that he is there.

My heart is beating so hard that I am afraid that I will have a heart attack. Or maybe I will hyperventilate and pass out or something. I must get my head together. Now is not the time to fall apart. Now is the time to strengthen my resolve and make up my mind to do what must be done. I will not worry about myself. I will try to be smart and not go to jail. Above all, I will not let this monster hurt Dawn, or anyone else in my family.

My goal is to make sure that he never hurts anyone again. Never.

When we get to the cabin, I try to act normal. I talk about the raft trip and what we will do tomorrow. I ask about my rock, knowing that it is in the trunk of my car. That is the perfect excuse to go out and make sure that my gun is in the console. My husband calls it the Enforcer. It is a large Derringer that shoots .410 shotgun shells and .44 longs, also. I can always hit my target with the Enforcer. It's fully loaded and ready to shoot.

I am calmer now. I keep asking God to help me. I know that sounds weird. You may think it's sac-religious to ask God's help to kill someone. Sorry, but I really need His help. I cannot fail. Our lives will be destroyed if he wins. I carry my rock into the cabin and start making plans for dinner. Everyone is hungry now, but I suggest snacks since it is too early to cook. In my mind, I think it will be better not to have a full stomach when I go after Dawn. My insides are churning right now. Every minute brings me closer to the moment when I will send Dawn out to get coffee. The little kids may want to go, but I will insist that she be allowed to go alone. She has been cooped up with us for way too long. She needs some time to listen to her own music and talk on her phone to her friends, etc... Whatever it takes to get her some time alone. I can only watch one person. She must be alone.

Dear God, Please, Please, Please do not let him hurt her.

I want to write this part as quickly as I possibly can. It's really a lot harder than I thought it would be, and I thought it would be

Impossible. Funny, but my fingers are stuck in the hovering position over the keyboard, refusing to type. You cannot imagine the absolute terror that I felt then… and I feel it even now. The memory of it is almost too fearful to deal with. I need to finish this story. You must know the truth. Let me say again, I will never regret this murder. I do regret the need to murder someone. There should be a better way to protect yourself from predators like him.

When I finally feel like I will explode if I don't do something, I say "Dawn, I sure would like to have some White Chocolate Hazelnut Espresso. Would you like to run down to the village and get us a Grande before we start dinner?" Of course, she is delighted. "Look, why don't you take the truck and get gas, too? My car seats may still be wet, and I don't need gas."

As expected, we must fight off a horde of hitchhiker cousins, but she is the oldest, and eventually, we prevail over them.

As I hand her the wrong credit card, she hugs me and whispers, "Thanks, MiMi, I really need this."

I hold her way too close, way too tight, for way too long.

She thinks I am crazy.

God forgive me because I am not crazy. However, if he hurts her, we will all be Insane. How can we recover from that kind of heart-ache? I know families that still have nightmares and guilt and grief from natural deaths. Who could bear the unbearable destruction of abduction...or worse? Dawn has been gone for about three minutes, now. Horror stories fill my brain, as I stand there with my wallet looking confused and frustrated.

I make eye contact with my husband "Holy Smokes! I gave her the wrong credit card! Dang it. She won't be able to get gas with an expired card. I should have cut it up last week. But I just forgot. She will be so embarrassed. I'll jump in the car and catch her. Or, maybe we can just sit outside and relax while we enjoy the mountain air for a minute?"

I turn to the younger cousins and say, "No, you guys just

stay here. She does not want us around when she's talking to her friends.... You'll understand when you get to be her age. I will be right back. OK? Bye-Byc, OK bye" ...I was babbling.

They all think I'm crazy. Maybe I am. I guess I am.

She is no more than five minutes ahead of me. But, I must be patient. I must give him time to find her. He must follow her without knowing that he is being followed, too. If I see the same vehicle, I will be amazed, but I watch, anyway. Mainly, she will be the one I focus on. Anyone that approaches her will become a suspect and a target. Anyone that could lure her, or trap her, or aid him in any way will draw fire from me. Nevertheless, I will not over-react or act too soon. God Help Me, Please. Slowly driving down the mountain, I watch every side road. I look at every place he might force her off the road. I suspect everything and everyone. Only God knows what he is planning to do. Where is he waiting? What will he do? I cannot think about Dawn right now. I absolutely cannot think about her right now. I know that this sounds stupid. This is only about her. She is the only one that counts. I cannot think about her fear or anything worse. I can only think about her being safe.

God keep her safe.

I am cautiously driving into the village now. It is a small town with only a couple of eating places. The coffee shop is the most modern place around this area. We spotted it as soon as we arrived. Luckily, there are lots of trees and shrubs and wilderness-type land-scapes near the coffee shop. I can park close but not in plain sight. Besides, he will be focused on stalking her. He will not even know that he is being stalked, too.

I drive around the parking lot from a block away. Suddenly, I spot her getting out of the car. She is on the phone. Good. Let her be oblivious. Don't let her feel the malevolent spirit around her.

I park and pick up the Enforcer. I have 911 on my speed dial. I do not want to even take the time to try to dial. It's cold in my car. Maybe I'm cold. Dear Lord, there he is. He has a cast on his arm!

How diabolical. His hair is pulled back into a neat ponytail. He's wearing glasses. This monster is trying to look like a normal human being who will need help with his coffee, his car door, and his laptop. He will need a helping hand from an innocent young person that will then be sacrificed on the altar of his demonic desires.

STOP! Do not think about any of that now. Focus on her. Watch her as she is standing in line. She is not ready to order. She is just wasting time as she visits and entertains her friends on the phone.

I must stay calm. Wait. Be sure. There must be evidence to support my innocence. There must be evidence of his guilt. They must not know that this was planned, pre-meditated. However, my future is not the most important issue. I want to live the rest of my life as I have always lived it...free and independent. Still, what must be done, will be done. Moreover, I will do it on my terms, not his. She is finally getting serious about ordering coffee. He is watching her. He is waiting by the door. I'm not sure what he plans to do. Dozens of scenarios are trying to crowd into my mind. It will be OK if I focus on her. When he moves, I will move. I pray that he is alone. God, please do not let him have an accomplice. I think he is by himself. He seems so solitary, like a lone wolf.

No matter what else happens today, his hunting days are over.

He will never hurt another living thing. I am sure of that.

Dawn hands the cashier the credit card. She runs it, shakes her head, and runs it again. She is explaining it to Dawn. Good. She will remember Dawn now. Two other customers are aware of what's going on, too. Dawn starts digging around in her purse. Talking and laughing about her crazy MiMi. Good. They will never forget how beautiful and charming she is. Finally, she comes up with some dollars and change to pay for the two cups on the counter.

He never takes his eyes off her. Everyone is focused on her. Good. It's as if she is on stage or something. Good. Everyone in this shop will remember her. It was smart for him to be innocuous and invisible. His eyes are smoldering, and I fear that she will FEEL the evil that is radiating from him.

At last, she starts for the door. He is not looking at her now. I step out of the car. I keep my eyes on Dawn. No matter what, I will not lose sight of her. He is fumbling with the cast, his laptop, and some change in his hand. She is almost face to face with him now. Many customers are still watching her. Good. She must be remembered. She must captivate everyone. They must be on her side. Everything hinges on her natural beauty and charm being imprinted on their minds.

Witnesses must remember how alive and vivacious she is.

He tries to open the door for her. He is still fumbling around with everything. I am walking in front of my car now. I put an old ball cap on and slip on some big, outdated sunglasses. Dawn will not immediately recognize me and foil my plans. He will not know me at all. I have the Enforcer in my pocket. It is comforting there. He will not hurt her. Suddenly, he loses his grip on the laptop, door, money, everything. As his stuff crashes to the floor, I see that she is totally dismayed. The evil genius has gotten her sympathy and concern.

She wants to help him. Just as he planned.

I am not far from the cover of trees now. She is fussing around, trying to decide what to do. He is hurriedly picking up his things. The clever predator is behaving as if he is embarrassed by not being able to be a gentleman for her. She is uncomfortable and completely disarmed by this unique situation. Her mind is racing. He is playing his part perfectly. However, nothing he does will compare to her youth and innocence. He is trying to get out of the door as quickly as he can now, as if he is worried about drawing any more attention to himself. They will remember only a blur, if they remember him at all. She does not want to cause him any more grief, but she thinks that she must do something. He is struggling as he makes his way toward an older model van. I knew it. He will need a van or SUV to take her.

Dear Lord, please let him be alone.

Please do not let him have an accomplice.

I am staying in the shadows parallel to them. I never take my eyes off her. Confused, she starts to follow him. She was reard to be polite and helpful. She will want to make sure that he knows that she is grateful for his efforts. This animal has perfected his technique. Now I am more convinced than ever that he has done this before… too many times. He has played this part too many times.

This will be his last performance.

Dawn stops, puts her cups on a table near the door, and hurries after him. For a split-second, I think I will scream "NOOO!" Nevertheless, I bite my tongue and move closer to his van. It is getting a little darker out here. His timing is perfect. He quickly slips the fake cast off his healthy arm. She is on the other side of the van. I am only twelve or fifteen feet from him now. He is calmly opening the sliding door and reaching into the darkness for something. There is no one else in the van. Thank God.

As she comes around to help him, he turns toward her, smiling awkwardly. I am still in shadows, closer than ten feet to him now.

He raises his arm as if to say, "I'm OK, don't worry about me." Brilliant.

It is as if he is beckoning her to his side. She cannot see the hand that he is hiding behind his back. I am close enough to step out now. But I must get this right. He must do more than menace her. There must be a deadly weapon. His intention to hurt or kill her must be evident to everyone. My mind is repelled by the fact that he will have to touch her. He has been so clever. My actions cannot be viewed as protection. This has to be a full-blown rescue.

Everything I do from this moment on will be scrutinized in the courts of the law.

She is a little hesitant to advance toward him when he is trying to ward her off. Good. The coffee shop doorbell tinkles, and Dawn looks back. He steps toward her so fast that I am alarmed. Both of his hands are in full view. He holds a syringe and a cloth of some kind. It is time for me to move. He cannot have the opportunity to put her between us, like a hostage. He is only a yard or so from her when she hears him approach. She turns. I must act NOW!

My mouth opens to yell a warning as the Enforcer fills my hand. But only indescribable sounds come out of me. It's enough. He turns around and sees me. As I look into his eyes, the evil darkness there bursts into flames of fury. Good. Come for me. Let her see him attacking me. She is screaming.

I am in control, now. "Run!" It's the only word I can say. "Run!"

He is on me, as I pull the trigger, once, twice… I lose count.

The truth is that I deliberately killed the predator.

No one would believe it of me. Honestly, I can hardly believe it myself. Others dialed 911 before I did. It seemed like only seconds passed before we were awash in a sea of red and blue lights. I was oblivious to everything...but Dawn. She was safe. She wept uncontrollably as she clung to me and tried to pull me further from the van and the despicable creature on the ground.

She kept crying, "Get away from him, MiMi. Get away from him. Get away from him..." I could not speak at all.

I guess I was in shock. Good. Everyone needed to see us as victims.

Truthfully, the following minutes, hours, and days were not as bad as I had feared.

I am not a suspicious looking murderer. I make no excuses for what happened. He was a killer that needed to be killed. Police and FBI officers quickly found proof that he was a serial killer. Good. I knew it. We both told exactly what had happened. Truthfully, I saw a man try to abduct my granddaughter from a public parking lot. I only had the gun in my pocket because it had fallen out of the car when I slid the wet towel out from under the console as I stood up. I was in a hurry to catch her with the good credit card before she was embarrassed at the coffee shop... so I just slipped it into my pocket. I am sure that I babbled. Our stories did not have to be perfect.

After all, we were the victims here.

We both told exactly what had happened to us. The law enforcement officials filled in all the blanks. Thank God.

My husband and sons and other grandchildren were terribly impressed with me. Good.

The truth is that Grandmothers are frequently underestimated.

Don't you think?

Truthfully?

God's Vision

MAY WE SHINE LIKE STARS IN A
DARKENED GENERATION...
LYNNE HYBELS

I had waited for that particular trip for years. I felt a very strong attraction to this place called "La Visiones de Dios," or God's Vision, ever since I first heard about it. It is a deep canyon in a remote area of the Sierra Madre Mountains in Mexico. The natives called it God's Vision because of the view from the top of the canyon. There is only barren, desert landscape at the top of the mesa. However, when you look down, there is a fabulous waterfall, which drops down a steep mountain into this beautiful green valley far below. You can only get there by following a trail through an area of huge boulders that do not look like they belong there. The Spanish villagers call it, "Piedras Estranas." Loosely translated, that means "Extraordinary Stones." They must have wondered where that water was coming from, too, because they named it "Aguas Perdidas." That means Lost Waters. I knew all about it from the many pictures I had seen. We have several friends that volunteer at a Mission called "Casa da la Verdad," or House of Truth, which is near God's Vision. They have shown us photos for years. Every time someone came back from a trip to that area, I renewed my efforts to get there myself.

My husband, Kevin, and I love to travel. However, he does not want to go to Mexico. He does not want to go to Canada, either. He is fundamentally opposed to leaving the United States. That is why it took such a long time to get him to agree to go down to God's Vision. Finally, Kevin agreed to make the journey. He is a "Jack of all Trades," with many useful skills. Everyone begged him to go help on one of the projects at the mission. He had made those kinds of trips before, just not to another country. I had not ever done anything like that. My "skills" are not that much in demand, by anyone. Luckily, people are always hungry, and I know how to cook. Strangely, Kevin made the decision to go because he felt like he needed to, not because I wanted to.

Our son, Jason, also wanted to go with us. He had just finished high school and would leave for college in the fall. He was one of the top Spanish students in Texas and had received a full scholarship to Southwest Texas State University. He tested into the middle of his junior year in Spanish. We were all amazed by that, since they placed him as a sophomore in English. How do you speak a second language better than your native tongue? Everyone teased him about that. It was amazing that he spoke, read, and wrote Spanish so fluently. My Spanish vocabulary consisted almost completely of names of food. You know enchilada, tortilla, burrito, the important words. I also knew bano-- bathroom. That could be very important, too. For the next couple of weeks, Jason gave Spanish lessons to his mom and dad every night. The Foreign Language Chair at Southwest had suggested a "Total Immersion Experience," and this trip to God's Vision could be it. We were thrilled to have Jason with us. It would be like another family vacation.

After weeks of planning, all of us were ready to go. The missionaries, Abel and Sierra, made the whole trip easy for us to organize because people had been going down to help at the mission for years. We did not have to figure anything out on our own. They gave us a list of toiletries and over- the-counter meds that their community did not offer. Our church helped us gather more than enough of those kinds of things. We also collected food to re-stock the pantry and clothing for those in need. The villagers always need shoes, too. Sometimes several family members will take turns wearing the same pair of shoes. We Americans cannot imagine such a thing! Each member of our family has many kinds of shoes. Every one of us has several pairs of "tennis" shoes that cost over a hundred dollars each. If you do not believe that we are a nation of excess, count how many pairs you have. Do not forget the ones that are in storage for the next season. Next time you help someone move, see how many boxes of shoes have to be carried out. Wow! I only mention this one article of dress to give you an example of how blessed we are. We are just as excessive with clothing, jewelry, furniture, cars, and every other kind of "stuff" that we can get our hands on.

Abel reminded us that we would be staying in a remote part

of a third- world-country. Things would be dramatically different from the ways we were accustomed to living. He said that it would seem like we had stepped backward in time. Most of his neighbors are only concerned with the most basic necessities, like food, water, and a place to sleep. Their food may be nothing more than a small, hand-made tortilla. Water may have to be carried from a well or a stream some distance away. A place to sleep may just be dirt with, or without, a blanket for padding or cover.

We Americans take all those things for granted. We are a nation that is consumed with "Stuff." We store "Stuff" to make room for more "Stuff." We throw away enough "Stuff" to feed and clothe a whole family in Mexico. My heart aches for those poor people. I have nothing but sympathy for them. I would be desperately trying to get out, too, if I lived there. Nevertheless, I would be the first person to say that America must secure her borders. Living in a "Border State" has taught me so much about illegal alien problems. It seems as if the issues have become too large to deal with. We need to find some solutions soon. In the meantime, I want to help hurting people whenever I can.

In rural Mexico, they do not have much "Stuff." They do not have money for "Stuff." Nor do they have any place to put "Stuff" that is not needed to survive. A large majority of the mountain people "live" in small adobe sheds. They spend most of their days outside, tending a few sheep or goats. The women cook outside and wash in a stream. Even younger children help the family survive by gathering wood and tending flocks. They do not have running water or electricity or telephones.

Most children do not go to school for more than a couple of years. The village probably does not have a school anyway. The Mexican government does not want to build schools or provide the utilities or teaching materials for education. If travel is required, neither parents nor children could do it for long. They would have to walk a very long way, barefooted, without proper clothing or shoes.

There may be only one running vehicle in the whole village. Vehicles are too rare and valuable to be used for children. Many vehicles are abandoned because there is no way to get fuel. Donkeys are the primary mode of transportation in rural Mexico. I know that we cannot imagine this life style. They cannot imagine our life styles, either. I have expounded on this because I want you to know what a culture shock this creates in people from affluent countries. In fact, that culture shock exists between rural and metropolitan Mexican citizens as well.

Since there is very little entertainment for the mountain villagers, they frequently go to the mission to see what those crazy gringos are doing over there. They think it is like going to an amusement park. There is always light, music, food, and fun at the House of Truth. These simple people love to laugh, and they are easily pleased. Work crews have built a nice house and a small chapel/schoolroom, too. Someone provided them with two huge generators that provide electricity for several hours in the evening. Several churches had arranged for the mission to have two satellite phones. Another company went down and drilled a great well. Everyone is always welcome to get water at the mission. They have built two large solar showers that are open to the public every other day. The whole family comes and makes a party out of bathing. It is a perfect time to sing, pray, and help them learn to read. Abel and Sierra have come to love and enjoy the hill folks. They are meek, gentle people with kind hearts.

Kevin, Jason, and I were all anxious to start our journey to God's Vision. We would enjoy helping at House of Truth Mission, but my main goal was to make that trip to God's Vision. At last we were driving south toward the Texas/Mexico border. Our church had hired an eighteen-wheeler to drive all the supplies on down to the mission. Abel had called two days ago to warn us that the "Federales" were known to be hi-jacking tourists and making them pay for safe passage. He talked to Jason in Spanish for a very long time that day. When they hung up, Kevin and I started asking questions immediately. We were greatly concerned by the seriousness of the conversation.

However, Jason summed it all up in a few sentences, which he often calls "loose translation." "Listen Mom and Dad, Abel told me how to handle anyone, Anyone that might try to intimidate us. Abel made sure that I know what to say to them and how to present our family to them. You two have to be polite and quiet when I'm interacting with whoever comes our way. I know that God will keep us safe. Do not be afraid. The criminal element preys on fear; it grows stronger by absorbing fear. We will not feed the beast. OK?"

I had never been prouder of him than I was at that moment. It was definitely God's plan for Jason to go with us to God's Vision.

The drive down was a wonderful time. We all wished that our oldest son, Shawn, could have been with us. He was in the Persian Gulf on the U. S. S. Abraham Lincoln. We all missed him more than I can say. Nevertheless, we all thoroughly enjoyed seeing this part of Texas because we had never been there before. I did not think that we would like the desert, but we did. It has its own quiet beauty. We found a peace there that is very different from other green landscapes. It is a place of stillness and solitude. The Big Bend has such awesome views that we cannot wait to come back here on a longer vacation.

Our border crossing was to be at La Jitas, a very small village right before you get to the tip of the bend in the Rio Grande. This river crossing turned out to be one of the highlights of our trip. There was no bridge in this poor village, so a local family had to ferry us across on a "barge" built of fifty-five-gallon barrels and wood! What a delightful experience that was. A friendly Mexican man was the captain, and his young daughter was his helper. She handed him the rope as he needed it. That is how he pulled us across the Rio Grande River. It is shallow there, without very much of a current. They were both thrilled when we paid the fee and gave them both a nice "Tip." It was truly a sweet ferry trip, unlike any that we had ever been on before.

As we began our drive in Mexico, I could almost feel the difference in our two countries. This is such a primitive, forbidding land. It is absolutely like stepping backward in time. There is a total absence of modern technology, or modern roads, or vehicles, or buildings. All of us were anxious to get to the mission in the mountains because there were no amenities for travelers out here. It would be around five hours of driving time through this harsh backcountry. The foothills ahead looked very inviting.

I was driving when we came upon the roadblock. As we passed through a field of large boulders, there was a Humvee blocking the narrow road. There were five men carrying machine-gun-like weapons all around us. I guess they had been watching us approach because each one was ready to fire if he needed to. You cannot imagine how fear instantly filled my heart. I gasped and quickly looked at Kevin for help.

In a heartbeat, Jason opened the back door, looked back at us, and said, "Stay here. Pray."

He was smiling without fear as he raised his hands and spoke to them in English. He said House of Truth and motioned toward the car; then he pointed toward the mountains, which were much closer now. Suddenly, another Humvee drove up behind us, totally blocking our way. Those men got out of their vehicle and started looking into the car windows and talking among themselves.

One soldier, who was obviously in charge, stepped forward to talk to Jason. He motioned for him to step farther away from the car. Many guns pointed at him, and some were still aimed at us, too. I was so terrified that I started crying.

Kevin said, "Pray," very softly to me.

We were literally afraid to move. I prayed for my son as only a Mother can.

The General or whatever he was asked, "May I see jour ID please? Where are jou going?"

He spoke slowly in heavily accented English. He looked into the car windshield intently, as if wondering why Kevin was not the one out there instead of this young boy. Jason looked at us too, as if to say, "Stay."

The General said, "Jason, is that the correct way to speak your name? Jason?"

Our son nodded and stuck his hand out to the General in a friendly manner and said, "Yes, si,r my name is Jason Carnes, and my parents are travelling with me, there in the car. May I know your name, sir, and what is your rank in this military unit?"

The General was surprised and a little intrigued by this polite, young, American boy.

He shook Jason's hand and said, "Federal Marshal Jesus Villalobos." The whole regiment seemed to relax then.

I know that I certainly felt a little bit better. Jason nodded, and Marshal Villalobos nodded back, and both men smiled at each other. Thank you, Jesus. Jason said something about being honored to meet him and how impressed his classmates would be when he tells of this moment. Again, the marshal nodded and smiled. He appeared to be pleased with our charming son.

Some of the men were getting bored, or restless, then. The marshal gave them a stern look and focused on Jason once more. He was all business as he asked again where we were going. When Jason told him that we were going to the Casa de la Verdad, the marshal nodded, and his shoulders seemed to relax some. He asked if we had seen anyone on the road or in the distance as we were driving. Jason told him that he and his troops are the only people that we had seen all day. The marshal looked off in the distance with some visible discomfort. Jason asked him if there was some danger out there. Marshal Villalobos really looked uncomfortable then and said something vague about reports of… merodeadores.

Our son looked into his face and quickly responded with, "Marauders?"

Then, without thinking, he began to ask questions in Spanish. We both smiled at the shocked expressions on the faces of those military men. Abel had cautioned us that some of them do not like Americans to try to speak Spanish to them. Sometimes it is wise not to let them know that we understand what they are saying about us. Presumably, Jason trusted this man enough to reveal this to him now.

Marshal Villalobos was quite surprised, but he recovered and began to speak to Jason at length about something. Kevin and I could only pick out a few words every now and then. Once, our son looked at us as if to say, "It's OK. Be cool." Both men's faces were serious, and Jason nodded and asked him several questions. As they spoke, I noticed that the men were looking out in the desert as if expecting someone else to come along at any moment. Jason and Villalobos were also glancing around nervously. At one point, the marshal shrugged and motioned all around the area vaguely as if to say, "What can I do?"

The military men were getting restless again, and Villalobos seemed to be ready to send us on our way. Thank God. Jason motioned to us and extended his hand in a clear invitation for Villalobos to come and meet us. The marshal looked over and gave us a smile and a nod before he approached the car. Kevin opened his door to stand, and some of the men aimed their guns at him. Jason walked over and opened my door for me, putting his arm around me in a protective manner. I know that he felt me trembling because he gave me a little squeeze, as if to say, "It's OK, Mom. I've got you." He introduced us, and Kevin shook hands with the Marshal. I did not offer my hand because Abel said that was not proper behavior in the Spanish culture. However, I smiled and nodded at him in a reserved manner. Women were not supposed to be too friendly or show too many teeth, you know. "When in Rome…"

Jason asked Villalobos to come to the mission with us and have some refreshments before they went back on patrol.

Kevin also said, "Marshal, you and your men are all welcome to come to The House of Truth. Our friends would be honored to have you share a meal with us. Please feel free to come there anytime. You will be our guest."

The marshal was nodding, but I could tell that he was reluctant to accompany us to the mission. He was probably a devout Catholic. It is the predominant religion in Mexico. At any rate, we certainly did not want to make them uncomfortable with us. After a short pause, the marshal said that we should get back on the road in order to arrive safely before dark. I was puzzled by that remark but hesitant to speak when I know that the custom is for women to be silent. All the men seemed to be waiting for something, also. However, for some reason, none of them wanted to say anything about what they were waiting for. Marshal Villalobos spoke to his men, and they began to prepare to leave.

The four of us remained for an awkward moment. There seemed to be something left unspoken.

Villalobos said, "Jason, you are a fine man. You have shown courage and wisdom today. I hope that my own sons will one day be as helpful to me as you are to your Mama and Papa. You honor them and the God that you serve. I speak as a father and as a friend. I ask your pardon if these words are too personal…"

I could not keep the tears in my eyes from spilling down my cheeks. I guess Kevin felt pretty much the same way, too. When Jason could speak, he thanked him and told him that his Mama and Papa had reared him to be a good man.

The marshal nodded to both of us and spoke one last time as he gripped Jason's hand in both of his. "Vaya Con Dios, mi Amigo."

We all waved to the military men assembled and drove on toward the mission. However, as soon as the car doors closed, we started asking Jason about what the marshal was telling him all that time. Jason gave us the, "Loose translation," which was much shorter than I expected. He said that the men were patrolling because there were report of some illegal activities out in this area. He said that many criminals think of American tourists as easy victims. He was concerned because this is such a large area, and there are not enough soldiers to protect everyone. He feels sure that the mission will be safe because all the villagers love Abel and Sierra, and they all look out for each other. That is why he wanted us to get there as quickly as we can. There is always safety in numbers. His dad and I both said how much we liked the marshal and that it was good to know that he was an honest, God-fearing man. Jason said that he was amazed to have felt such a strong connection to Villalobos. It was like he already knew him or something.

We both encouraged him to pray for the Marshal and to expect those kinds of meetings throughout his whole lifetime. God definitely brings people into our lives for His purposes. Sometimes we only get a few short minutes to smile, or nod, or speak the words that someone desperately needs to hear at that very time in their lives. Jason nodded thoughtfully and added that he thought the marshal was looking for something out there today.

Kevin said, "He was, son. He was looking for God. Marshal Villalobos saw Him in you, just as your Mama and I did. I think you will see him again."

None of us spoke for a while after that, but I felt as if there were a lot more going on that we did not know about.

The rest of our drive to the mission was uneventful, and we made it to the mission with plenty of daylight left. When Jason told the story of the roadblock, our friends were shocked into silence. Some meaningful glances that passed between the three of them that made me wonder if something else was going on. However, I trusted my son's judgement and we were all safe and sound now. Abel suggested that we eat early and get to bed early, so we would be rested and ready to begin working in the morning. As he prayed over our food, he asked God to bless the marshal and his men for his kindness to us that day. He prayed for Villalobos to prosper and for God to protect him as he served in such a dangerous job. We all agreed, but I silently asked God to help the marshal find everything he was looking for. After a delicious meal, we each went to our rooms and got ready for bed. It was a beautiful, cool, starlit night that made us truly thankful to be there.

Bright and early the next morning, the men began working on the addition to the small chapel. They were to build another room that would serve as a children's church on Sunday. During the week, it would be used as a schoolroom. The missionaries would leave two bedrolls and some fresh water there every night. They often had some stranger sleep in the small chapel. Most of them left long before anyone saw them. They are shy and do not want to draw attention to themselves. More importantly, they were afraid they would get in trouble for being there. Nothing could be further from the truth. Abel and Sierra had such kind hearts that they would only try to help any wayfaring stranger. On occasion, parents had brought sick children to the mission in the middle of the night. In cases like that, the chapel was used as a hospital unit where the whole family could stay as long as needed. The new room would serve as an infirmary, a homeless shelter, and many other purposes to benefit the whole community. Kevin was able to do everything from designing the room, to digging the foundation, to building the structure, and finally roofing it. However, he does not like to do plumbing and electrical. That part was not necessary because of the lack of power and facilities for those things.

After three days of hard manual labor, my two guys were ready for some R and R. We got detailed instructions on when and where to find everything we wanted to see. They told us to be at God's Vision late in the evening because of the fabulous sunsets. We had flashlights and lanterns to help us get back to the car safely. In addition, there would be a full moon tonight, giving us even more light.

Tourists and locals had been successfully making this pilgrimage for years without a single incident, so we had no reason to worry. You cannot imagine how excited I was to be on my way to God's Vision.

We left the mission around three o'clock in the afternoon because we wanted to make another stop on the way. At last, I was going to see the wonderful place that had been drawing me down here for years. When we got to an area that looked like a lunar landscape, I knew that we were at Piedras Extranas, the Extraordinary Rocks. We all climbed on them and took many pictures of the unique formations. They looked like they were literally from another world or something. There is nothing else like these huge rocks anywhere. After we had been there for thirty or forty-five minutes, I began to feel… "Uneasy." I cannot really explain how I was feeling or why I felt I felt that way. I just know that something was "Wrong" with me. When I reminded the guys about the time, we got back in the car and headed on toward God's Vision. You will be shocked to know that I was not feeling excitement as I should have been. This trip was my dream come true, and yet I was filled with a sense of foreboding.

Kevin must have sensed that something was wrong because he looked at me quizzically and said, "Are you going to Barf?"

I have world-class motion sickness and have even had to pull over when I was the one driving. I looked at him, and tears filled my eyes as I tried to explain that something was wrong. He slowed down really slow and asked again if I needed to pull over. I just shook my head no and tried to self-talk myself out of the dreadful anxiety that was overwhelming me.

Jason said that he could tell something was wrong because I was not as happy as I should have been to finally get to see God's Vision with my own two eyes. I tried to reassure him (and myself) that everything was fine, but we all knew that was not true. However, I did not want to ruin this trip for anyone when we had waited for so long and so many people knew what a big deal this was for us. Kevin came to Mexico, for goodness sake! That in itself was an enormous sacrifice for him. Then those two had worked like rented Army Mules for days, doing the work of five grown men, just so I could come here now. What in the world was wrong with me? Why was my skin goose-pimpled and my hair standing on end? Dear Lord, please help me understand and/or feel better.

A Jackrabbit jumped out from the side of the road and I jumped and screamed a little bit. My poor husband slammed on the brakes and almost wrecked the car, looking at me like I had suddenly grown a second or third head.

Jason said, "Dad, can you just find a place to stop for a minute?" He took off his seat belt and leaned way forward to search my face.

Trying to hide my fear (fear?) and embarrassment from him was unwise and unsuccessful. He said that he could tell something was really upsetting me because I was so pale, and my hands were trembling, too. He put his left hand on my arm and asked me to please step out of the car for a minute and get some air. Maybe it was not car sickness… Maybe I was coming down with Montezuma's Revenge or some other South of the Border sickness? He suggested that we all get out into the cool evening air and relax, just relax.

He nodded at me and said, "Come on, Mom. It's OK. Everything is OK. Let's get some air. OK? I'll get your door. Dad, do we have any cold water left in that ice chest? Could it be too much sun or maybe this altitude bothering you, Mom?"

Kevin had pulled over between two large boulders and was opening the trunk to get cold water. Jason opened my door and held out his hand to help me get up, as if I were terminally ill or something. I hated to see him so worried about me. Why couldn't I shake this terrible feeling of impending doom that was looming over me? What was wrong with me? If there is one thing I cannot stand, it's some hypochondria -type person ruining everyone else's good time! Now here I was doing the very thing I hate. There was nothing wrong with me, physically, and I hated to be a wet blanket on our good time. Standing out in the cool air, so close to the trail that would lead us to God's Vision, my whole body just began to shiver. Please Lord, I prayed, take this terrible feeling of death away from me! Death? Why did I pray that?

Without warning, I felt like something large and black swoop down over me! I actually ducked down and cried out in horror as it passed above my head. Kevin and Jason had been standing several feet away from me looking toward the setting sun. They were having a rock -throwing contest, trying to hit a certain rock a certain distance away. Kevin can throw like a major leaguer, and Jason had now surpassed his dad in speed. Kevin was still a better shot, though. When I screamed, they both turned toward me and saw me crouching down by the car as if something was trying to attack me.

"Get in the car. Get in the car! Now!" I yelled.

As I opened the passenger door, I literally felt something dark and evil coming toward us from the canyon. The boys were hurrying now, and Jason kept looking back over his shoulder, toward God's Vision.

Kevin jumped in the car, and even though my voice was shaking and I was semi-crying, I said, "Get us out of here fast! Don't stop for anything. I mean it, Kevin. I don't care what happens; do not stop this car for anyone or anything!"

Thank God, he did not need an explanation; Thank God, he did not want to try to reason with me. Thank God, he drove like a bat out of Hell to get us as far away from there as fast as he could.

Jason had turned completely around in the back seat and was watching...something? What had he seen?

His voice was deadly calm when he said, "Dad, if someone steps out in the road and tries to stop us, You Keep Going. Do not stop, Dad. Even if you have to take him out, you gotta just keep going. Mom, be watching for anything that might be coming from the rocks. If you see anything, anything at all, you tell Dad, so we can get ready. I'm watching the back in case...IT (?) follows us... But Dad, no matter what happens, do not stop this car."

While watching the rocks on both sides of the road, I fumbled around in the glove compartment for some kind of weapon. In Texas, we always have guns in the vehicle. Sadly, in Mexico, only the criminals are armed. I found a Buck Knife, which I opened and placed on the console between Kevin and me. Then I found another one under my car seat. When I tried to hand it to Jason, he already had one open in his hand.

He said, "Great, Mom, now we are all armed. Do not be afraid to use that if you have to."

Kevin asked what in the Blue Blazes was going on. What had we seen? Who, or what, was out there? Neither of us had any answers to those questions, but I knew that I had to say something to help my husband understand what had happened to me. Just as I gathered some words of explanation, I caught a glimpse of a vehicle up ahead. There was a red pick-up parked off the road among the boulders. Again, both Jason and I told Kevin not to stop, Even if he had to run over a person, we urged him to keep on going until we were safe. He gripped the wheel with great resolve and never took his eyes off the road ahead. We all braced ourselves for whatever might occur in the next few seconds. Certainly, we all prayed for God's protection from whatever Satan was trying to do to us. There was no doubt in my mind that there was something evil out there, and it had targeted us. We flew by that truck like we had been shot out of a cannon! All three of us remained hyper-vigilant for the next several miles, until Jason turned around in his seat and heaved a sigh of relief.

There are no words to describe what had spooked me so badly back in the Extraordinary Stones. My son and spouse seemed to be waiting for me to speak, so words just began to gush out of my mouth. I cried while telling them how that Dark Presence had rushed over me, trying to destroy me. In my spirit, I knew it wanted to destroy all of us. Kevin asked me if it was gone now. I nodded and said I was feeling calmer now that we were safe from it. He asked how I knew that we were safe, and all I could say was that I just knew, in my spirit that IT was gone now. My husband looked intently at our son and asked him what he saw.

Jason met his eyes in the rear-view mirror and said, "Dad, I didn't really see anything at all. But, I felt something. I felt something coming toward us from the canyon. It was something big and black, like a bear or a dinosaur or something." He stopped talking and looked back over his shoulder again. "Mom's right; it's gone now, though. I feel safer here, too."

Kevin asked if that red pick-up had anything to do with anything. Neither one of us could answer that truthfully, but all three of us had some kind of bad feeling associated with it. Jason said that he thought someone would have come out of the rocks there by the truck and try to stop us and kill us. As strange as it sounds, we all agreed that Death had stalked us today. We talked about it all the way back to the House of Truth. Periodically, one of us would look back or ask if anyone felt IT again. We thanked God repeatedly for giving us the discernment to get away from that evil thing out there. I asked Jason why he had said it was black and why he said it was like a bear or dinosaur. He explained that those two images came to him when they were throwing rocks.

"Weren't you scared?" I asked.

He thought for a minute and said that he felt worried, maybe anxiety, but he was not truly afraid until I screamed. "When I saw that black thing swoop down over you, Mom, I was terrified."

I gaped at him and asked him how he saw it. Again, he said he did not actually see it, but he knew that it had swooped down on me, trying to drive me toward the canyon. That is when he knew that death was coming over the canyon wall toward us!

All of this was just too much for us to believe. Nevertheless, we knew that it was true. Kevin checked the rear-view one more time and asked if Jason would drive for a while. He was just totally wiped out by all that had transpired in the last few hours.

When he had stretched out in the back seat, he asked us to tell him the whole thing again. "Slowly this time, and say everything that comes into your minds. Even if it sounds stupid, tell us about it. OK? Tell us anything that you saw, heard, or felt when it was happening. Also, tell us any conclusions that you have come to about the whole thing. I want both of you to take your time and tell us as much as you can about this EVIL/DEATH thing back there. OK?"

We both agreed, and as I told my part, they both listened intently. Then Jason told his part while we absorbed all we could from his description of events. Again, Kevin asked us both if we felt safe now that we had gotten so far away from IT. Both of us agreed that we felt safe now, Thank God.

For some reason, I felt like Kevin knew something that he had not told us yet. I asked him, "Honey, what about you? What did you see, or hear, or feel back there?"

Jason looked at his dad in the rear-view mirror, and then he pulled off to the side of that narrow road and stopped. We both turned around to look at Kevin, waiting for him to speak. The car was in park, but the motor was running, so the headlights were on, and all the dash lights, also.

Kevin said, "I could hear something weird. It was like a heavy breathing, coming from the canyon. I thought it was the wind, or waterfalls, or…something. When I threw the first rock, I just wanted to hear it rattle around to see if it sounded natural. I also wanted to see if there was anything over there. I mean, like animals or something. I sensed that something was coming, but I refused to believe that anything was wrong. I did not want to ruin this trip for you. You have wanted to go to God's Vision for so many years… I could not imagine not going there now. Then when you screamed for us to get in the car, something like a black cape flew at me and tried to push me toward the canyon. That… thing (?) was pure evil. Jason, I know you felt something, too, because when Mom screamed, we both knew that we had to get out of there. We knew, in our spirits, that our lives were in danger. Thank God that we ran when we did.

I only wish that I had been more in tune to the spirits there. I should have protected you better, Honey, but I just could not believe that anything evil could be at God's Vision."

Jason and I both assured him that he did not need to feel so bad, because neither of us had said anything either. We all felt exactly the same way about God's Vision, that nothing evil could be out there. It was getting late, and all of us were very exhausted from that terrible experience. Kevin said for Jason to go ahead and get back on the road while he prayed. My husband gave thanks to God for getting us out of there safely and for His love and protection, not just today, but always. It was a beautiful prayer, and we all felt His peace come over us. In a while, Jason said that from now on, all of us have to agree to tell others when there is something wrong in the spiritual world. We agreed that we would always listen to and respect each other's Feelings.

We were very close to the mission when I asked the boys what we were going to tell Abel and Sierra. How could we tell them that we did not even go to God's Vision because some evil spirit had tried to kill us? There is no way to ease into that conversation, but we knew that we had to tell them the truth. My son and I told Kevin to start the explanation and then both of us would tell our parts, too. We were ready, but when we drove up, all the lights were out in their rooms, so we just went on to bed. We had a big family hug first, and said how much we love each other. After Kevin turned out the lights, he asked me if I felt OK, and if I felt safe now. I told him that everything was fine, now and I did not feel any evil spirits or anything wrong. We fell asleep right away.

It seemed like it was just a matter of minutes when I woke up with Abel knocking on the door. He was calling for us to come down quickly. He asked if we were OK, and Kevin told him that we were fine and would be down in a minute. Abel immediately started banging on Jason's door asking him to come down right away, also. Our son stepped out of his room just as we walked out of ours. We all looked sleepy-eyed and tired as we mumbled, asking about what could be going on at this hour of the morning. Maybe someone was sick or needed help?

When we opened the outside door, we saw the Humvee with three military men fanning out across the field in front of the mission. One other man was walking around toward the back of the house. We could hear Abel talking to someone as we walked down the porch toward the front door. Marshal Villalobos had removed his hat and was wringing it in his hands as we came into his line of sight. Jason was leading the way, and the marshal rushed forward and hugged him as if he would his own son! Jason embraced the older man and acted as if this was a common occurrence.

"Madre de Dios," gasped Villalobos, and he immediately began to ask him questions… in Spanish.

Our son had placed his hand on the marshal's arm and was motioning for him to go into the house and sit down.

When Jason turned to us, he said, "Let me find out what all this is about, and then I can tell you guys in a minute… OK? Just give me some time to figure things out. I'm sure it is all going to be all right."

Abel and Sierra were coming out of the kitchen with coffee and water, asking for everyone to please sit down and explain what had happened last evening. We three looked at the marshal, but all three of them were looking at us! They wanted us to tell them what had happened! Now all three of us were looking at each other, too, wondering what we could possibly know that would matter to Villalobos. All six of us started trying to speak at the same time. We were all asking questions and looking at each other for help. This had turned into a madhouse.

Finally, Abel stood up and said to Kevin, "Please tell us what happened when you went to God's Vision yesterday afternoon. Marshal Villalobos came here at two o'clock in the morning asking me if you three were safe. He is investigating some murders and thinks that you three may have seen something that can help him solve this case. He wants to know where you were every moment, and why you got back here so late. You must tell him every detail of the evening. Kevin; this is very serious. Do you understand?"

You could have knocked me over with a feather! What in the world, could we possibly have seen? What could we know about these murderers? Surely, we are not suspects. Dear Lord.

Some invisible communication must have passed between the four men, because Kevin nodded at Abel and stood to tell where we were, at what time, and what occurred there. He spoke slowly and clearly, wanting to make sure that the marshal was understanding everything he said. When he got to the part about my feeling, "Bad," he said that he wanted me to explain this part, and then, he wanted Jason to tell his part after I was finished. We were all nervous about explaining the "evil spirit" events, but we had to tell everything now. When I finished talking, all of them had dumbfounded looks on their faces. Like Kevin, I had been speaking very slowly to make sure the marshal was clear about what I was saying. They all were sitting in shocked silence when Jason began his narrative.

We had all mentioned the red pick-up truck, but our son told the marshal that we wondered if the truck had anything to do with the "death" spirit at God's Vision. Villalobos was silent for a minute before he said that he could not comment on that red pick-up truck. He said that he had to speak very carefully because he did not want to suggest anything to us. We could be the only people alive who saw anything out there.

Kevin said, "But, sir, we told you the truth. We did not see anything. We did not witness anything. We left God's Vision like our hair was on fire! There was no other human being in sight when we flew out of there."

Sierra took that moment to ask the marshal if she could prepare breakfast for his men and the rest of us while we finished talking. He was very grateful and gave her permission to go and cook.

I knew that I had to stay and answer questions, but I wanted to help her out in the kitchen. Jason asked the marshal to explain everything he could to us, assuring him that we had told him all we knew about being at God's Vision.

He looked him in the face and asked, "Marshal, how did you know that we were there yesterday? Why did you come here to check up on us? How did you know that we were out late last night? Have you been following us? Are we suspects in these murders that we know nothing about? We don't even know who was murdered, or when, or anything else. Please tell us what is happening, sir." All of us were looking at him like little lost sheep. Surely he knew that we were not murderers!

Marshal Villalobos stood up and cleared his throat before he began to speak. "Friends, I am very sorry to come here like this. It is not my desire to cause any of you fear or sorrow. I have not followed you, and I do not think anyone in this house is a murderer. Our regiment is investigating several murders in this area. We believe that some sort of... diablo (?) devil clan is... killing people for... some terrible ritual. Your pardon, Senora. I try to be...delicate for you. Do not let these words cause you to fear. We have apprehended someone believed to be the leader of this evil group. Last evening, we watched two places that we believed to be target areas. God's Vision was one of those isolated places from which innocent people could easily be abducted. One of our first victims was last seen alive there. That is the reason for my regiment to be stationed out here. You see, we have been trying to patrol a very large area, watching and searching for these devil people. My general ordered us all to keep silent because he did not want too much panic.

When we met at the roadblock, I wanted to warn you, but I must be obedient to my superiors. I thought you would all be safe here at House of Truth. When I heard them describe your automobile over the radio, I was filled with fear for your lives. I left my hiding place to intercept you, and that is when I found the suspects. They were creeping up the canyon trail to abduct you when I arrested them.

It took me hours to get all the things done so that I could leave. I asked the stakeout officers where you had gone, and no one knew. Therefore, I drove out here to see if you all were safe. My deepest apologies to you for not telling you about this danger. My heart would break if you had been harmed by these devils." Most of this speech was made in English; however, Jason had to translate part of it, too.

All of us felt gratified by this man's concern for our safety. Kevin stood and reached out to place his hand on the marshal's shoulder. He told him that God had protected us. God was trying to warn us not to go to God's Vision, but we refused to listen to Him. It was God that had led him to find and capture those devils before they could harm anyone else.

He looked into the marshal's eyes and said, "Be at peace, my friend. Do not concern yourself about warning us any longer. Everything has worked out for our good and God's glory. You are a true friend to come out here, and we deeply appreciate it"

Marshal Villalobos was moved by this speech, as we all were.

In a moment, he said to Kevin, "Senor Carnes, that evil black thing that flew at each one of you… It flew at me, also."

We all gazed at him open-mouthed. Jason said, "Marshal, you mean to say that you knew about that black thing? We were afraid you would think we were crazy if we told you about it. What did you do?" The marshal said that he cried out to God. Wow.

Sierra opened the door with two pans of biscuits and said breakfast was ready. I went to the kitchen to help her carry the food, while the men put out more chairs. The marshal went to the door and whistled for his men to come and eat. When we had all gathered around the table, Abel said a lovely prayer thanking God for the marshal and his men. It was a wonderful meal, and all of us were just so thankful to be safe, in God's hands, and in His Vision.

We did get to go back to God's Vision at the end of our visit. None of us felt anything evil out there this time. We stayed there most of the day with Abel and Sierra. That evening, Marshal Villalobos came out with his beautiful wife, Gabriella, and two sons. Those two boys were completely fascinated with Jason, and they talked and laughed like best friends. He really enjoyed their company after two weeks of hard work at the mission. The marshal told us that his superiors had recommended him for a promotion and a substantial raise. Everyone in his department was awestruck by his single-handed capture of the two ringleaders of that evil group. He is confident that all of them would be apprehended very soon, as there were several regiments searching for them. We congratulated him and assured him that he and his men, and his lovely family, would always be in our prayers.

Gabriella spoke softly to Sierra and said that she had heard many wonderful things about The House of Truth, and they wanted to come out and help next weekend. Of course, they were both delighted to hear that. She said that Jesus wanted the boys to learn to help those less fortunate than they are. She told us that he was stunned by Jason's willingness to travel so far and work so hard to help the Mexican villagers.

"We wish for our sons to follow this example of your son. We wish to follow, also. These terrible crimes have shown us how much our people need God." You cannot imagine how blessed we were to hear her say those words.

The sunset over God's Vision was truly magnificent that evening.

As we were getting ready to leave, Jesus said, "Senor Carnes, on that first day, at the roadblock, Jason told me that he wanted to come here for many reasons. He spoke of the mission and wanting to serve God. He also said that his university degree requires a certain months living in a Spanish speaking culture. If you wish for him to come back here, it would be my honor to have him stay with my family, in my home… for as long as he wants to stay. We would be honored to have him. I give you my word that he will be safe with us. I seek your permission to extend this invitation to him before we go from this place tonight."

Wow. Of course, we agreed, and I hugged Gabriella as our husbands shook hands.

Jesus walked over to the edge of the canyon and spoke to the boys. Both shook hands with Jason and began walking back to their mother. Jesus put his hand on Jason's shoulder and spoke to him for a moment. He nodded and the huge smile on his face told us that he liked the idea of spending more time down here with the marshal.

The American Way

SOMETIMES YOUR ONLY AVAILABLE
TRANSPORTATION IS A LEAP OF FAITH...
MARGARET SHEPHERD

I work for the Department of Defense, but I just call it the DOD. It sounds military, like maybe weapons, ammunition, or something intriguing. However, my job is not intriguing. I am a bus driver. That's right; the DOD pays me to drive a bus to their job site. It's out in a remote desert area where they used to "dump" stuff. When I say "stuff," I mean lots of stuff. None of us really knows how many thousands of acres of stuff are dumped out there. I love the desert and take my family camping out there as often as I can. Until I took this job, I never knew about this dangerous dumpsite. It has been a well-kept secret until just recently.

We have been told that it's all old military stuff but not weapons or explosives or anything like that. It is supposedly detritus from military bases all over the world. People are quite upset about a Nuclear Waste section. You know, people are afraid of things they do not understand. Mainstream America certainly does not understand anything about Nuclear Waste. Some people do not even realize how Einstein, Hiroshima, and Nuclear power plants are related. I did not know either…before I applied for this position. Because of the nature of risk associated with any type of nuclear activity, we are all required to have a "Q" level security clearance to enter the facility. Basically, that means that you have led a "clean" life with no felony drug or alcohol charges. In general, they do not allow criminal records, or too many tickets (of any kind), or even bad credit. Getting a security clearance to be around Nuclear Waste is evidently hard for most people. Over sixty percent of Americans cannot pass the drug tests required to get into nuclear facilities. Imagine that.

Regardless of all that, The U. S. government wants this whole area cleaned up and the president has thrown millions of dollars at this particular dump ground. Believe me when I say he never lets anyone forget it either. This clean-up/recovery has created thousands of jobs in this state, and we are all grateful for it. There are employees from all over the globe on my bus every day. It is pretty awesome for me to be involved in this whole thing. On top of all that, who doesn't want our "Back Forty" to be reclaimed and useful? It is a real good thing for all of us.

As I said, I am a bus driver. My company wants me to be polite and respectful to everyone at all times. I always am. My Mom taught me that; it used to be The American Way. According to company policy, I can be "friendly," but I must remain impersonal with our clients. It is my opinion that they do not want personal relationships to cause us to compromise their rules. When someone says, "Good morning," or "How are you?" or "Thank you" I respond appropriately, but I do not initiate lengthy conversations. I recognize people, but I do not know their names. I must walk the line between friendly and aloof. I don't mind not talking while I drive. Not talking allows me to listen more.

I listen to people talk all day long. Of course, I don't let them know that I'm listening. I have heard some hysterical snippets of conversation from time to time.

One guy was on the phone with his wife and said, "A WHAT? She put a what? In her ear? Good Lord! Where in the Hell did she even find a garbanzo bean?"

I had to laugh remembering some of the stunts my own kids had pulled. Another man had been whispering very intensely into his flip phone for several minutes. Suddenly, he just broke the thing in half and stuffed the pieces in his backpack. You could have heard a pin drop on that bus. There was another time when one lady was in line to get on the bus. After a few minutes of furious whispering, she threw her phone down, stomped on it and then threw the pieces out into the desert. Some of us nearly fell out laughing. Others clapped and whistled. We all wished we had the grit to do the same thing. When she got on the bus, she dropped into a perfect curtsy and earned another round of applause. It was fantastic.

I sympathize with these people. It is stressful to be working out here in the middle of nowhere. Not to mention all the razor wire fences, security guards, and restricted areas. This is not your average work environment. My employers are concerned about stress and its effects on us. Every bus has a hidden camera and a microphone that looks like a pair of ear buds. It is hanging right behind me.

My passengers all seem to be so important and full of mysterious facts about all that stuff out there. They are living the great American Dream and working on the president's high-level special project. I am just the bus driver that picks them up and drives them through forty-five miles of desert every morning at 5 a. m. I am not complaining. This is a wonderful job, and they are paying me big bucks to do it. There is no traffic, and the worst thing that can happen is some kind of vehicle failure. We all feel comfortable and safe working here.

The DOD is extremely focused on safety. We are required to attend a Safety Meeting every week. It is usually only about an hour long and painless. I will have to admit that I have gotten a lot out of those meetings. This is my first driving job, so I have plenty of things to learn. You cannot believe all the checks we make on our "coaches" each day. We do much more than kick a tire and check the oil. We have lists of self-checks and peer checks that require conscious effort on my part. My employers send Safety Observers on "ride-longs" regularly. We have extensive training programs and Fail-Safe scenarios for any kind of emergency that any deviant mind might come up with. I am responsible for my passengers, my coach, and myself. I take all of those things very seriously. It seems unlikely that anyone could present a security threat out here.

It is still dark as night when I get to the bus lot at 4:30 in the morning. The night shift has my coach gassed up, inspected, and ready to go before I ever arrive. They allow us thirty minutes a day for early check-in. I guess some wise guy may have tried being there an hour or more before time. Oh, one more thing about being on site at 4:30… we must be awake. That's right; some joker also claimed time for sleeping on site. Wow! What will they think of next?

My bus leaves the lot at exactly five a. m. Do not be late because that is part of my contractual agreement. I am sworn to leave at that time, no matter what. Now, if someone is desperately trying to get to me as I'm leaving, I will stop. It's my judgment call. I want to be fair to everyone, and so far, I have not had any complaints. However, I am a punctual person, and I expect others to be also. There are four bus runs each day for each bus driver. This means that when someone misses a bus, they will lose two hours of pay...guaranteed. Each company has their own policies, but there is an oversight committee that strictly regulates tardiness. My schedule is to leave the lot at five, seven thirty, nine thirty, and my last run is at eleven thirty. I get back to the lot around one p. m., and I am free to leave then. I drive these four runs six days a week. But, the crews operate 24/7. That is right; most companies do not ever let their whole crew off for even one day a week. There is always someone from every crew working. They are deadly serious about cleaning this mess up.

There are four buses running outside the gate and four that run inside, too. With eight drivers on days and four alternates, we have not had any buses fail to run yet. Our company is very professional and thorough. Our coaches are relatively new and well-maintained. They are clean and comfortable, too. Thank God, because as you well know, eight hours is a long time to drive. So far, everything has run smoothly on all shifts.

People do get upset if they forget something because I cannot turn around. This bus absolutely will not turn around. No matter what you forget, I am not turning around. I can be fired if I do. It is only a big deal if you forget your badge. You cannot work without your badge. In fact, you cannot even get inside the gate without it. So, I feel really sorry for anyone who does not have it with them.

They have signs all over the place that say **Do You Have Your Badge?**

Your badge is the key to your paycheck. I try to remember to ask before I leave for the work site. I wear a badge myself. It is a requirement for every employee, even the bus drivers.

The whole badge thing is very ingenious because it is more than an ID. It has your picture and name, the company you work for, your employee ID Number, and two supervisors' names with their phone numbers. It also has a code that will allow you to enter places that you have been granted clearance for. Isn't it incredible how much information is contained in that little silver strip? I am constantly amazed by the modern technological advances of the last twenty years. This is basically a huge construction/demolition site, even though it is much more complicated than that. Along with some type of radioactive trash, there are harmful chemicals leaching into the earth and dangerous metals decomposing out here, too. It must be cleaned up. Some people call it remediation. I like that term because it implies that they are fixing things up like new.

We are all intrigued by the idea of radioactive materials being stored out there. Back in the old days, the scientists had no idea what a Pandora's Box the Atomic Bomb really was. The military did not realize how to use that power for anything other than destruction. Thank God, we are now able to produce electricity with it. Anyway, they brought in Radiation Protection Technicians; (we call them RPs) which are required to be present whenever there might be any radioactivity in anything they dig up. They control access to those areas, and everyone entering must be closely monitored.

Every time I hear something that I do not understand, I look it up on the internet. I want to know as much as I can about this whole operation. When I look up things about this site, they say there are nuclear, biological, and chemical concerns out here. They are always extremely vigilant about all of them, but nuclear takes precedence over everything else. There are special concerns about locating, containing, and disposing of all radioactive materials because of the danger of "Dirty Bombs." Some nut case could, (theoretically), gather up some stuff and contaminate the whole southwestern United States. Scary.

We all take safety and security very seriously. We get continuing training about security breaches and unauthorized intruders every other month. I have never seen so much security in my life. We have guards everywhere. The whole perimeter fence is electrified with little "Booby-Traps," ever so many feet. Every square inch of fence line is under constant surveillance by cameras, drones, and human eyes. It is the most intense scrutiny I have ever heard of. Those security guards do drills all the time, and it is quite impressive. They even have the helicopters and black Suburbans show up out here. I really like this D. O. D. stuff. It makes me feel like I am a part of something important. It is safe and fun. The workers are happy and thankful to have such good paying jobs in this economy. We never hear of problems or injuries. Thank God.

My company has some very strict rules about protocol. Any time anything out of the ordinary happens, I am required to report it. We have training about aberrant behavior all the time. I wear a tiny microphone at all times, and every coach has a camera mounted on the front dashboard. Nobody is supposed to know about the microphone or camera. Of course, everyone knows that nothing goes unnoticed. We are always told that if we see something, say something. They also tell us not to proceed in the face of uncertainty. Always have a questioning attitude. Do not accept things just because that is the way we always do it. At the same time, always follow procedure. Do not improvise. Follow the procedure at all times. Those things are drilled into our heads.

So, if someone seems to be unusually stressed, angry, or belligerent, I must report it to my company via the microphone on my collar. Every coach has a different code word that signals distress. That code word changes without notice. Pretty smart. I have never had any problems to report. If someone gets rowdy, all I do is look at them in the rearview mirror. They settle right down. Our company will not tolerate any profanity or off-color comments about anything. It is common knowledge that if a worker is reported for a bus violation, he will be escorted off-site immediately. It is tough to get your foot in the door here, so most everyone wants to stay in their company's good graces. Good behavior makes my job easier.

I certainly do not want to be responsible for anyone losing his job. Nevertheless, I will do what I have to do. Ultimately, I am responsible for what happens on this bus. and I want everything to end up well. So, I may as well get on with the story of the Bus Ride from Hell. I will give you all the information that I can remember. You can draw your own conclusions. Remember, information does not always equal knowledge. No one can really know what that ride was like for me. I have a hard time explaining how I feel about it, myself. Everyone on the bus recalls something different. There were even five or six different descriptions of the same terrorist. Looking back on the Day of Disaster, I promise you that I did my best. I was just juggling as fast as I could.

That day started off just like any other. Then, at the last minute, Doug, one of the night shift drivers, jumped on my five a.m. run. He immediately sat down right behind me and moved my little earbuds, so he could lean close and talk to me. I must have been giving him some "What the???" looks because he said that he forgot some stuff on his bus inside. He looked very tired and distracted.

I murmured some sympathetic "Doesn't that just figure?" and "What a Bummer" comments.

Doug sat back and started texting on his phone. I assumed that he was telling his wife that he would be late. Do not forget, it is forty-five minutes to the site. Then, its forty-five minutes back to the depot, and then at least thirty more minutes back to the outskirts of town. We do not ever want to forget anything.

I had only driven about ten minutes when Doug got up from his seat moved closer to the door.

He kind of crouched down into the stairwell, looked me in the eyes and said, "Sandra, I don't want to hurt anyone. But, I will kill you and every person on this bus if you do not do exactly as I tell you to. Your cameras and microphones are disabled. Do you understand me?"

Dear God. I instantly understood what he was saying and a whole lot more. My heart started banging out of my chest, and fear clouded all my reason.

I guess that I was instinctively slowing down because he told me "Get back up to speed. Right now." He was talking in a low, steady voice that only I could hear. "Sandra, I do not need you to drive this bus. I can drive it myself and do what I have to do without you. Do you understand me? If you try anything, I will kill you. No matter what else happens, you will be dead. Do you believe me, Sandra? It is absolutely imperative that you know that I will kill you if you do anything that I don't like. I will shoot you and the two people behind you if you try anything. Nod your head if you believe me."

I nodded and looked into his eyes for a second. There were no lights on, and nobody was home, either. He meant every word he was saying. His voice was completely devoid of emotion. Like a robot.

Full realization of Doug's intentions hit me like a bolt of lightning, and I was horrified beyond belief. We were all dead. I just knew that we were not going to be hostages. We were going to be headlines. He was going to kill us all, no matter what I did, or did not do. We were all dead. He was looking at his phone periodically. Maybe other terrorists were on other buses and we had to rendezvous out here somewhere? He was talking to me again, so I tried to act as if I knew what he had said.

God forbid that my actions would cause him to kill other people...."So when I tell you to turn, girl, you had better turn without any crap. You understand me? Do not try to be a hero, Sandra. You will not live long enough to enjoy it. If you want to live long enough to see your family again, you just do exactly what I tell you to do exactly when I tell you to do it. You had better believe what I'm saying to you. Nod your head if you want to keep on breathing." I nodded.

My mind was racing like mad. What should I do? I could not think, but I could not stop thinking either. I tried to keep my eyes veiled so he would not snap and start killing people. I prayed in a wildly hysterical manner that God probably hears all the time. Hopefully, He would hear and understand and work some miracle in the next few seconds. Doug was texting someone, now. I suspected that Doug was just a puppet. Someone else was probably pulling his strings. He was expendable to these people. They would sacrifice anyone for their own purposes. We saw it on the news all the time. Our time was running out. There was no way off this bus. We were all dead. What could I do?

Doug looked at me as if trying to read my thoughts. I just kept my eyes on the road and tried to act as if I was being compliant. He spoke quietly again telling me that I was doing really well, and if I just kept on being good, everything would be fine. Just fine. I wish I could believe him. I can't. He seemed so calm that no one else would ever suspect that he wass threatening all our lives. He simply appeared to be visiting with the other bus driver.

Now, he looked at his phone again and said to me, "In a couple of minutes, I'm going to tell you to take your foot off the gas. Do it slowly and get ready to turn right when I say. I do not care what any of these passengers says or does. I am watching you; I only care what you do. You do exactly as I say, and I will take care of the passengers. Do not try to screw around, Sandra. I will kill you and those two people behind you. Believe what I say. Your life depends on it. You understand?" I nodded.

I did not know how many seconds or minutes we had left. Why was I turning right? There was absolutely nothing out here but sand and cactus. It was not even daylight yet. When I looked at the clock on my dashboard, I was shocked to see that I had only been driving for thirteen minutes. Unbelievable. I looked at Doug quickly and he was intent on his phone. I made a fast glance in my rearview mirror, too. No one seemed to be aware of this crisis. However, one passenger was staring at me as I looked back. I saw that man all the time, but I did not know him. I made sure that no expression crossed my face. I did not want to cause any harm to him or anyone else. Let these people stay calm as long as possible.

Part of me wanted to try to reason with Doug. However, I knew that I could not trust my voice or my eyes to be obedient long enough to fool him. If I asked him, "Why are you doing this, Doug?" He might shoot people just to shut me up. I kept driving in silence.

His right hand moved toward his waist. No! God No! Not now, please. I was still trying to pray.

He put his phone in his coat pocket and said, "Sandra, it's almost time for you to take your foot off the gas. When I stand up, you do it. You understand me? When I stand up, you take your foot off the gas. Nice and slow."

He started unzipping his coat, and my heart almost burst out of my chest. Now, I could see the wires and something metal. Tears filled my eyes, and my hands shook so badly that I could hardly hold onto the wheel. God, Please help...I blinked the tears out of my eyes and glanced back again. The guy behind me was still looking at me, and this time he nodded; as if he was saying, "Go ahead, Sandra." He cut his eyes toward Doug and nodded again.

I quickly looked away from him before my eyes or face could give me away. Oh My God. He knows. This guy knows.

I blinked tears out of my eyes again, and Doug looked at me closely. "You are doing very well, Sandra. It's OK. We are almost ready to turn off. When I stand up, you just take your foot off the gas, nice and slow. OK? It's almost over. Get ready. Ok?"

I wanted to believe him. Surely, they were not going to kill all of these people. I was just being hysterical. I must be wrong. Then he unzipped his coat some more, and I knew that we were all dead. This man was going to destroy all our lives and sacrifice his own, too.

He started to get up, and a small sob escaped from my throat. He instantly turned his dark, empty eyes on me and said, "You believe what I told you?" I nodded.

When he stood up, I slowly took my foot off the gas. Doug opened his coat, and I saw all the explosives and blinking red lights on his chest. He kept looking at me and said, "Turn right, Sandra. Nice and easy. Do just like I told you." Slowly, I started to turn the wheel right. We were bumping over the sandy shoulder, but I was afraid to put on the brakes.

Now, I was hearing some of the passengers' voices, and I sensed some movement behind me.

Doug suddenly yelled, "Allah be praised!"

Then he held up some kind of a detonator in his right hand. When he raised his right arm, I hit the gas pedal as hard as I could and turned the wheel left as hard as I could. At the same time, I opened the door and Doug rolled out. He was grabbing at the air frantically, but he hit the bottom step hard and bounced out. Some bloodthirsty revenge part of me wanted to run over him, too. However, I was afraid that he would grab onto the bus and still blow us all up. So, I turned the wheel until we were back on the road and drove as fast as I could away from him. Almost immediately, there was an ear-shattering explosion and the brightest light I have ever seen. The whole sky was lit up as dust and sand filled the air around us. Some of the bus windows blew out, and the whole bus rocked from side to side. I drove even faster, cried, and prayed while total chaos erupted among my passengers.

I could hear people screaming, now. Some were yelling into their phones, but some were just screaming. I am sure that I was in shock, but I just kept driving. I guess God helped me keep the bus on the road until all the emergency vehicles got to us. I was shaking so badly that I thought I would have a stroke or something. Suddenly, I realized that one of my passengers was standing behind me with his hands on my shoulders. He bent low and spoke quietly to me. His lips were almost touching my ear. How long had he been there?

He was just saying soothing things like, "We're OK, now. Everything is OK. You did so good. You saved us all. It's OK. Everyone is safe. He's gone and we're all OK."

When his words finally sunk into my brain, and I realized that dozens of cop cars had surrounded us, I took my foot off the gas and coasted to a stop.

You know, all these things had happened in a matter of minutes. It seemed like hours since Doug had jumped on my bus. But when I looked at the clock, it had only been twenty minutes. My passengers were still screaming and sobbing, just like I was, myself. I was shaking like a leaf in a hailstorm. The whole world around us had filled up with cop cars. There were helicopters circling us from the air, too. I felt even more frightened when I saw all the guns aimed at us. Again, the guy behind me held my shoulders firmly and kept saying those calming things about all of us being safe now. He shifted around until he was crouched beside me.

He was looking into my eyes now. "You are OK. Everyone is OK. You saved us all. Thank you. You saved us all. It's all OK now. We just have to calm down and help the cops understand what happened to us. Those guys out there don't know who to trust yet. They don't know what's been going on out here. We have to tell them about the terrorist. Ok? Don't be scared. Ok? We are all going to get through this. The worst is over. Just calm down and tell the cops what happened. I'll help you. OK?"

He stood up in front of the bus and yelled real loud, "Everybody be quiet. Stop yelling. Everybody calm down. Calm down. We all need to get off this bus safely. Do what the cops say to do. They don't know what's going on, so don't spook them…"

He was cut short by an extremely loud bullhorn telling us all to put our hands behind our heads and stay seated. He sat back down behind me again and told me to relax because this could take some time. They made their announcement several times before they ordered me to open the door, keep my hands up, and sit back down. I obeyed immediately.

There must have been two hundred guns and lights trained on us the whole time. I was so wiped out that I could barely keep my arms up. However, I certainly did not want to get shot now. The bullhorn was screeching about identities being verified and when our names are called, to answer the officer, but nobody move. These instructions were repeated again, and again. I was still crying as quietly as possible. We were all scared and did not know what to expect next. This was quite obviously going to take hours to resolve. None of the officers was getting close to the bus. My guess is that they were afraid that one of us was going to shoot them. What a mess. They had no idea who was friend or foe.

After a minute or so, the bullhorn guy said "Sandra Blanchard." I answered, "Here." He told me to keep my hands behind my head and give my ID number. Next, he wanted the bus number and a secret code word for all clear. He asked for my supervisor's name and call number. The next inquiries were about whether we were safe, now. After I answered about twenty more questions, the bullhorn said for me to slowly get to my feet and stand in the doorway with my hands behind my head. When he yelled for me to stop, I stood there with two hundred guns pointed at me. I was blinded by all those lights and trembling all over. The bullhorn said for me to slowly step down to the ground. Again, he asked me if we were all safe, and when I said yes, strong arms lifted me swiftly out of the lights.

I was literally carried away from the bus and put into a black suburban where my supervisor was waiting to identify me. Then I was finally able to relax a little. I blurted out that the terrorist was Doug and that I thought he blew himself up in the desert. At least I hoped that he had blown himself up. I asked if my passengers were all OK. I asked if there were other buses hi-jacked. I ask them to please let my passengers off the bus and take us all home. I was worried about some of them being injured. People could have been cut by flying glass when those windows shattered. Some of them are older; what if they needed medical attention? I told them repeatedly that none of my passengers was dangerous and that Doug was the terrorist.

I had no idea how long it took, but they finally started letting people get off the bus. Every ID was checked, and every badge was swiped on a portable badge reader. Each person was asked several questions and led away from the bus. None of us could take anything off the bus with us. I had to answer about seven million more inquiries, too. I asked again for them to please take my passengers home because we were all exhausted and everyone needed to go potty for sure. One of the FBI guys asked me how I could be sure that none of my passengers was involved with Doug. How could I be sure?

I said, "Look, I really don't know that for one hundred percent sure. But, we have been through a terrible ordeal, and you guys can figure stuff out while we are going potty and getting drinks. You are supposed to be helping us… not making things worse. Please take us back to the bus depot and help us all get home. We need to call our families… Please…" By that time, I was blubbering like a baby.

Our ordeal had begun at five a.m. It was a little after eight when we were told that we could board the police buses that were to take us back to the depot. I had been talked to by so many different officers that my head was just spinning. I had answered the same questions forty or more times. We had been allowed to use the restrooms on alternate buses and given coffee, tea, Gatorade, and water. Now, we were supposed to be allowed to go back to the bus depot. They were not ready to let us go home yet, but we were one step closer, now. Thank God.

They told me that I could ride in the suburban, if I wanted to. However, I said I would rather see my passengers safe and sound before we all went our separate ways.

My supervisor came back over to my Suburban and said "Sandra, two things I need to ask you. Number one is someone is asking to speak to you. Do you feel up to it? And number two is I would like to ride back with you, if you don't mind."

Of course, I said yes to both. We walked over to where the police buses were parked. When I stepped around the first one, all of my passengers were standing there waiting for me. They clapped and cheered and shouted and cried for me for a long time. I hoped they did not want me to say anything…because I could not. I also could not stop crying… for a long time.

After a few minutes, the wonderful man that had helped me stepped out of the crowd and came toward me. He's crying, I was crying, everybody was crying.

I put my trembling hand out to him, and when he took it, we both said "Thank You" at the same exact time.

We hugged, and he held me up and supported me, again. Everybody was cheering and clapping like it was the Super Bowl or something.

I stepped back to look into his eyes as I mumbled something like, "I'm Sandra, I feel like we know each other, but what's your name?" He answered something like, "Hey Sandra, it's really good to know you. I'm Daniel." We smiled, and Daniel helped me climb the steps onto the bus that will take us all "Home."

MONTHS LATER

You cannot begin to know how this terrorist changed all our lives. Doug was a lonely, depressed man with some emotional problems. He had been recruited by a radical Muslim group that was pressuring him to steal some nuclear stuff to build a "dirty bomb." This group rejected him when he failed to gain access to those restricted areas. He then decided to end his own life, and ours, to achieve his fifteen minutes of fame.

It would take forever for me to tell you about the months following that Bus Ride from Hell. We were thrust into a media frenzy that day, which invaded our private lives for months. We have been on the news many times. We have had lots of counseling. Almost all of us have recurring nightmares. Some people have quit their jobs; others have been fired because they cannot bear to get on a bus and go back to work. The Site is requiring all work groups to take additional trauma training. Even the Security Guards have to take some sensitivity training because everyone was so stressed. Even our families were offered psychological counseling.

There have been hundreds of lawsuits. I think that most of them are stupid, greedy, and frivolous. I had to hire a tough lawyer just to keep me from having to testify in every one of those cases. Turns out that I needed a lawyer to protect me from suits blaming me for allowing Doug to get on my bus that day.

Although no one was seriously injured, there were millions of dollars of medical bills. After a few cuts and bruises were treated and released that day, the ambulance chasers had a field day. Local doctors banded together and had a big meeting trying to defuse that situation. Some people dropped their lawsuits after that.

I cannot even begin to tell you the names of all the political groups that were entangled in our case. Every law enforcement agency in the world got involved, and we had to be interrogated by all of them. They even contacted our relatives and friends and started investigating us to see if any of us had been recruited.

It was insanity around here for a while. Things are better, now.

Most of the Medical stuff is quieter.

Most of the Legal stuff is quieter.

Most of the Political stuff is quieter.

Most of the Insurance stuff is quieter.

Most of the Media stuff is quieter.

I am going back to work today.

I have to get my life back.

When a horse throws you, you have to get right back in the saddle.

It's the American Way.

As I drive into the parking lot, dozens of buses start flashing their lights and honking their horns. Hundreds of people clap, whistle, and yell. A huge banner says:

WELCOME BACK SANDRA
WE LOVE YOU

I love them too.

Justice

IF YOU WANT TO CHANGE THE WORLD,
GO HOME AND LOVE YOUR FAMILY...
MOTHER TERESA

Those of you that have worked night shift will identify with my experience here. However, everyone can relate to some degree because the time of day or night is not really relative to the pursuit of justice. All of us must be aware of the world around us. They say that justice is blind, but we certainly cannot afford to live our lives in darkness. Wake up. Pay attention to those around you. Be aware that you can make a difference. You must make a difference. When the bell tolls, it is tolling for you, and for me.

I work for an inventory company. We travel all over the United States taking inventory of various retail businesses. There is quite a large demand for our services because we keep everything on computer. Clients can access their information at any time without having to update or change anything. When they scan their newly delivered products, everything automatically goes into current inventory. This system is very effective and foolproof. We store and backup millions of dollars' worth of inventory for every type of business you can imagine.

Lots of us choose to work nights. There are not as many people to deal with at night. There are not as many customers or personnel to interfere with our jobs. When people see someone that looks like they are working, they pounce like ducks on a June bug. You and I have done it ourselves, dozens of times. We all need help finding the gluten-free cookies, or the natural toothpaste, or whatever it is that is hiding from us at that particular time. Most retail stores are no longer concerned with customer service or satisfaction. They no longer hire enough people to serve the public. They staff for one purpose only, to make money. You know what I'm saying.

After many years of doing this job, I have a specialty. It seems that I am the resident health and beauty aid expert. Do not ask me why. It is very tedious. However, I guess I am one of the ones that care about doing my job well. You know that some do, and some do not. So, my nights consist of scanning the aisles of toiletries, vitamins, make-up, hair care products, and everything else that's over there in that section of the store. You would not believe all the stuff that companies make that are supposed to help us feel better, look better, and smell better. This world is so focused on being young and beautiful and thin … it's kind of scary. Every child thinks he or she has to look like Barbie or Ken. This generation may not realize who Barbie and Ken are, but they know what they look like. They look perfect. Perfect is tough, impossible, unattainable, and expensive.

My division is even more specialized than most. We only work for the Big Triple S stores. You know, Stop, Shop, and Save. Every town with a population over ten thousand has one. Since I live near a huge metropolitan area, we service over one hundred of them. I travelled a lot when I was younger, but, now, I only have to go if I ask to go. Some years I do want to get away from here. Others, I like to be close to home. Most of my clients ask for me. That is gratifying. It's probably because I help their customers find stuff. Who would know better than I would? After all, I have been walking these aisles counting their products for years. I know where it all is. I do not mind helping people out. That is just common courtesy.

Each store that we work in has its own personality. They all have the same basic line of goods, but some are more ethnically diverse than others are. This one may have a lot more Oriental, Spanish, or Middle Eastern things than some of the others do. Depends on where each store is located. Naturally, everything hinges on the law of supply and demand. Our company does not just offer a yearly inventory. We also do one every three months for the most successful businesses. If something has not sold for three months, get rid of it, and do not order it again. It's survival of the fittest. There is a certain Justice in that.

Night shoppers are unique. If you pay attention, you can learn a lot about what they do and what they need. It just so happens that I pay attention. I am usually very focused on the content of my shelves and what's around them. However, in recent years, we have had to become more conscious of the people that are out at night while we are out at night. I do not have to tell you about the crime rate in the big cities. It is hard to believe that rapists, murders, thieves, and even terrorists need toothpaste and fingernail files, too. Nevertheless, they do. By their very nature, they are night crawlers, and never get the justice they deserve. Those kinds of people hide from the light and shop in the darkness.

I am definitely not saying that all night shoppers are criminals. I have to shop at night myself, since I sleep the biggest part of the day. We do see some weird and scary individuals out late at night. My company is very concerned for our safety. Management takes every opportunity to present us with safety programs. Situational awareness is a big key to preventing a crime. You all know about pepper spray and whistles, and all those kinds of personal protection devices. However, if you fail to see a perpetrator approaching, you may not have time to use any of those things. If you are going to survive the night shift, you must learn to identify dangerous people, places, and things.

While working near the hair-coloring aisle one night, I saw a man studying all the different shades available. Curiously, he was not looking at blondes or browns. He was checking out all the colors on the whole row. Now, a man's wife may send him out in the middle of the night to buy a shade of hair color for an emergency do-over. However, this guy was not looking for an emergency repair. He was picking a color. Any color. Strange. I thought it was very strange. He was out of place, in the wrong place at the wrong time. He stuck out like a sore thumb. I noticed him, but I did not want him to notice me.

Any time I have a check in my spirit about talking to someone, I pay attention, and you should, too. That night, I felt like I needed to be invisible to that man. He was absorbed in his search, so, I quietly blended back into the next aisle and went on about my business. He was just an unremarkable man looking at hair color in the wee hours of the morning. Ok. Stranger things happened all the time. Still, it stuck in my mind.

I never expected to see him again. Of course, over a period of years, I have started to recognize some regular customers. They are mostly hospital/medical employees, and food service workers. You know, the usual day sleepers that fall into a routine of shopping at particular stores at particular times. Few of them have ever caused me to scratch my head and ask, "Why?" Even fewer have made me feel like I needed to be invisible. This incident stuck with me.

After a couple of weeks, at a different location, Mr. X showed up again. He was picking out a hair color again. WHY? It occurred to me that I needed to find out why. Why was he so intent on his task when his own hair was not colored at that moment? Was he acting out some fantasy? What was he doing with this stuff? What woman was behind his behavior? Could he be involved in some type of role-playing game? For some reason, I did not feel like this guy was playing. He was too serious about dyeing someone's hair in the middle of the night… but it was not his own.

Once again, I had a bad feeling about him. So, once again, I watched him closely. He was probably in his thirties. There was nothing significant about him…nothing about him attracted attention. He was practically invisible with his non-descript hair, skin-tone, eyes, and clothes. Nobody would notice him at any hour of the day or the night. So, why had I? What was it about him that kept my attention? All I can say is that I had "The Feeling" about him. Always pay attention to "The Feeling." Always. I am thankful that I decided to pay attention this time.

I am no hero, believe me. I am just like everyone else in the world. I just want to be OK, and I want everyone else to be OK, too. Not being a hero is the normal way to live, but, in fact, we are all heroes. So, having said that, I can tell you that I did not want to pursue "The Feeling," and where it was going to lead me. However, I knew that I had to find out what this man was doing out late at night, picking out hair colors. I had to find out why he made me so uncomfortable. I was not ready to admit that he was actually scaring me. Nevertheless, he was.

That night, I made myself promise that if I ever saw him again, I would follow him and try to get a name and address for him. Then, I went back to work and tried to forget about him. I did not forget him. I could not forget him. In fact, I thought about him more and more. Why doesn't he show up again? I questioned myself about him constantly. I was obsessed with finding him again. I was crazy. I knew it. Nothing ever affected me like this before. I hope and pray that nothing ever will again. Still, when he appeared weeks later, I was as confused and frightened as I was the first time I saw him. I was totally unprepared to deal with how he made me feel.

There he was, at three o'clock in the morning, looking for a new hair color. My knees started knocking, my hands were shaking, I was sweating, and I felt like I was going to cry. Not to mention that I felt like I had been kicked in the stomach by an army mule. Somehow, I had to get my act together and figure this whole thing out. I watched him pick out his hair color, pay for it, and scuttle out of the store toward his non-descript little car.

I called my supervisor and told him that I needed to leave. When I got to my car, I behaved exactly as all the TV detectives did. I followed several car lengths behind him, slumped down in the seat. I knew that I was in way over my head here, and I swim like a rock. God help me…Frantically trying to stay hidden from him, I lagged farther and farther behind his car. He must not see me or suspect anything. This night must end right. Nothing can go wrong. I made mental notes on my internal GPS as I followed him.

He drove to another Triple S and went inside quickly. I was too terrified to follow him, but I did slink around the parking lot and investigate his car. There were two shopping bags on the front seat. Both were from Triple S. One thing for sure, he was a loyal customer. Of course, I wrote down the license plate number, the year, and make of the car as well as the color and everything else that I could learn about it. I was so nervous that I was shaking and almost crying. I never took my eyes off the exit doors as I crept around his car. I wanted to make sure that I saw him coming out long before he saw me. My car was parked between two big SUVs where no one would notice it. It was close enough for me to get into it quickly without being seen.

In one pocket, I had my phone; in the other, I had my .41 Magnum Revolver. My prayer was that both would remain silent and unused all night. I have seen the movies where the phone rings and leads the crazed killer straight to the terrified victim. How stupid is that? I am probably crazy to do this, but I am trying not to be too stupid about it.

When he came out the door, I almost jumped out of my hair. He never saw me get into my car. He never saw me turn onto the street several blocks behind him. Hopefully, he would never know about this escapade. Hopefully, he was a doll maker, or a sculptor, or maybe he used hair color for some kind of art project. Hopefully, he was some eccentric that never harmed anyone in his life. He probably was not a dangerous criminal. I was probably not in any danger of anything but feeling like a fool tomorrow. Right now, "The Feeling" was driving me forward with more force than the fear that was pushing me backward. At least I had the .41 for protection if things went really wrong.

I knew that I could use it – kill – if I had to. Many years before, I was in a situation where I could have killed a man if he had taken one more step toward me. When he opened my door, I was standing there with a .44 Magnum pointed straight at his vital parts. When I told him to drop the key and get out, he did not hesitate. My hands were not shaking, and I was not scared. I was steady as a rock and ready to kill him on the spot. He knew it. When the police got there, I told them that I would kill him if he ever came near me again. They advised me to shoot to kill and do not stop pulling the trigger until the cylinder was empty. That is exactly what I intended to do if I ever face a situation like that again. Magnum Justice.

Honestly, I could not imagine this unassuming little man

menacing me…but I could not dismiss "The Feeling" either. He was involved in something unnerving, illegal, and maybe even evil. I didn't know what he was doing. Heck, I didn't even know what I was doing. He was invisible to everyone but me. I would be just as invisible as he was until I discovered whatever it took to bring me peace about him.

He was driving through an area that I was slightly familiar with. It was a lower middle-class housing development. All the people in this area worked a lot and did not have much time or money to spend at home. It was exactly like a million other streets in this town. It was a perfect place to hide in plain sight. He was clever. I felt sure that he was much smarter than I am and that I must be extremely careful, now.

Instinctively, I turned my headlights off. I slowed down even more. Now, his headlights were all I saw. They reflected off a window, and shone onto a row of shrubs, leading me from several streets away. What if he turned into a garage and I lost him? Maybe I should close the gap a little tighter…get closer to his car and not lose him now. It made me sick to think of losing him and not knowing what he was doing and what was going on with him.

Suddenly, I decided to park and follow his lights on foot. This was a good idea if he is actually living here in this neighborhood. Terrible idea if he was just picking up drugs or something like that. He must not see me creeping around this deserted street that night. There was a For Sale sign in the yard in front of me. With great uncertainty, I parked and got out without a sound. Wouldn't it be a hoot if someone called the cops on me? What would I say? "Oh, thank God you guys are here! You've got to arrest that guy… for excessive hair coloring." "Sure thing lady; assume the position." That would be Poetic Justice.

The foolishness of my quest almost overwhelmed me. A short distance away, his headlights turned into a driveway and the garage door started to roll up. Now, it was absolutely necessary for me to see where he was, get the address, and find out as much as I possibly could before it got daylight. Dear Lord, help me do this thing... whatever this thing is. He closed the garage door as I slinked behind a hedge on the corner. Now, I knew the street number and I felt better that he was inside.

In the darkness, my presence was unknown to him and the sleeping neighbors around us. I prayed that no insomniacs saw me and decide to dial 911 now. He must use black out blinds or something because there was only the thinnest line of light around two windows. Getting close enough to see into those windows was causing me to believe that my heart really might attack me now. Nevertheless, there would be no turning back. This must end now, tonight. I simply did not have the heart, the guts, or the brains to pursue him again. I am just an Inventory Control Tech. Not James Bond.

O.K. Settle Down and Think... Just settle down and think about how they do this on T.V. Turn the phone to vibrate. If it rings, the crazed maniac would not know exactly where I was. As I pressed close to the side of the house, I heard the snap and crackle of the car engine cooling in the garage. That made me aware of how loud my heart was beating and how deathly silent everything else was. Why was there no sound from this house? No TV, radio, or wife to greet him? He was a shadow living in a shadow land. Finally, a slit in the blinds allowed me a skinny peek into a vacant looking kitchen area.

Although it seemed like hours had passed, it had been only a few short minutes since I parked and snuck up here. Dawn will start creeping into the blackness at any moment. Whether I like it or not, my escapade is rapidly ending. Several cars have driven away from other homes in the past half hour, causing terrible shaking, and quaking on my part. Soon, people would be stirring, and someone would see me. In a way, that's good, because I need to leave. How much more fear and anxiety could this heart take before it rattled right out of my chest?

Muffled voices were coming from inside the semi-empty kitchen! Dear God. It's him… and a child. Isn't this what I was really dreading all along? Every time we see a creepy, disgusting derelict, don't we all think "Child Molester"? Slow, painful death and everlasting hell are too good for anyone who could ever harm a child. Hell is true Justice for people that hurt children.

If only I could prove something, right now. I want to call the Police or Child Protection or F.B.I. or anyone right now. The sad truth is that I cannot prove anything. For all I know, this is his child and he is a perfectly acceptable parent who is doing nothing wrong. It is absolutely necessary for me to calm the heck down! I will try to see as much as I can through this tiny slit of light before the whole neighborhood wakes up and sends me to jail instead of him.

Help me, Jesus. The little one had a cast on her right arm and a bruise on her cheek! Her little body was thin and pale. Surely, a call to the Police would be some kind of deterrent to him. They would come in a heartbeat if the slightest hint of child abuse was mentioned. You do not even have to give your name or anything. There was a Phone Booth a few blocks away. No one will ever know it was me. She will be safe as soon as I call. This is what "the Feeling" was about…saving this child. Justice would be done this very day.

Just as I was ready to slink away, he surprised me. He held up the three boxes of hair color for the child to see. What? The blinds limited my vision and I could only see a sliver of the whole room. His hands were holding the boxes out for the girl to look at. Now, I was intrigued. If only I knew what they were saying or doing. It appeared that she was going to choose her new hair color. She was being invited to be a part of this deception. But, who was being deceived? Who is this man? Who is this child? What am I doing here? Why aren't I racing to the phone to dial 911?

A very, very wise person from the 70's once said for us to believe none of what we hear and only half of what we see! In my spirit, I know there was a major truth hidden in this house somewhere, but

I may not be able to find it. It was going to be too dangerous for me to be here in a matter of minutes. The tiny girl's finger pointed and he held the chosen box out to her as she came closer to him. The little towhead nodded as she touched the box with one hand and her own hair with the other. Uncertainty flooded her eyes and my own mind. She is not afraid of him. She is not trying to escape from him. She is telling him what color she wants her hair to be! She is a part of what he is doing!

There seemed to be no menace here at all. Muffled voices again, and suddenly a little boy came tearing into the room as only little boys can. A sweet looking Grammaw - type was following close behind him. They were talking and laughing with each other as relaxed as anyone could be at this hour of the morning. I was shocked to realize that this looked like a family unit here. It was not what I thought at all. The four of them are happy and comfortable together. I am so relieved to see that I have been on the wrong track about this whole thing.

I could not see or hear enough to know what to think or do now. All I was sure of was that I must go. I must get out of here before the sky gets any lighter. I know that I am not going to call any Law Enforcement officers today. Something has changed in my perspective since I started this trip tonight. There was more here than I ever imagined. And I imagined a whole lot. However, this was not at all what I suspected.

Seeing this helpless, wounded child here with this man has changed everything in my mind. She and the boy are obviously siblings. The old woman was obviously their Grammaw. They were going to get their hair dyed. They all wanted to look different…Why do they want to look different? Who are they trying to hide from? Why are they on the run? Oh, Dear Lord, I have to run out of here, myself, before someone sees me.

I started creeping back to my car as quickly and as quietly as possible. I guess no one noticed me because I made it home without incident. Actually, I got home earlier than I usually do. It was tempting for me to discuss all of this with someone, but not my husband. He would go ballistic and probably try to kill someone – anyone – maybe even me for scaring him. I set the alarm and got ready to sleep while everyone else was getting ready to start his or her workday. I was exhausted and hopefully would be able to relax and rest for several hours before I had to go back to the House. As I drifted off to sleep, it occurred to me that I had already decided to call in sick again.

My plan was to go back to the House sometime around midnight. Common sense told me that they were sleeping in the day also. How could they not be? When you stay up all night, you must sleep some time. Surely, they were all on the same sleep schedule. A few minutes ago, I felt confident that this mystery was all but solved. Now, I felt more confused than ever. I wondered if this is too much for me. Have I mentioned that I might be crazy?

No matter what else happens tonight, the police or some other official agency will be called before I go to sleep again. Right, wrong, or indifferent, this decision has brought me comfort and even a little peace. I have the power to see Justice done. I have the power to change these kid's lives tonight. I knew that I was going to call someone to help them.

Being anti-techno in a super techno world is a very large handicap. However, for a few dollars I was able to find a web site for identifying license plates. When I typed those letters and numbers into the proper places… Bingo! Right away I knew the owner's name, age, address, and of course, I saw her photo. The car belonged to the Grammaw that I saw last night. It is surprising what all we can discover about people nowadays. For someone like me it is a bit frightening, too. Our whole lives can be accessed by anyone with any type of computer or even a cell phone. My youngest grandson has some kind of a game that can do anything you can imagine. To me, this whole information generation is invasive and intrusive.

However, at this' point, I was thankful to learn anything I could about this woman because she was my first clue.

Her name was Sophia, but I could only think of her as Grammaw. She just seemed to embody that name. On another web site, I entered her name and address looking for more information about her, the "color man" and the two kids. In a short time, a photo of her appeared with a biography-type write-up that was several pages long. This lady was quite lovely in her younger years. In fact, she was a beautician before she met and married a young, wealthy shipping magnate. She was beautiful, and rich and evidently extremely philanthropic. She was frequently in the news for doing something kind and good for other families. She had a particular interest in some orphanages and missions in Australia. Both she and her hubby built and supported several church-run facilities that helped children in crises. I continued to peruse the internet articles that chronicled her life for an hour or more. It was amazing how this sweet little lady had such a powerful influence on those around her. However, after the birth of her daughter, Natalie, she really faded into the background. I suppose that she was totally focused on caring for her only child.

Holy jumped up bald headed palomino! Five years ago, Sophia's daughter was killed in a car accident, leaving two children, Matthew and Makayla behind her. Scrolling down for the next five years, I learned a whole lot about Grammaw and her love for her two grandchildren. It is the same old story that we have all heard too many times. A wealthy, stupid young girl got hooked up with the wrong guy and got pregnant. He married her for her family's money, and they all lived miserably ever after...

Unfortunately, for this Grammaw, Natalie was tragically killed before she could get her away from that parasite. Now, the two children's lives were hanging in the balance. The local media recorded all the gory details and publicly revealed the whole sordid custody battle. Grammaw had to fight with her son-in-law for months just to get visitation rights. In spite of her money, or maybe even because of it, the judge seemed to favor the kids Dad's wishes over those of their Grammaw. Certainly, there had been no Justice there, not for Grammaw or the two children.

As soon as he could make his escape, the dad disappeared from the scene, and Matthew and Makayla were lost to Sophia. What a disgusting piece of trash he must have been to torture his own innocent children like this. I hated him instantly. According to the local newspaper, Grammaw was devastated by losing her family. Her dear husband had passed away before Natalie married that scum ball. She made numerous public appeals and offered a substantial reward for information about the missing children. Grammaw had great sympathy from the locals, but, the kids were gone, and she was left alone and broken hearted. Very shortly after all this, Grammaw seemed to have disappeared, herself.

Whoa! Hold the phone! This cannot be right... the latest news clipping said that Grammaw had died. Died? Dead? Seriously? Her face was looking up at me from the obituary in the paper. It was her all right...It was the sweet little Grammaw that I saw right here last night with my own eyes. She is no more dead than I am. However, the news clippings recount the horrible trial and the subsequent events that took a terrible toll on the old woman's health. She is said to have died from her broken heart while visiting an orphanage in Australia. Her ashes were spread over a beautiful garden there that is dedicated to her memory.

Again, I was totally perplexed by all this news. I just saw Grammaw last night. I saw her and the "color man" with the two kids at the House last night. Those kids must be her grandchildren. Somehow, she and the "color man" had rescued them from their despicable father. That was a pretty neat trick for a dead woman. Now, I was more intrigued than ever. I had to know who the "color man" was, and how the four of them got here...and why.

My mind told me to concentrate on what I did know about them. The one thing I knew was that he buys hair color in the middle of the night. He, (or she) was going to change all of their hair colors! Hey…maybe he was a hairdresser too? I felt sure that he was. After all, he was the one who bought and presented the colors to Makayla. She was choosing a new hair color for him to apply. He must be a beautician. OK. Now, how in the heck do I find a beautician's license on the internet? Amazing how easy it is to just Ask.com!

My best choice was to search the city where Grammaw lived, married, and raised Natalie. The "color man" appeared to be young enough to be her son, so I began to search on a public record site for that area. I figured he had to be close to Natalie's age, so I fast-forward twenty years from her birth year to start my investigation. The site offered several helpful hints about age, sex, ethnicity, and other pertinent things to simplify my search. This whole internet thing is just incredibly informative. Everything you ever wanted to know about everything and did not know who to ask is now available to us all.

After another hour and a half of flipping from screen to screen, I was very shocked to see the "color man" on the computer screen right before my eyes. Can you believe this? I absolutely cannot believe it myself, yet, there he was. The beautician's license gave me his name, which was Evan, his age, his address, and even where he graduated from Beauty College. I realized that Evan was thirty-two years old when he got his Beauticians license. Surely, that was a little bit older than usual? That made him forty-three, now. There were many other useful facts as well. As I suspected, he was from the same small town where Grammaw and Natalie lived. This is so excellent!

Now, I just had to go back to the newspaper from their hometown and type in his name and address, too. Through the miracle of modern technology, Evan's whole life was shortly presented to me. I was hoping for another small piece of the puzzle and now I got the whole cannoli!

Evan was only twelve years old in the sensational cover story in front of me. My heart broke as I read about the horror of his young life... Evan and his two little sisters, Alexa and Alysa, were objects of abuse and neglect by a pair of lousy parents. Both drank, drugged, and fought way too much. The children were frequently left alone with little or nothing to eat. Evan was often the only parent that the girls had at home. He comforted them by brushing or braiding their hair and telling them how pretty they looked. I suspect that he was also trying to keep them quiet and out of sight of their abusive father.

According to this account, a terrible brawl was going on with Evan's parents as all three kids cowered under the girls' bed. The children related how their Mother's final scream was so terrifying that Evan crept out of hiding to help her. When his father saw him, he charged after Evan bellowing threats at the boy. Evan got to the top of the stairs just as his father made a wild lunge for him. Evidently, he was too stoned to manage himself well and lost his balance as he swung his fist at his son. Evan tells how he scrambled to safety as his father plunged headfirst down the stairs. Momentum and stupidity resulted in a broken neck that mercifully ended his reign of terror. Poetic Justice?

Of course, the children were placed into foster care, and later they were transferred to the local orphanage that Grammaw frequented. Evan was the same age as Natalie, and they went to school together. Sitting in front of the computer screen, I began to like and respect young Evan. There were numerous articles about his athletic abilities. In the newspaper clippings, he always looked serious and uncomfortable in the spotlight. The girls were always in the pictures too. He is their very own real-life hero. I really liked this kid now. He was very bright and such an accomplished student and athlete that the townsfolk loved him too. One article relates how gifted he was with foreign languages. His natural ear for dialects got him an appointment to West Point. Wow! West Point. Now, he could travel and learn all the Languages he wanted to learn, knowing that the girls were safe with Grammaw. He gave her all the credit for saving his life and those of his two sisters. They were little beauties that

Grammaw and Natalie loved and enjoyed. In fact, they were all living together, as a family when Evan left to begin his military career.

He was gone for several years, but his accomplishments came home to roost with Grammaw and the girls. He was always being presented with a medal or commendation for some heroic act. His military career took him to several foreign countries, but he never lost sight of home and the family he loved. Why would this bright accomplished young athlete come back home to be a beautician? The story tells how Evan began doing hair in his barracks for friends. His military "clients" said that he always made them feel better about themselves and gave them confidence in their appearance. He was as adept at fixing hair as everything else he turned his hand to. This Home Town Hero had been cutting hair all over the world for years. The article said that Evan was more comfortable as a barber than he was as a decorated soldier.

It seemed appropriate for Evan to go back home and make a life with Grammaw and his sisters. He was doing something that he loved, and people loved him for it. He had developed a ministry in hairdressing. I imagined that he became a true hero when he was combing and braiding his sisters' hair so many years ago. Grammaw appointed him as chairman of several of her orphanages. He was successful in every aspect of his life.

After several years, Evan and Alexa, with Alyssa and her husband, all moved to Australia to oversee the Agape House Foundation there. Agape means God's Love. Evan and his family oversaw three orphanages and a very large foster care facility. They not only survived many challenges, they thrived, just as their young charges did. There were several articles about their tremendous success, and their campuses were expanded several times. Alexa married a former military chaplain that had served with Evan. He was also a decorated veteran, and their wedding was highly publicized, which was great for Agape House. All of them remained faithful to their cause - Taking care of kids in need. True justice.

That compound in Australia is reportedly where Grammaw had "died" last year. Now I understand what must have happened. These people, (this family) had developed their own Justice System for kids that were in desperate need of help. Not the conventional legal mumbo-jumbo type of help but real, life-changing help. I suspected that Grammaw somehow learned where Matthew and Makayla had been taken. Holy Smokes, I bet their nasty dad had been hiding out right here in my hometown! She must have gone to Evan, in Australia, for help. After she "Died," no one would be looking for her, and Evan would inherit a large fortune. He would then be free to travel, as he needed to. If what I was thinking was true, Grammaw and Evan have found ways to evade the legal red tape that paralyzes so much of our Justice system. I hope so.

I was just sad that no one else would ever know this story. My "feeling" about a night shopper had brought me a long way. I am so glad that I know a little bit of the truth now. I want to know more, and I want to help. Not just these two kids. They are OK with Grammaw and will be for the rest of their lives. However, I do want to help with the other hurting kids that the world passes by. Can't we find some Justice for them, too?

Did I mention that I am crazy?

This is how crazy I am...

I will write a letter and take it to the House tonight.

Dear Evan and Grammaw-

I am a friend.

I am a Mom and a Sister.

I want to help.

I want to see Justice done, too.

You can trust me.

Where can I volunteer?

Contact me via Phileo@gmail.com

I used Phileo because it means Brotherly Love in Greek.

Agape means God's Love in Greek.

When they get my message, they will know that I have figured out some things about them. Their first instincts will be to flee as quickly as they can. They may be gone now. I know that they have been here for at least six or seven weeks. They must be getting ready to flee at any moment! I hope and pray that I can get this letter to them before they disappear. Evan has probably developed a foolproof escape plan. They will all live happily ever after. I really do want to help them and other children in need as well. I am deeply inspired by their courage and commitment to save these two kids. How many others have they rescued? I sit in front of my computer screen for a while longer as I think about what I have learned in the past couple of hours. How amazing this whole thing has turned out to be!

I finally went to bed and tried to sleep for a few hours before I go back to the House. My family still thinks that I am sick, and they pretty much leave me alone, so I can rest. See, I must stay on my night shift schedule, because if I get off I will be too messed up to go back to work in a couple of nights.

I printed my short note and intend to try to stick it some place where they will see it when they get ready to leave. God, I hope they have not already gone. Where do I put my note? I cannot get to the car and I was terrified to go to the front of the house. What if they didn't find it? How could I make sure that they would find it? I was wearing a disguise again. After all, Evan is a military man who won a lot of medals for killing people. He may be a danger to me. Again, fear gripped my heart.

Did I mention that I am crazy?

I ftel better as soon as I saw that they were still at the House. I could still reach out to them before they disappeared forever. I do not know why I was so Hell Bent on talking to them. I just had to let them know that I want to help save little kids, too. Have you ever felt driven to do something insane like this? Of course you have. Everyone has crazy compulsions. Just look at all the marriages that end in divorce…or worse.

I was still having a hard time deciding where to put my letter. Finally, I stuck the paper in the last slat of the garage door itself. I hoped that when Evan opened it, the paper would fall out and he would read it without wanting to kill me. After I wedged the note lightly in place, I was shaking with fear and anticipation of what might happen next. I was afraid to look through the screen again. I decided to just go home and try to get some sleep. I was totally exhausted.

Of course, I could not sleep. I was too nervous and excited to sleep. I wanted to go back over there and ring the bell and say, "Hi, don't kill me. I'm just a friend who wants to help." That probably would not end well for me. After all, there was no sign of that evil father that took the kids away from Grammaw. My guess is that he is paying his dues in hell right now. That would be Justice, Right? Do not forget Makayla's' broken arm and bruised face. No kid should ever be hurt like that. We should all be willing to make sure it does not ever happen to any one of them, ever again. I want to help.

I was an emotional train wreck. Anxiety had kept me from sleeping for more than an hour or two for days. My husband and kids think I am sick. I am sick… sick with worry. What if Evan tracks me down like I tracked him? What if some neighbor saw me and or my car and told him about it? What if I have drawn fire to my own home? Could my husband or kids be in danger now? How far will Evan go to remain invisible? What have I done?

I worried.

I cried.

I prayed.

I waited.

After going back through the information I found on the internet, I felt better. Once again, I was impressed with Evan. He stuck me as a man of integrity. He must be a good person to help all those orphans and street kids. Surely, he would appreciate the fact that I am the only person that had figured any of this out. He should realize that I could be a great asset to their cause. I hoped that he would understand that I know enough to keep quiet.

I worried.

I cried.

I prayed.

I waited.

Finally, after two more days I went back to work. On the third day, I logged on to my Phileo email account and found that I had a message from Agape Foundation. It read:

THE JUST SHALL LIVE BY FAITH

Is this my Beginning or my End?

Waiting

THEY THAT WAIT UPON THE LORD
SHALL RENEW THEIR STRENGTH.
THEY SHALL MOUNT UP WITH WINGS LIKE EAGLES
ISAIAH 40:31

I have entertained an Angel...Unaware. That is what the Bible says in Hebrews 13, verses 1 and 2. God says for us to let Brotherly Love continue and to entertain, or welcome, strangers, because we may be entertaining Angels...unaware that they are Angels.

Now, I personally am not very big on strangers. I am not extremely friendly with very many people. I try not to be un-friendly without exactly being friendly either. Often, I do not succeed at either one of those things. See, I have to travel a lot for my job, and it is exhausting to make and maintain friendships while on the road. Consequently, I will read or do Cryptograms when I am in the breakroom. By withdrawing from everyone around me, I do not have to worry about being friendly to, or entertaining strangers. I especially do not ever flirt or get "touchy-feely" with anyone.

I do not like people to touch me at all. You know how some people are always walking up behind you and massaging your neck or shoulders. I hate that. I am not open to the bear hug or dancing, either. I have my own private little "Space Bubble" which I do not like for anyone to violate. It is like Sacred Ground to me. I have always been this way. That is why this whole Angel experience is so incredible.

Let me begin my story by saying that my husband and I usually work nightshift when on the road. We get up around three PM and must be at work by six. We work a twelve-hour shift and get back home around seven AM the next day. Then we go to sleep and start the whole thing over again. It is an exhausting seventy-two-hour workweek. That is much too long for someone my age. From the day I start the job, I am literally just waiting for it to end so I can get back to my real life at home.

We were down on the Texas gulf coast and, my husband wanted to go fishing on our night off. Therefore, after we had eaten and bought enough groceries for the coming week, we got some bait, grabbed the rods, and headed out. The RV Park we were staying at was right on the water. They have nice boat slips, fishing piers, benches, umbrellas, and everything else that you could possibly want or need to be comfortable while fishing.

We started walking along by the boat slips looking for the perfect spot to catch fish. I was really enjoying the evening because it was cool. There was a beautiful full moon, a light breeze sighing in the sails, and hardly any mosquitos. You could say it was a perfect night. The moon, stars, and lights were reflecting off the water in a dazzling light show. All the bulbs had developed some kind of rainbow type auras too. There were multi-colored halos emanating from each fixture. The evening had suddenly become Mysterious and Beautiful. Maybe it was the humidity. I'm sure there is a scientific reason for rainbow auras; but I do not know what that explanation is. All I can tell you is that it was a perfectly beautiful night.

Seems like we were having a great time just walking along – not fishing. I almost felt like I was waiting for something to happen. We had only seen a few people along the way, which was OK with me.

I guess my hubby felt compelled to ask the age-old questions, "Been here long? Catching anything? What are you using for bait?" You know the inane angler talk between strangers on a pier? I just kept strolling along, not fish-talking, not being friendly, and not entertaining strangers.

Funny how I can still see and remember everything about that evening so clearly. My hubby was about a block behind me, as I strolled slowly along the water line by myself. Waiting? But what was I waiting for? Why did I have that feeling of anticipation in my spirit? It was really strange for me because I was very tired and stressed by my job. I still had six days of laundry to do before I could even go to bed. Dominic was still listening to the fellas down the way, so I just leaned on the rail and relaxed. I do not do "relaxed" very well, but it was so peaceful that I decided I would find a bench and get comfortable. Waiting.

Looking to my right, I saw an old man just six or eight feet behind me. Waiting? When our eyes met, he slowly got to his feet, smiled, took off his hat, and made a small bow to me! His eyes held mine the whole time, and I felt like he was welcoming me to some place special. He was quite old. However, his eyes were young and blue, a deep midnight blue like the Texas sky above us. They had a timeless quality that illuminated his whole countenance. His hair was white and somewhat fluffy around his head like a soft crown or halo. I was drawn to him instantly. Without knowing why, I started walking toward him.

He put his hat back on, took a step toward me, and of all things, he opened his arms to hug me! Of all things-,this stranger saw me coming, stood, smiled, took off his hat, bowed, and opened his arms to embrace me. He was waiting for me! Me, the one who does not like strangers and does not want to be friendly. I am the one with the space bubble who does not like to be touched. Wow. I never hesitated for a second. I walked into his arms and we hugged like long-lost kin. I felt goodness and comfort and many other nice things just flowing out of him. Wow. I felt like hugging him was the most natural thing in the world.

We did not speak for a minute or so; apparently, we just hugged in silence. When we parted, we instinctively reached for each other's hands and held them in front of us as we stood looking into each other's eyes. He nodded to the bench beside us and we sat facing each other... still holding hands between us. I could not let go of him. After all, I had been waiting for him, for a long time. You cannot know how much this whole thing was not like me at all. However, I was not nervous or uncomfortable with him at all. As matter of fact, I felt so lucky, so blessed to have found him here tonight.

This sounds crazy, but it is the gospel truth. I had never seen him before, but it felt like I had known him forever. My heart was at home with him. He seemed to feel the same way about me too. On this moonlit night with the rainbow halos around soft lights, we experienced a small miracle. A stranger had been transformed into a lifelong friend. Isn't that a miracle? Especially for someone like me?

I am not sure how long we sat there; it could have been sixty seconds or fifteen minutes. Maybe time had been suspended for us. I just knew that he had been sent down there to that pier, on that night, specifically for me. We had a divine appointment. At that moment, I knew that I had been waiting for this meeting all my life. Even though I had not been particularly good or faithful to God at that time, He had blessed me with this visitation.

After a period of time, Dominic saw us sitting there, and he must have been quite shocked. He started walking our way, and The Angel began to talk about his life. He told me that his wife had died recently and that he was going to move in with his son. He had been a very successful clothier, owning two upscale men's shops. He had gone to college and to war. When he had finished fighting Nazis, he married his high school sweetheart and began his personal and professional journey. They raised three children together,r and all of them went to college, too. He had an infant daughter that had died in childbirth many years ago. We both wept when he told me that. In spite of many tragedies and hardships, he said that he was always blessed, and always thankful for the contentment and joy he experienced in his life.

Now, my husband was standing there giving me looks that asked "What the??? And Huh??? Who are you, and what have you done with my wife?" I pointed to The Angel and said, "Dominic, this is my friend" … I looked askance at him and he said, "Amos Bishop, I am so pleased to meet you."

They shook hands, and Dominic could tell there was something very special about him. I learned later that Amos means Burden Bearer and Bishop means Elder or Overseer.

When Dominic sat down, I asked Amos how long he had lived in this area. He replied that it had been over fifty years. "Where does your son live?"

He explained that his son lived down on the Louisiana Gulf Coast. "Wow small world. My father was raised in Pineville, LA., and I still have lots of family there, even though it has been many years since I have heard from any of them."

Amos said that he, too, had lived in Pineville when he was a young man. Small world?

When I spoke my maiden name, he gasped delightedly and hugged me again. It seems that Amos had often helped my Grandfather and his brothers harvest tobacco and sugar cane on the old home place there. One of my early childhood memories was of those cane fields during "boiling off" time. I will never forget the smell of that sugar cane being processed. As a little girl, I could not understand how those hard sticks would become the sweet white sugar that I put in my oatmeal every morning. My father cut some pieces of it off and gave all three of us a chunk. We chewed on them for hours. I also remembered the beautiful big tobacco leaves and how great they smelled in the huge drying rack sheds.

My father died when I was seven. We lost contact with all his family after my grandparents passed away. My mom was a young widow with five children to feed. She worked two jobs, and we never had the money to travel back to Louisiana again. All those family members were just gone from our lives… and we never really knew them. All those things had happened so long ago. I was shocked by the depth of emotion that sprang up in my heart when I recounted these facts to Amos. I felt an even closer kinship to him now. He knew my family of origin. No wonder my heart felt at home with him.

Amos looked deep into my eyes and said, "You come from a wonderful family. It is such a blessing for me to meet the granddaughter of my old friend. He is certainly so very proud of you today."

Somehow, I knew that he spoke the truth. I also realized that I had been waiting to hear those words all my life. What an amazing encounter this had turned out to be! A total stranger had stepped into my path and changed my life forever. He had spoken words of life to me. There was some kind of a supernatural connection between us that could not be explained or denied.

In a moment or two, we knew that it was time for Amos to go on his way. Other people were waiting to meet him also.

Our hands were still clasped between us as he slowly stood and said, "There are my son and daughter in law." Sure enough, a middle-aged man and woman were standing in a pool of rainbow colored light several feet away.

Waiting.

Amos once again drew me into his warm embrace and said, "I am so honored to have met you tonight. We will surely see each other again one day."

I felt like crying. I did not want him to leave. However, I knew that I would see him again. I knew that I would recognize him, even if he were an old farmer's wife, or a young black student, or whoever he might become next.

I would know his eyes, his heart, and the gentle spirit in him.

We are family, after all.

"Amos, thank you for sharing your life with me tonight.

I will never forget you.

I hope and pray that we will meet again very soon."

He smiled at me with twinkling eyes and said, "I'll be waiting."

High Valley

SHE'S BEEN THROUGH HELL. TRUST ME
WHEN I SAY... BE AFRAID OF HER... SHE
LOOKS INTO THE FIRE AND SMILES.
E. CORONA

No one was supposed to see the Black Helicopters that evening. No one was even supposed to be anywhere near their flight path. It was just a fluke for me to be there, myself. Seeing those choppers changed my life-forever. They appeared well after midnight, in a remote area of an even remoter area of central Texas. This was a dark, overcast night, with some patchy fog in the low-lying areas. Not a fit night for man, beast, or this lonely, emotionally drained woman to be out on that deserted road.

I was only there because of grief. Sometimes, grief overwhelms us and makes us do strange, even desperate things. I had been overwhelmed for a long time, but it is not in my nature do strange stuff. I keep a low profile and try not to draw fire. Driving out there that night was completely out of character for me. It seems like some things are just meant to be.

Probably, you need to know some facts about me, in order to understand why things happened the way they did. First, let me tell you about the grief. I learned about death when my Dad died at forty-eight years of age. I was only seven, but I understood that he was gone from earth forever. After he passed, our family survived and grew to be very closely knit. We faced everything together. Then, when I was forty-nine, my world started crumbling beneath my feet. In a six-year period, I buried my Mom, two brothers, a sister, my brother-in-law, a niece, and a young nephew. In addition to my immediate family, several close friends had died during that same time. My husband's sister, who was like a mother to both of us, had helped me through everything. She died suddenly, less than one year after my own sweet sis. Good Lord, no wonder I was losing my mind. Usually, it takes more than five years to recover from one of those deaths! I could not grieve, as I needed to, because someone else was dying or dead within in a few months.

They say that what doesn't kill us makes us stronger. I should have been a real Samson, or Hercules by that time. However, I was not stronger. I could barely put one foot in front of the other. Most of the time, I felt like an orphan- lonely, scared, and lost. It is terrible to lose your whole family in such a short time. My oldest sister and I were the only two of five children that were still alive. We had always been very close and were alike in many ways. She was having heart problems, and I was afraid that her husband's death would kill her. Both of us tried to help and encourage each other, but it was too hard. I always said that I was going to do better, but she was my oldest sister, and I was just too broken and needy.

One night, one of my dearest friends said to me, "Look, you're really scaring me with this thousand-yard stare. Are you going to be ok? Maybe you should get help. You know that you will see your family again, but for now, you need to come back to the land of the living."

She thought I was going to kill myself. I had thought about it, because I literally could not imagine growing older without my siblings. However, I could not bear to deliberately hurt my own kids and other family members by ending my own life. I needed help.

That next day, I started seeing a grief counselor. He was about my age, but he seemed much younger. He was extremely helpful to me. He told me to start allowing myself to remember the happy stuff and not just the death scenes. I was appalled by that. How could I ever be happy again? There were several "Projects" that this guy wanted me to do, but I could not even make myself try. On my third visit, I finally told him that I was not able to look at a photo album… any album… because I was afraid that I would see one of them. If I had to drive through the town where my youngest brother had lived, and died, I would have a full-blown anxiety attack.

When I told him those things, he looked at me for a couple of heartbeats; then, he started rummaging through his desk drawers.

In a minute, he said, "Oh yeah, here it is."

With that, he held up a new, pink pencil with a nice, sharp point. He started telling me that this was his favorite pencil, and that he had it for a long time. He said that he really needed that pencil, and it was the only one he ever used. Even if there were other pencils available, he always picked that pencil.

He really loved that pink pencil. "Let's say that there is no other pencil, OK? Let's say that this is the only pencil…OK?"

I shrugged, as if to say "OK, big deal."

Apathy was all I could feel at that time in my life. He played with it in the air for a short time, like a metronome, back-forth, back-forth…as if he was trying to hypnotize me.

When I finally focused on it, he calmly snapped his pencil in half and laid it on the desk right in front of me. He never said a word; he sat back and looked at me, waiting. You cannot believe how much I did not want to talk to him. Nevertheless, he was expecting me to say or do something.

"It's broken," I said, "You broke it."

He nodded, looked at me some more, and waited some more. A small earthquake had begun to tremor its way into my consciousness. Now, I knew that I needed to pay close attention here, because a major truth was coming toward me, at light-speed.

Even though words would not come out of my mouth at that exact second, I was thinking and putting some puzzle pieces together. You know how you put a jigsaw puzzle together? You have to put the edges together, first. Then, you fill-in-the-blanks, by looking at the picture on the box . What does any of this have to do with the counselor and the pencil? What did he want from me? Think. I had to think and speak, or he might keep looking at me for the whole hour. I did not want him to look at me. I did not want to look at myself. I did not want to know what I looked like when everyone else was dead. I knew that I was ugly, broken, ruined, and useless.

That earthquake hit me when I reached out to pick up the broken pencil. I held onto those pencil pieces as if they were solid gold lifesavers. He let me cry for a while. Some part of me was coming back to the land of the living. He knew that I knew the truth about the pencil. I will tell you what blew me away. I am the pencil. Yes, I am broken. Part of me is jagged and dangerous to others and myself. Still, I am one of a kind. There is only one of me. I am greatly loved and desperately needed. I am broken, but I am not gone. I am still here. Part of me is shattered, but I can still be useful, if handled properly. A broken pencil is better than no pencil at all.

He spoke quietly to me. "Will you keep the pencil for a while?"

Yes! Of course, I will keep the pencil. It holds so much truth for me. He stood and escorted me out of his office. The healing had begun. When I went back the following week, he asked me where the pencil was. I opened my purse, took it out, and showed it to him. He smiled and asked me what I wanted to tell him. I talked; he listened. He talked; I listened. In time, I was better. The pencil stayed in my purse for weeks. Then, I put it on the console of my car. For a while, I kept it by my easy chair. When it started to get in the way, I put it on my bedside table. Eventually, I put it the bottom drawer of my dresser. I do not know where it is, now, but I still keep it in my heart for the times when I need it.

This man is a genius. He literally brought me back to life, back to the land of the living. Now, I will not bore you with all the details of my treatment in the months that followed. However, you need to know that he is the one that sent me on the journey to High Valley, where I saw the black choppers. This whole story is about that time when I was broken and jagged, and not sure if I would ever feel completely whole again. I knew that my family were all at a reunion, having the best time of their lives. They all knew that I was coming to join them; but none of us knew when I would get there. I think that every now and then my Mom, or Dad, or, maybe my youngest brother would look over at the door; anticipating my arrival. In the meantime, I was still here, in the land of the living.

Why was I out there, in the middle of nowhere, by myself, in the middle of a dark and dreary night? I was going to an old cemetery where many of my older family members were buried. When I say old, I mean old. My grandparents' parents, brothers, sisters, and cousins were all buried there. The place was called High Valley. It was just a small, white clapboard church and cemetery where our family gathered to sing, pray, weep, and say good-bye. It was a time to visit other graves and talk about loved ones that had gone on before. We laughed there at High Valley. We always reminded each other of the funny, eccentric things that those old characters did. We loved and enjoyed High Valley. It was a place of laughter and tears. I had not been there in many years because my own grandparents were gone, now. There was no more room for any more graves.

When I told my counsellor about the comfort and peace that I always felt when we gathered there, he suggested that maybe I should go back, now. I was astonished by his suggestion because my sweet sister had made that trip, right before she died. She was quite ill when we talked about her journey. I will never forget how animated her face became as she told me how someone had updated the church and grounds. She smiled and said she had a good visit when she was there. She told me that I should go visit, too. I think I told her I would. Even then, something was drawing me back. I promised myself that this time, when I went to High Valley; I would be looking for life. My life.

My work schedule kept me from getting an early start. I was literally running late before I even started the car. However, this was the only time I would be able to get away for several months. Better late than never, right? Even though I thought that I knew where I was going, I was soon lost. All the old landmarks were gone, and nothing looked the same. I was sure that I could find High Valley as soon as I found my Auntie's house. I could not even find her old place. She was the glue that kept our family together. I had not been back since she died many years ago. Her home was like something between Gunsmoke and Mayberry. Her two older brothers lived with her and they were the greatest old scallywags ever born. Auntie had been trying to keep them straight since they were toddlers. She never succeeded, but she never gave up. They were the best of friends, and each one would have given his life for the others. They continued to play jokes on each other until they died...laughing all the way to High Valley. When the last of those three died, my Grandparents were gone, too. I never went back to High Valley. I couldn't.

When I was a young wife and mother, I thought that I could not handle all of my family ties. In fact, we could barely keep up with our immediate family birthdays, holidays, and daily crises. At that time, my husband and I made the unconscious decision to cut some of those ties that were binding us. Then, it seemed prudent. Now it seems unwise. I wish I knew then what I know now. I had kept some of those cousins, but many just slipped away. They were gone, and I was out here lost and lonely. Too soon old...too late smart.

After I drove down a couple of country roads, looking for something familiar, I was very frustrated. There was only one family member still in this area that I could call to ask for directions. He was an older cousin that was as deaf as a post. Talking to him was such an ordeal, and I did not want to have to explain why I was there. He was deaf...not stupid. He would need some explanation, and I could not give him something that I did not have. Therefore, I had to start asking questions...at the Pecan Valley Chamber of Commerce. It turns out that the improvements at High Valley were a very big deal in this area. Seems there had been many upgrades in recent years. Movie stars had purchased thousands of acres in those hills, all of which needed to be beautified... Hollywood.

The Chambermaid was quite a talker, and I was semi-interested, which cost me another forty-five minutes. By that time, I had to have something to eat, and the sun was setting when I finally got on the road again. When I crossed the bridge over the Colorado River, I knew that it would only be a few more minutes to High Valley. That was a good thing because the last three road signs said, County Maintenance ends, State Maintenance Ends, and Loose Livestock, (with a picture of a cow). That made me smile remembering milking, making butter, and cottage cheese all summer. I swear that if you put a cow in front of me right now, I could milk her.

Surprisingly, this was still a wild and undeveloped section of Texas. All the talk about movie stars made me think that there would be million-dollar mansions and BMWs everywhere. Nothing could be further from the truth. I had not passed another vehicle in a very long time, but I did see deer and a variety of small wildlife, as well. Common sense told me that some farm or ranch houses were out there, somewhere, but I could not see any signs of human habitations from the road. There was no cell phone signal, either.

At the top of the next hill, I could see lights through the trees. This must be it! My sis had said that this whole place was lit up the evening that she was here. Why? Who was paying for this? That church was painted a brilliant white, and there was a charming white picket fence around it, as well. Everything was sparkling, clean, and inviting. Even though I knew about these improvements, I was still moved to tears when I saw how beautiful everything looked. It was exactly as I remembered it… except none of my family was there. No one was hugging, or crying, or laughing in the churchyard. I was alone.

After driving for five hours, I intended to get out, look at some headstones, and remember the good times. My sister and counsellor would both be proud of me. I was proud of me. The caretakers had placed benches and lights all over the churchyard and the cemetery. How thoughtful of them to do that. It was obvious that whoever put those lights out here had been here often enough to know where they were needed. Who could that be? Even though it was a mystery to me, I was grateful for this opportunity so sit and relax after my long trip. I would do some research tomorrow, but tonight, I wanted to talk to God here. I needed God to talk back to me.

When I tried the door, it opened right up! I was shocked that anyone could come here at any time and go into the house of the Lord. What a great idea. My heart was thankful for whoever did this. Could it be one of the movie stars? Surely, it had to be, but Who? And Why? I guess it does not really matter about any of that.

Someone was providing me with this wonderful opportunity, and if I could find out more about him; that would be great. I would even want to help with this project, myself. I would definitely investigate more tomorrow. For right now, I was feeling a warm spiritual welcome here. I knew that it was the right thing for me to come out here. Thank God that I listened to my sister and my counselor. I could feel the love and warmth of the Lord, and those that had gone on before me. My family's love had always been like an umbrella that sheltered me from the harsh world outside. It was great to feel that way again. There in High Valley, my heart felt peace and comfort just like I had as a child. Once again, I told myself that our Circle will not be Broken. I was getting better.

Walking to the cemetery, I found our family plot quickly. There were three names that I needed to find that night. Alfred Tennyson March, Joseph Fielding March, and Emma Jane March- my Auntie, and her two crusty old brothers. I knelt and ran my hands over their names as soon as I got to them. The stones were cool and smooth, but it seemed as if I could feel warmth in them. They were right next to each other in death, even as they had been in life. Alfred had always been called Uncle Buddy, Joseph was Uncle Joe, and Emma Jane was always Auntie. These three had been the Heart and Soul of my grandmother's family. They were the three oldest of eleven children. Not one of them had ever married. Each one had some adventures when younger, but never found the right mate. Auntie once told me that marriage and family was just too hard if you didn't find that Special Someone to commit your life to. Uncle Buddy had Lady Friends until he died. He was a Heartbreaker, and a Loose Cannon all the days of his life.

He and Uncle Joe and some other boys had once trapped some "revenooers" in a tiny cabin near their "moonshine still." They kept those two men penned down for a couple of days. However, when my Auntie found out about it, she sent the rest of the brothers up there to get those boys and bring them home immediately. She claimed that she taught them some manners that day, but they denied it. She still scolded them about that when they were eighty years old. I had wonderful memories of these folks, and I thanked God that I came here tonight. Once again, I imagined that great family reunion in the sky. My sweet little "Mammaw" would be surrounded by her huge rough and tumble family once again. She and Auntie had been bright, twinkling lights in my life. These memories were cathartic for me, more than just healing. I felt "Whole" for the first time in many years. After a while I felt ready to head back.

I came here to find my life, and I did. Now, I am the Mom, the Auntie, the Mmmaw. Now, I am the umbrella. God will help me be who He created me to be. I was ready to start my journey home. Before I could start the car, I saw two lights in the sky, barely above the treetops. They were some distance away, but flying low, and fast. They had to be helicopters. Planes would never fly so close to the ground. Why were they there? Where were they going? The night was dark and cloudy, and this was the middle of nowhere. In a couple of seconds, I heard the muffled "Whump! Whump!" of the choppers, but I still could not see them. My natural instinct was to lay low and not draw attention to myself. Better to be safe than sorry, right? We had all heard the conspiracy theories about the black choppers, and I knew that they were cruising over my head that night.

Suddenly, I realized that I had not come here by accident. This was so much more than a sentimental journey. It was my destiny to be here tonight; it was my fate. Without knowing why, I was doing it, I manually turned all my vehicle's lights off. I did not want the dash or dome lights coming on when I started the engine. I did not want any lights on as I followed the black choppers through the darkened countryside. Yes, I had decided to follow them as far as I possibly could. In my heart, I suspected that they would disappear quickly. Nevertheless, I would try to find out where they were going and what they were doing. This would be the adventure of a lifetime.

Keeping the helos in sight as best I could, I started driving slowly down the country lane in the pitch-blackness. They had come up from the south, but we were moving in a northerly direction, now. Thank God for the small running light on each one of them, because that is all that I could see most of the time. After approximately ten minutes, two more lights appeared on the left side of my car, also. Those two choppers had flown in from the west, and they were heading north, parallel to the first two. I took my foot off the gas and rolled to a stop without touching my brakes. I did not want the brake lights to come on and alert them to my presence. Why would four black helos be flying in tandem, below the radar, out here in the wee hours after midnight? It was obviously some kind of rendezvous... With that thought, all four of them started shining some kind of spotlights toward the ground below. Simultaneously, they began to turn in a very wide circle. Apparently, they were looking for a place to land. I had been following them for close to twenty minutes, now. Of course, I was hopelessly lost, but, if I turned back south, I would eventually get back to High Valley Church. It was so well lit up at night that I should be able to see it from any high point around here.

When I noticed that the choppers were slowly descending, I drove off the road and hid my car the best that I could in a dense tangle of shrubbery. I was seriously nervous about this whole thing now. However, I opened the door and jumped out as quickly as I could. I was afraid that something would reflect off of my vehicle and bring them over here, with their guns blazing. Good Lord! I did not even know if they had guns to blaze. I had better get a grip. The four choppers were gradually getting closer and closer to the ground as I slunk around the side of my car toward them. Without any light of my own, I was trying to make the most of their searchlights to keep from falling on my face in the tangled undergrowth.

I was surprised to realize that those choppers had almost dropped out of sight. They had descended into a small cup-shaped valley that was several stories lower than the little rise where I was. They had effectively disappeared from the road and the surrounding area. What a perfect hiding place. These people were smart, very smart. Who are they? Dear Lord, please do not let them be drug smugglers, or terrorists, or something horrible like that. I wanted to see everything that was going on down there, but I was afraid of snakes, spiders, poison ivy, and just about everything else that I could not see in the darkness. Whether I wanted to or not, I had to crawl on my belly, like an army man, up to the edge of their landing basin. There was a lot of thick vegetation out there, and I was thankful for it, in spite of my fear. In fact, there was almost zero visibility thwn, because of the foggy mist that had been creeping up on me all evening. Hopefully, it would cover me and my vehicle to keep us hidden for a while.

As the first helicopter settled down onto the valley floor below, the other three hovered protectively above it. As soon as the door opened, armed men began jumping out of it; and formed a circle around it. The door closed quickly, and the rotor slowed to a stop. All the men were dressed in black, with those earphone things, and maybe body armor, too. Each one of them was searching the darkness intently… looking for anyone who did not belong there. Gulp… that would be me? I fervently hoped that they would not find me, or anyone else. They did not appear to be friendly. I shrank slowly back and lowered my head into the tall grass. How could I make myself smaller and less visible? I slid my arms down to my sides, and quietly pulled some weeds and held them in front of my eyes. I was just terrified that they were going to see me. What could be going on?

I was about half-convinced that there might be political figures on those choppers. This might be some type of extremely top-secret meeting of some kind. In a minute or so, the next helo landed and followed the same process as the first. After the third and fourth ones landed, sixteen armed guards formed a human shield around the landing site. I was very impressed with the precision of this whole sequence of events. They were obviously trained professionals. I could not tell if they were men or women. Nor could I tell if they were military. It seemed to be a military unit, because of their weapons and the way they operated. But, how could I know for sure. Some para-military organizations were staffed by former soldiers. Many mercenaries were also former military men (or women).

I am such a conventional thinker that I do not think of women as soldiers. When I was young, only men served in that capacity. Now, my middle granddaughter is in the police academy and will probably serve in the military as well. One of my oldest and dearest friends was a Highway Patrol Officer for over twenty years. She was a highly decorated officer and received several medals for valor. She was shot three times before she retired. Still, I am old fashioned, and often forget that this is not totally a man's world anymore. Maybe just ninety-five percent? Regardless, I was assuming that they were all men, when they could be women. I think that a part of me wanted them to be women. I do not know why.

After several intense minutes, the door on the first helicopter opened again, and some steps slid out from the bottom of the frame. Two more black-clad figures came slowly down the steps. Each one appeared to be talking on their earphones. The doors on the second, third, and fourth choppers opened, and two people came out of each one of them also. Almost all of them were speaking into those little microphones on their heads. At first, I thought that maybe they were communicating with each other. However, I soon realized that they were talking to other people, somewhere else. What in the heck could be going on out here? Why all this secrecy and security? Maybe the President of the United States was on one of those black choppers?

Man, the suspense was killing me, and my mind was running wild, too. Someone else was coming out of number one, and she was definitely female. The woman wore a black skirt, beige shirt, and black vest. She also wore the headphone thing, but she was not speaking into hers. She was speaking to someone behind her. She was holding hands with a child…leading her toward the steps. It was obvious that the little one was frightened and needed coaxing to step out into the night. I wondered why the woman didn't just pick that little girl up and carry her down. Then, I realized that there was more than one child on board. She was trying to get several more children out the door. The lighting was poor, and I was a good distance away, which made my vision poor, also. It appeared to me that the children were not Caucasian. They all appeared to be darker skinned, Hispanic, or maybe black kids, and they were all dressed in black, also. The girls had on little jumpers, and the boys wore knee shorts. To say that I was shocked is quite an understatement. I was flabbergasted. There were kids on that chopper... Kids! I guess the woman asked for light, because, all four of the Black Helicopters turned on those spot lights and aimed them into the middle of the circle of armed guards. They created quite a bit of light, which seemed to encourage the little guys to venture out.

My guess is that they were between the ages of two and five. When the next woman stepped out, she was carrying one little girl that was too terrified to walk. Then, the pilot and co-pilot stepped out and left all the doors open. Now, six children, two women, and two male pilots joined the sixteen armed guards and eight other men who first came down those steps. For some reason, I felt compelled to keep a count of how many people were in the circle. There were thirty-four out there, now. One of the soldiers went into number one and apparently searched to see if there was anyone else inside. He came back out and gave the universal thumbs-up sign as he talked on his headset.

The door to number two opened, and I expected more kids to come out, but there were twelve adults on this one. The two pilots exited, along with two flight attendants. Guess what? They were all dressed in black. There was no significant difference in any of them. One thing was obvious, though... they were couples, and they were waiting for these children. This was some kind of adoption ring or black-market babies, or something. Whatever it was, it certainly was well-funded. I cannot imagine how much all this cost. Even very wealthy people would be hard-pressed to afford this kind of operation. I was more intrigued than ever. The parents knew exactly which child was theirs; because they paired off immediately and knelt down to speak comforting words to the little ones. The kids all looked healthy and reasonably happy. I mean to say that they did not appear to be victims of some disaster or anything like that. Most of the children were allowing the adults to hold their hands or even hug them and pick them up. That was a good sign. Traumatized children usually will not respond that way. At this point, there were fifty people in the circle of light.

The four flight attendants began to divide the families between the two choppers, presumably to fly them out of there. The third and fourth choppers went through the same process, with the same results. All the children were met by excited, happy parents and loaded onto the black helicopters in an amazingly short period of time. All the armed guards loaded up, the engines roared, and, one-by-one, they lifted up and took off. This time, they all went in four different directions, very rapidly. They were still flying below the radar, and without lights. I did not move at all until they were completely out of sight. Even then, I was afraid that they might circle back to make sure that no one was out here. No one was supposed to see those black helicopters.

After about ten minutes, I started to slowly creep back to my car. What I had just witnessed with these people convinced me that they would spare no expense to make sure that no one discovered that secret meeting. Once again, I started and drove off without any lights. I was correct about High Valley Church. It was lit up like a beacon, and I saw it from the first high point on the way south. Even though it was quite foggy now, the church lights, which were the only ones visible, gave me the direction I needed to go. Wait… wait a minute; what if that was the whole point of the church being lit up like it was? What if the church was the beacon for those choppers as well? Maybe someone upgraded High Valley for the express purpose of using it as a directional signal for vessels flying without lights on dark, foggy nights? Whatever I had seen tonight was creating more questions than I could provide answers for. Nevertheless, I had to figure this out.

When I had been back on the road for another ten minutes, I turned my lights on and looked at my watch. It was four o'clock in the morning, now. My body was exhausted, but my brain was electrified. I kept thinking about everything that I had observed that night, and what it could mean. This was no conspiracy theory. The helicopters were real, and they were right there, in south central Texas that night. I just did not dare tell anyone else the truth about them. Truth, like beauty, is often in the eye of the beholder. Someone else would certainly tell me what I had seen and what it meant, but I did not know who to trust, yet. Therefore, I would tell no one at all. One thing was for sure, I needed to get off this road quickly. They might be monitoring traffic out there to ensure complete privacy. I had to be extremely careful from then on out.

The nicest motel that I could find was a full hour away from High Valley. There were others, closer, but I wanted it to look like I had been coming from the opposite direction when I checked in. After some sleep, I would begin some serious research on the internet. I asked for a wake-up call at eleven, telling the night-shift man that I was on my way to Dallas for a business meeting tomorrow night. A last-minute deal for me because a colleague had gotten sick and could not make the trip, himself. I would stay until checkout tomorrow, because I needed to spend some time preparing for my presentation. That was bound to be a common enough occurrence to make a plausible cover story for my presence there. When my head hit that pillow, I was sound asleep.

Luckily, for me, five or six hours of sleep is all I ever require. So, when the phone rang at eleven, I was ready to start my day. The public library is still a perfect place to go for local news and historical information. I wrote down the name and address of a large construction company that was making repairs on the interstate out-side of town. I told the library staff that I worked for that company and wanted to study some topographical maps for a different project that we might be interested in later. I was just trying not to draw attention to High Valley or myself. In a couple of hours, I learned a lot more about this area than I hoped I could. It turned out that two prominent movie stars had, in fact, bought the sections of land around the church, and landing site. Those two were widely known for their humanitarian efforts. They were not only extremely wealthy, but philanthropic, as well. I read a lot about the black choppers, too. People around there had seen them a couple of years ago. There were several reports then, but nothing had made it into the official records since. In addition to those subjects, I searched topics dealing with refugee children and adoptions of all kinds. Then, I did a cross reference with all of those things. Jackpot! I got an Information Overload on that.

Newspaper articles from three different continents claimed that children were being "Abducted" with those black choppers. Jiminy crickets! Did you get that? The newspaper articles said, "Kids and black choppers!" in the same sentence! According to those that were being interviewed, the children in question were all orphans. Some of them had been "Working" together to support their large families. Of course, we know about the "Sweat Shops" where those little ones were exploited to the point of slavery and death. The U. S. government refused to give credence to any of those rumors. To this very day, no one will answer questions about those helicopters. In fact, officials claim that they are just urban legends that do not really exist. Truth to tell, I thought that myself... until I saw them flying into Mexico over fifteen years ago.

That is correct I have seen them on two separate occasions, now. The first time, my husband, my oldest son, and I were working on some property about forty-five minutes from the border town of Del Rio, Texas. We were out in the boondocks, alone, clearing some land for a fence line. We heard those powerful engines and humongous rotors from miles away. It scared the livers out of all of us. It seemed like the ground was vibrating under our feet. There were five of them flying very low, and very fast, down a narrow canyon, straight into Mexico. I guarantee you that they were well below the radar and not on any designated flight plan. The helos that I saw last night were much, much quieter than the first ones we saw and heard years ago. There had been a definite improvement in that area.

I could not help but wonder if there were kids on board when they flew back out of Mexico, then. What if they were rescuing little kids that were being abused, neglected, or abandoned? Maybe they were bringing starving kids from India, Ethiopia, or anywhere else on the globe. Gosh, I hoped they were. I hope that people are adopting them and saving their lives. I hope they increase the number of the little guys like the ones I saw last night. I hope forty or fifty choppers bring loads of them over here every single night. I hope all of those kids get parents, and brothers, and sisters, and aunts, and uncles, and whole families that want them, love them, and give them nice homes to grow up in. Kids need their families.

You do not need to be a trained grief counselor to see where my mind was going with all that. I was seeing a whole bunch of broken pencils that could still be loved and needed. Even those parents last night had probably been shattered and jagged at one time. Taking a broken child into their broken hearts would be the very best kind of glue known to God and man.

They would all be stronger in their broken places.

I will be stronger where I have been broken, too.

So will you.

Do you have a High Valley in your past, or in your heart?

Find a place of Comfort and Hope.

Go there now.

God Speed.

The Geek

VIRAGO- A STRONG, BRAVE, WARLIKE
WOMAN THAT DEMONSTRATES
EXEMPLARY, AND HEROIC QUALITIES

My husband, Derek, does many things that drive me insane. One of those things is constantly going to Thrift Shops. Yes, he is one of those crazy "Thrift Shoppers." He has dragged the kids and me to every Goodwill, Salvation Army, and resale shop in every town that we have ever been to. Seriously, we even had to go thrift shopping when we were on vacation. For years, we also had to stop at garage sales and estate sales. However, we finally made him stop that because of the crappy houses and scary neighborhoods that he would take us to. Once, we got covered in fleas and had to fumigate our car, and the house. The kids had several large fits about that incident. Dad agreed to give us a break from garage sales after that. He just about never lived it down.

I have told him many times that he is "killing me" with all his thrift shop stuff. Well, last month, a thrift shopper literally nearly killed me. Let me tell you how this whole thing started. We were on vacation in Florida, at a large Goodwill Store in an upscale urban area. He was looking at shirts, because he has an unfortunate shirt fetish. So, he was in the men's department, and I decided to go look at the lamps. I needed a lamp in the RV, and I have seen many great household products at thrift shops. You know that one man's trash is another man's treasure.

While I was over in the electronics department, I could not help but notice all the computers, printers, and copiers stacked everywhere. We know many people that buy things like that all the time. We have one friend that built his own computer from old ones he bought at thrift shops. Our nephew has a computer/copier/printer repair shop, and he routinely uses parts from old machines. He once bought an old copier for two hundred and fifty dollars. He used one part from it and made a four-hundred-dollar profit. I am telling you about this because I want you to know that many people buy and use the old computers that we consider junk.

I found a small lamp that looked to be the right size, so I carried it to the back wall to plug it in. I wanted to make sure it would work, before I paid for it. There were several power strips along there for people to use. The lamp would not come on, so I crouched down to see if the power strip was plugged in and turned on. As I looked around for the wall plug, a laptop screen on the floor suddenly came to life. I was a couple of aisles away and did not see anyone at first. However, when I bent further down and looked under the display tables, I spotted a man kneeling with another computer on the floor in front of him. Both of them were working. How amazing! This fellow must be one of those "Geeks" that we are always hearing about. I started to say, "Good work; you have resurrected two of them from the dead" … or something witty like that. However, my sixth sense told me to stay down and stay quiet. I was not sure why, but for some reason, I did not want The Geek to know that anyone was watching him. His back was to me, and I slowly moved a couple of feet to my left where a solid shelf could hide me.

I spied on him for a minute or two. He was a young man, with swarthy skin and long dark hair. He was dressed in dark clothes and was wearing black gloves. Imagine that…black gloves in the middle of the day…in Florida. My full attention was riveted on him as he continued to tinker around on the floor with both computers. I could not see what was going on, but this whole thing made me very suspicious. Maybe he was going to steal them. Maybe he was just going to steal some parts off them. Wait… both of them were working, so maybe he had already stolen what he needed…Truthfully, I had no idea what he was doing, had done, or was going to do. He was very intense and moving very fast, and he seemed to be doing something wrong. He stuck one of those little flash things in the side of one of the laptops and both of them started going like crazy. I do not know or understand anything about modern technology, but The Geek was doing something; that much was clear. He pulled his cell phone out of his pocket and plugged a wire from it to one of the computers, and that screen lit up and started scrolling down, also.

This was quite impressive to me, because of my lack of ability in this area. I was impressed, but my nerves had suddenly developed "The Frizzies." Something was just not right with The Geek. I pulled out my cell phone and snapped a couple of pictures of him and the whole scene in front of me. I decided that I had better find my husband, before he started looking for me. As I gazed over the tops of displays, I caught his eye. I made the universal "Be Quiet" sign by putting my finger to my lips. Then, because I know him so well, I slowly drew my finger across my throat and cut my eyes down toward The Geek. He could not see down there, but I slowly put my finger back to my lips again and held the other hand up like "Stop." I hoped I was not waving the red flag in front of the bull, but you never know with my husband. He looked around, really confused, and mouthed, "What the…?" I slowly put both hands in the air in front of me like those football referees do. (I guess that means get back, or stop, or something like that.) I keep saying slowly because I was afraid that just the movement of my clothes would scare The Geek and cause him to leave before I could figure out what he was doing.

Well, the bull was charging my way, now. However, he was doing it slowly, with a puzzled look on his face. Once again, I put both hands in front of me and mouthed, "Wait," while giving him a killer evil eye. He finally stopped and looked at me like he was going to do something… anything, even if it was wrong. I cut my eyes down toward The Geek again, and mouthed, "WAIT. STOP." He did stop then. Thank God.

There is something you should know about Derek…He is a man that was born in the wrong century. He is a Daniel Boone type that is always "Packin' Heat." Which means he carries a gun at all times. We are both Native Texans, and guns are a way of life for us. He has never even pulled a gun on anyone before. I guess he looks like the type that no one should mess with. On the other hand, I have pointed a gun at two different people; and would not hesitate to do it again, if the need should arise. I am not a violent or mean person, but I am not a victim, either. Both times that I felt as if I needed to kill someone, my children were with me, and I feared for their safety. No one will ever hurt my kids or me as long as I can prevent it.

Nevertheless, I did not want Derek to shoot The Geek or anyone else today. I did not want to be on the evening news. So, I continued to hold up one finger in his direction as if I was saying, "Just one minute." All of this had happened in a few seconds, even though it seemed a lot longer. When I turned back to look at The Geek, I was shocked to see him walking rapidly toward the back of the store where the volunteers go to price merchandise! He was carrying a large backpack, which probably contained the two laptops. They were not on the floor or the table where he had been. Maybe he was working here? He was probably running diagnostics or loading programs or something important like that. But, I thought he was doing something wrong or illegal.

I motioned to Derek to come with me, and when he got close enough I whispered for him to be quiet and just act like nothing was going on.

He wanted to ask me a million questions, but I cut my eyes toward The Geek and said, "SHHH- just follow me. Quietly."

We both made our way toward the back of the store where I opened the door with the Employees Only sign and looked around. There were several volunteers looking back at me in a somewhat hostile manner, but, no Geek there. Derek could not stand one more second of silence and asked me what was going on.

I explained everything that had happened in the last few minutes. Of course, he thought I was crazy for wanting to know what The Geek was doing. He told me to mind my own business, and threw in several other pieces of advice, as well. I was shushing him as we walked back through the store and out the door to leave. When we got to the car, I asked him why he was not curious about someone wearing black gloves in the middle of the summer…in Florida. He sighed heavily and said that he was not curious about the stupid things that young people were wearing, doing, and saying. You certainly cannot argue with that.

"Derek, I just KNOW that The Geek is doing something TERRIBLE. I KNOW IT. He is creeping around, and secretly using The Internet at Thrift Shops! He's hiding because he doesn't want anyone to know what he's doing! I'm telling you that he's doing something illegal and TERRIBLE! I just FEEL it in my Gut. Please, Honey, just Trust me, Honey. Please just help me find out what he's doing? PLEASE?"

My husband looked at me very intently for a minute before he put the truck in reverse. He was mumbling about "Crazy Female Tuition Crap" while he was backing out of the parking lot. The Geek drove right past us on a bicycle. He was wearing the backpack, but the gloves were gone.

I calmly said, "Derek if you will follow him, I will go to a thrift shop every single day next week. I promise I will, if you will just follow him. Please, don't let him get away."

"Oh, Hell No!" he yelled. "I am definitely not following this Geek. How long do you think we are going to follow him? How many miles or minutes do I have to follow him? What else do you plan to do besides follow him? I hope to God that you don't make me have to shoot someone today. If he were following me, I would sure as hell shoot him."

I was watching The Geek turn left into another parking lot.

"Just slow down and stay way back away from him. Let's just see where he's going."

He came to a full stop and looked me in the eyes, and said, "How many minutes do you think I am going to follow this guy?"

I answered, "Well, how about thirty minutes? That's not very long and I will go to one of your favorite stores every single day for a week. I will stay for thirty minutes for you. OK? Please, Derek, just humor me, OK? I think he is doing something illegal, and wrong." I had never taken my eyes off The Geek during the whole negotiation.

He pulled into the parking lot and parked far away from where The Geek was locking his bike.

"Now what?" he growled.

I asked him to just be still, and quiet until we see where he goes next. I got nothing but more heavy sighs from my husband. I still kept my eyes on the geek and waited to see what he was going to do next. I guess that he had those two laptops in his backpack, because it looked heavy. In a minute, he started walking toward a store at the other end of the strip mall. You will not believe this. He was going into another resale shop!

"Now, Derek, I need for you to go in that shop and watch him for me. I do not know if he saw me at Goodwill or not, but I cannot let him see me here, or he will get suspicious and hide. But, Honey, he could not have seen you, because you were over in the men's department. You want to go in there, and shop anyway. Don't you? You can just watch where he goes and what he does from the corner of your eye. He won't even know you're watching him. You know how to creep around and hunt and stuff…"

After he thought about it for a minute, he asked me if this counted as one of his weeklong thrift shop rewards for following The Geek for thirty minutes. Oh, dear Lord, sometimes he can drive a saint to drink. I assured him that I would still go with him every single day next week, and he finally got out of the car and headed into the resale shop.

We are major bird watchers, so we keep binoculars in every one of our vehicles. I grabbed mine and tried to find out something about his bicycle. How smart he was to use a bike instead of a car or motorcycle. It is very difficult to trace, he can weave in and out of traffic, and even ride on the sidewalk if he wanted to. I sure hoped my crazy husband was watching him. It seemed like a long time before The Geek came out and got on his bike to leave. It was twenty-two minutes. Time really drags when you are sitting in a car waiting for someone. I watched him through my binoculars, while slinking way down in my car seat. Surely, Derek would hurry right on out here before the geek could escape? He was probably buying five or six more shirts...

Just then, he jerked open the door and scared me to death. I screamed, and I guess that scared him, because he also screamed (like a little girl). Then, he tried to run, jump, and get in the car all at the same time. He practically fell into the driver's seat and started yelling in a hushed voice.

"What the Hell? You scared the crap outta me. Are you crazy? Do you want me to lose him? Dammit woman, we gotta be real incognito with this guy. You better lay low and watch him before he gets away. Why were you yelling, anyway?"

Keeping The Geek in sight, I answered, "Well you scared me so bad that I nearly jumped out of my hair. Why are you so frantic, now? What happened that made you change your mind about following him? Tell me everything. He is only about a block ahead on the right side of the road. Just go slow, and don't let him see us. Come on; tell me what happened in that store."

Derek was strangely silent for a minute, which really freaked me out. When he stopped at a red light, he turned to me and said, "He did exactly the same thing there that he did at Goodwill."

I was stunned. My voice quavered when I asked, "What does that mean? Why is he doing this? Don't you think all this stuff is illegal? What should we do? Should we call someone? Who should we call? Should we be scared?"

Evidently, only one question was going to be answered because my Daniel Boone said, "Hell no, we are not going to be scared. That Geek is the one who should be scared. I think the little freak is Al-Qaeda or something. Why else is he creeping around using other people's internet, without them knowing it? If he is sending some kind of secret code about the U.S.A. I'll teach him a real secret code-the one that starts with, Smith and ends with Wesson."

His outburst caused me to ask many more questions. "Honey,

why did you say that about Al-Qaeda? Did you see or hear anything that seemed to be Arabic, or Muslim? Did you see anything on the computer screen that looked like it was Middle Eastern? Seriously, why did you say that?"

I was terribly worried about him jumping to some kind of conclusion and making things a whole lot worse. We all knew that every terrorist/mass murderer in recent history had been recruited and nurtured through the internet. The Geek was accessing the world-wide-web in a sneaky manner, as if he did not want anyone to be able to track his internet time. Truthfully, I think that if this thing is all about trying to kill Americans, I will shoot him myself. Just last month four unarmed soldiers were slaughtered at a recruiting center. If this geek is one of the people who commit those acts of terrorism, I want to stop him.

I wondered if we should call Homeland Security and tell them what we had seen. Derek was one hundred percent against that because he thinks they are incompetent and would only spook him into hiding. We certainly were not any more competent than any of them. I cannot imagine why he thinks we would be more successful than government employees that are specifically trained for this. They have satellites and telephone bugging devices for goodness sake. I plan to find a pay phone and make an anonymous phone call to several official agencies tomorrow. What if they trace my call and started looking for me, too? Thinking about what might happen was scaring me to death. I really did not want to be on the evening news. How in the heck did I get in the middle of this thing with a terrorist Geek and a Daniel Boone whose motto is "Remember the Alamo?" You know… nobody survived The Alamo.

Now, Derek, was thoroughly enjoying this little escapade. He was talking about trading vehicles, so our quarry would not know that he was being tailed. He seemed to have forgotten our deal about only following this person for thirty minutes. In fact, he was making plans to stake him out that whole evening, and see where he went the next day, too. I did not want to ignore a potential terrorist threat, but I did not want to make a life-changing decision based on faulty reasoning, either.

"Seriously, how do we know that The Geek is doing anything wrong at all," I asked him. "Right now, we are the ones breaking the law. Following him is a crime, it's called stalking. Maybe we should just go home and call the authorities."

Derek was muttering things like, "How do I keep the geek in sight, and stay out of sight myself? Now I understand why the T V detectives always have two or three cars following the murderer. One car is too obvious if you have to go more than a few minutes. He is on a bicycle, for Pete's sake. Doesn't he ever look behind that bike? I know that I would recognize a car that was following me…"

Naturally, when he said that, I looked in the side mirror to see what was behind us. It was just an automatic reaction to his grumbling, but still a good idea. So, I made a mental note of the vehicles back there. Once or twice, I tried to get him to talk about calling the authorities, but he was not interested in anything like that. However, he promised that we would call Homeland Security as soon as we found out what The Geek was doing. That was no comfort to me. I secretly vowed to make that call as soon as I could, without my husband ever knowing about it.

We had made several turns while I was worrying about appearing on the evening news, or America's Most Wanted. Without thinking, I glanced in the side mirror again. To my surprise, one of the cars I had noticed earlier was still back there. We had gone a couple of miles in heavy traffic since my first look. What were the odds that the same car would still be behind us? I told myself to relax. I needed to see if that car stayed with us or turned off. Why in the world would I even think that someone was following us? I guess because we were following someone else? Regardless of what my mind was screaming, I kept quiet and began to watch the vehicles behind us. When we passed a big window, I looked intently at the reflection of the gray sedan that was staying three cars behind us. There were two men in the front seat, but that was really all that I could tell about it. I made a mental note of the time and realized that we had been on this quest for a little over an hour and a half. It seemed a lot longer, because my emotions were just wearing me out. Derek continued to twist and turn along the way, never losing sight of The Geek. To my horror, the gray car stayed right with us.

Seriously shaken up now, my voice quavered when I spoke. "Umm, Honey, let's just go on back to the RV Park now. OK? Please?"

Derek shot me a look and said, "Woman, are you crazy? You need to barf or something? Now is not the time to be carsick. If you are, just hurl into one of those plastic bags. I am not stopping or turning off now. If I do, we will lose The Geek, and all of this will count for nothing. I have a bad feeling that this guy is some kind of radical terrorist that intends to do something to kill Americans. You feel that way, too. Why are you crying? You're gettin' scared, aren't you? You always cry when you're scared. Don't be scared. What if we can stop him from hurting people? You know we gotta try. Don't be a sissy-baby-girl. You're scared, and you wanna go home. But, you know I'm right about trying to stop him from hurting anyone? Tell the truth. Am I right about this?"

Strangely enough, he was right. I was scared. Everything he said was right, but he did not know that someone was tailing us, too. Truthfully, I was scared to tell him that. I was afraid of what he would do to them. I Really did not want to be on the evening news... not now, not ever.

Without any warning, The Geek turned very sharply and quickly into a tiny alley that looked like it was too skinny for his handlebars to fit. Derek shot through the orange light above us yelling obscenities about losing him after all this time. My eyes immediately flicked to the car behind us, and I was gratified to see them stuck at that intersection. We were speeding toward the next block where we could turn around and find that bicycle again. Thank God there were no cops around, because we had broken several laws in the last few seconds. All I could do was hold on and pray that we would come out of this crazy adventure unharmed. After making two fast left turns, Derek slowed to a snail's pace and continuously urged me to find the geek before he totally disappeared. He was now moving so slowly that I could have run circles around our car. However, I was also terrified that the gray car was going to catch up to us again any second. We did not see our suspect anywhere, and the alley was empty except for dumpsters overflowing with garbage. Derek asked me if I thought he knew that he had a tail. Without waiting for my answer, he asked where I would go to lose a tail. Then, he immediately raced to the next cross street and flew around two more blocks on the other side of the road. My husband had remained extremely focused during this whole afternoon. Of course, he did not know that we had a tail, ourselves. Ignorance really is bliss.

Derek had made so many random turns that we were hopelessly lost. He had also lost our tail, without even realizing what he was doing. I glanced at a road sign that said we were only three blocks from the Downtown Auditorium. The very next sign was a lighted marquee that advertised The Messianic Mosaic at the auditorium today. I enjoyed their music because it was both Christian and Jewish.

"There he is! I cannot believe it! I found him! Look! He's coming out of that pawn shop!" Derek yelled.

Sure enough, The Geek was walking away from the Downtown Dough Pawn Shop with a guitar case on his back. The backpack full of laptops had evidently been exchanged for a… guitar? My stomach lurched into my throat and my heart pounded so hard that my whole body shook. In Texas, men go to pawnshops for one main thing… guns. What if he had one of those machine gun things? You know that AK47 gun that was supposed to be outlawed because it could automatically fire a zillion and nine bullets in a Nano-second. As soon as my mind processed these ideas, I turned to look at Derek and saw that his whole complexion had turned ashen.

Looking right into my eyes, he croaked one syllable, "Gun."

Tears began to run down my face again as the truth settled into my brain.

"Oh, Dear Jesus. No. Please, God. No."

I had spoken aloud without even knowing it.

Daniel Boone reached over, grabbed my shaking hands, and said, "It's OK. Don't freak out. We are here for a reason. God has us right here right now for a reason. We can do whatever we have to do. He doesn't know that we know about him. Honey, we have to stop him. Help me think… How do we handle this? Where is he going? What's he going to do? Who's the target?"

Words almost refused to come out of my mouth, so I pointed toward the huge building in front of us. "It's the Auditorium. He's going to kill people at the concert. They will all be Jews and Christians. Infidels. He's going to that concert to kill Infidels. Dear God…"

Derek jammed the car into park and jerked his door open so fast that I gasped in fear. He just ran right around to my door and started pulling me out.

"You gotta go park this car and come in as fast as you can. I'll call you and tell you where I am. Come on, Baby. Go park. You have your gun. Keep your hand on it at all times. Keep your phone in your other hand. I'll call you, and we will make sure that he can't hurt anyone. Nobody is going to get hurt here today."

He had shoved me under the steering wheel and slammed the door. He bent down and looked into my eyes; his left hand held my trembling chin.

"Go park. I love you." He was gone, running into the crowd, my Daniel Boone.

Horns were honking all around me as I shakily turned into the nearest valet parking lot. When I slammed on the brakes and jumped out, the attendant knew that something was terribly wrong. He tore off a claim stub without any questions, and I grabbed it from him as I ran into the auditorium. It took several minutes to get my ticket.

While I was running up the stairs, my phone rang. "Where are you? Are you in the building yet? Have you seen him or anyone else suspicious?"

Anyone else??? Oh My God. What if there were others? What if he had help? What do they call them? Cells? Terrorist cells? What if they all started shooting at one time? How many people were going to be shot or killed?

"Talk to me, Bev, Bev... BEVERLY! Where are you?"

I gulped and answered him, "I'm at the top of the stairs on aisle E. Where are you? Have you called 911? We can't possibly find him in this crowd. He has probably already gotten into his firing position. Derek, he has been planning this for months, and he knows every nook and cranny of this place. We gotta call 911. We can't do this."

Derek's voice crackled, "OK. You're at the top of the stairs. Good. Now, start walking on the outside of the crowd. Walk along the outside wall. There will be doors leading into electrical maintenance areas and A/C vents, and stuff like that. You know what I mean? He needs to be high up and hidden. You have the skills and training for this. We both know what we're doing. We have gone to classes and gotten certified for this exact scenario. We have urged our friends and family to do the same thing, Honey. Stop saying you can't! You can, and you will! Peoples' lives are at stake here... Where is your Enforcer? You have your hand on it?" I could barely understand all of that because the reception in here was awful.

We had been involved with several N R A-type groups that "trained" civilians to protect themselves. I was a good shot. God, please help me remember what to do, and do not let anyone get hurt here tonight.

I spoke quietly into the phone, "I see him. Derek, I see him. He just went into a door. Just like you said. I can't tell what letter is nearest to him because it's darker over there. I'm by aisle J, now. Everything past me is dark and empty. Where are you?"

Our phones were full of static, "Oh crap! I'm all the way over at aisle T! Bev, I'm..." Snap, crackle, and pop. He was gone.

His phone must have died because mine still had a signal and a charge. Immediately re-dialing him did me no good. His voice mail answered. I tried to look across the building to find aisle T, but my terrible vision made it impossible for me to see much of anything. I moved toward that room arguing with myself about the necessity to proceed without Derek. I was a wreck.

My entire body was cold and shaking as I made my way along that back wall. There were no lights on back there, and all this whole section had been blocked off. Strobe lights and fake smoke began to streak across the stage. Messianic music floated through the chilly darkness, and the house lights dimmed even more in preparation for the concert to start. Part of my brain was screaming for me to dial 911 and run out of there as fast as I could. Another voice was quietly trying to reason with myself to just find out what The Geek was doing. Reason said to open the door and see if he had a gun or not. If he were just another musician/computer geek, I would tell him that I was a security guard and then run out. If he had a gun… I could not hesitate to kill him, or he would kill me. There was a weak light strip under the door, and I could hear a low, muffled voice inside.

Once again, I tried to call Derek. No answer, so I crept closer to the room. I took my gun out of my pocket, squatted down, (to make a smaller target), breathed a quick (and confusing) prayer, and quickly jerked the door open. The Geek whirled around, wide-eyed. He had a tiny bright light on his forehead, like a coal miner. He was also wearing one of those little earplugs with the microphone coming around to his mouth. He had a radio or walkie-talkie in his right hand. My voice was firm as I told him to put his hands up and keep that light on the ceiling. While he was doing those two things, I stepped into the room and closed the door.

To my shock, The Geek spoke into the microphone, "Chief, she's here! She just pointed a gun in my face."

I stepped closer to him and rapidly jerked that microphone and light off his head.

He kept his hands high and said, "Lady, who the hell are you and why are you here? You are interfering with a Top-Secret CIA operation. I am a Government Agent working undercover here. Lady…"

He started to lower his head, and I said, "Keep those hands and your head real high. I will shoot you if you move again. Believe me; I will not hesitate to put six shots right into your heart. I will not miss. What…?"

My phone began to ring, but I was afraid to answer it. If I was distracted for a split-second, he could grab my gun and it would all be over for me.

My phone vibrated with a text message and then began to ring again. I prayed that it was Derek, because he was the only living person who had any idea where I was and what was going on here. The Geek tried to talk again, but I told him to shut up and lay down on the floor with his hands behind his head. I stayed far away from him and made sure that he could not reach me or anything else on the floor. I was now using the little light thing to see what he was doing in there. When he was flat on the floor with his fingers laced behind his head, I could see the open guitar case lying on a low table in the corner. Dear God, he had one of those AK guns in there. Thankfully, it was in two pieces, and not ready to be fired. The little microphone thing had been squeaking continuously since I took it from him. His radio crackled with static every few seconds. My phone rang and vibrated without stopping, too.

Time seems to stand still when you are stressed out. Doesn't it? We had only been in there together for a minute or two, but it seemed like such a long time to me. The concert had also begun which added to my confusion and stress. This little room was almost vibrating from the huge speakers that were mounted along that outside wall.

The man on the floor said, "Please, Lady, please…"

I kicked his foot and told him to shut up or I would shoot him right then. I wanted to ask him what he was going to do with that gun, but I decided to wait for Derek. A foreign language started breaking through the static on his radio.

"I'm a CIA Agent... I have to answer him Right now... or I'm blown. Lady, people are going to die! You have to let me answer that radio. They will start shooting people any minute now. Please give me..."

Someone outside the door said, "Beverly Day, this is Chief Brandon of the Central Intelligence Agency. Please stand down. Do not shoot. I am going to open the door..."

"NO! Do not touch that doo,r or I will kill him and you and anyone else who tries to help him..."

I looked at the door as I screamed, and The Geek flipped over onto his back with a gun in his hand. "Please lady, just let me answer that radio call..." I don't want to have to shoot you...Please, for God's sake... Give me that radio..."

I tried to make myself start shooting, but it was not as easy to kill someone as I had been trained to believe it would be. I had been arguing with myself about him all day. Now, we were pointing guns at each other and I could not make myself shoot. He did not shoot me, either. He continued to babble about the CIA, and moved very slowly into a crouch while begging me to let him answer his radio before they started killing people...

Derek's voice came through the door, "Bev, it's me. Do not shoot The Geek. He's really CIA, really, Don't Shoot. Bev, you hear me?" I knew it was my husband out there, but how did I know that he was not under duress to tell me not to shoot?

I was so confused and scared. However, The Geek was not shooting, and he was on his feet now, looking into my eyes as he told me that he had to have the radio Right Now.

He held out his hand and nodded at me as he said, "Please just give me that radio and we can sort all of this out later. Please...Look, we both want to walk out of here alive, and we both want all these other people to be okay. Right? I do not want to shoot you. Please, give me the radio, and I can stop them from hurting anyone here to-day." His hand was shaking, and he sounded sincere about wanting to save people. Something in his eyes made me want to believe him.

I said to him, "OK. OK… But how do I know…"

Outside the door, Derek said, "Bev, I'm opening the door now. It's me, Bev, I'm coming in, now… Honey…"

My voice was shaking badly as I told him to come in alone and hurry up. The Geek/CIA Agent was still holding out his hand for the radio, so I just gave it to him and waited for my husband to help me straighten this mess out. The Geek turned his back to me and immediately began to speak into the radio in that foreign language.

As Derek came through the door, he whispered, "Bev, Honey, he really is CIA. Put your gun on the floor and come over here. Chief Brandon is coming in now. The other two gunmen have already been arrested. The Geek is talking to the person that recruited him… They want to get him, too, but he's hiding somewhere and…"

To be honest, I just tuned him and everything else out for a while.

They tell me that I was in shock, then. I was so exhausted that I literally felt like I could not stand on my own for two more minutes. My brain was spinning, and my heart was still pounding out of my chest. I think I had been crying for a long time. Derek had pulled me into a far corner and was standing in front of me holding my shoulders as he tried to make sure that I was OK.

Three more men squeezed into that little room with us. They all had the ear/microphone things and radios, and telephones and little blinking lighted things on their wrists. Derek turned and stood protectively in front of me with his arms folded across his chest. It made me realize that I was in big trouble, mega big trouble. They would put me in prison and throw away the key for threatening a Federal Agent with a gun. I was keeping him from his undercover assignment of saving this auditorium full of people. I was pretty sure that there would be something about a Parking Violation, too. Oh, yes, let us not forget that whole stalking thing that went on earlier today, either. It was beginning to look like I would be on the evening news after all.

I allowed myself to slowly slide down the wall and sit with my back against it while all those men listened to The Geek on the radio. He kept his back to all of us as he spoke. He was certainly convincing me that he was desperately in need of that recruiter's help. I felt sure that they would find out where he was and catch him, also. Perhaps we could share a cell… somewhere terrible and degrading. I was probably going to be charged with treason. I zoned out again because it was too much for me to deal with. No one made a sound for the longest time.

One of the other agents had picked up my gun as soon as he opened the door. He was now quietly closing the gun case and picking up everything that was lying around in the room. One of the other men suddenly turned around and put his hand over his ear, listening to some urgent communication from someone important. We all knew it was important by the way he concentrated on it.

The Geek was talking much louder now and seemed to be arguing as well as pleading. Every person in that room was listening intently to a conversation in a language that we did not even understand. What an amazing world we live in. Derek and I had become involved in an anti-terrorism scenario that was run by the C I A. Who would have thought that such a thing was possible? Not me.

The man with his hand over his ear mumbled into his microphone and one of the others mumbled into his radio. Believe it or not, the third man spoke into the blinking light on his wrist. The Geek turned to face us and held the radio at arm's length, so we could hear the unmistakable sound of gunfire.

They got him.

LATER

Technically, this whole thing is classified as Top Secret. However, pieces of it were reported on the evening news channels all over the world. Derek and I were not on the evening news, however, our three CIA Agents were interviewed for weeks after that. Thankfully, we are not ever going to be connected to any part of it. We are just two of the concert-goers that were escorted outside after the terrorist plot was discovered. Everyone was evacuated from the auditorium, and the authorities conducted a thorough search for explosives and additional assassins. We saw all of that on T V, later, because we were being interrogated at that time.

Believe me when I say that interrogation is an extremely unpleasant experience. It was pretty much like what you have seen in the movies all your life. First, they separated us, and then they left us alone and miserable for two hours. It was after midnight when two government officials finally came in to talk to me. I was terrified and exhausted long before they rushed into the room and started intimidating me. Trying to be polite and respectful, I immediately told them that I wanted an attorney. You could have heard a pin drop in that room. Clearly, they did not expect me to say that. However, I had watched The Closer for years and knew not to say anything without an attorney present.

I told Derek about a million times to say only one word if he was ever arrested…Lawyer. I also told him Not to say one single other word after he asked for said lawyer. Just to be on the safe side, I repeated my instructions to him at least twice as we were being hustled out of the auditorium and into the waiting Police cars. There is a good chance that I threatened his life before we were separated at the door.

After a little period of silence, I told the two that I would speak to an attorney, or Chief Brandon, or they could charge me with something, or I was going home. "Do not waste one more minute of my time. I'm tired. I know that the Chief is waiting out there, so just get him in here. I will only talk to him or The Geek. Sorry, I mean the undercover agent that's working with the chief. Come on, Guys, I mean it. Enough is enough." I looked around the room and spoke loudly, "Chief Brandon, please come and talk to me. I don't think you want me telling my story to the press right now. Do you sir?"

This was not a bluff. They had left me alone long enough to figure some things out. It was time to get everything settled and go home. The two flunkies mumbled and grumbled while stalling for time.

Finally, they left, and the Chief and The Geek came in. I stood and thanked both of them for coming. I asked for permission to make some statements to them. Then, I told them that I was so proud and thankful for their service to our country.

"You saved hundreds of lives tonight. I want you to know that I will agree to any conditions that you would like for me to. I will agree with whatever you say, and I will do whatever you want me to do. You can trust me to keep quiet about everything that happened today. I am intensely patriotic. I would never knowingly do anything to threaten my country's security. You have a monumental task to perform and I support you in every way possible. Please just tell me what you want me to do and let us go home. Please."

As an afterthought, I told The Geek that I was extremely sorry for threatening to kill him, and the Chief, too.

I sat down and listened as the Chief told me how things were going to be… From that point forward. His plan was for Derek and Beverly Day to disappear from this scene Totally. No one outside of these walls would ever know about our involvement in this Take Down. We would never speak of this incident again. Derek and I immediately agreed to keep silent… Until the Chief gave us permission to do so. That last part was my idea. I Really needed to let the whole world know how Dangerous this THRIFT SHOP COMPULSION can be. It's my Civic Duty.

YOU HAVE NOW BEEN WARNED

Relatively Seeking

MAMA'S STRENGTH COULD MOVE
MOUNTAINS, BOTH BIG AND SMALL.
MAMA'S STRENGTH COULD DO IT ALL...
CHRISTINA PATTERSON

I stepped out from behind the tree as the County patrol car turned into my gate. I walked up as the sheriff rolled his window down and looked at me expectantly.

"Hey, Jeffreaux. He went past here about four minutes ago, so he will be coming back in a minute or two. What are you going to do?"

He turned on his lights and backed across the two-lane road in front of my gate, effectively blocking traffic both ways. He got out, laid his shotgun on the trunk of the cruiser, unstrapped his sidearm, and crossed his arms over his torso. He spread his legs, gave me half a wink and half of a Nod.

"What do you want me to do, Kassie?"

"Well, I want you to find out why he keeps driving by here all day. Is he looking for a place to rob? Is he a murderer, looking for his next victim? Is he a criminal looking for a place to hide out from the law? What is he doing out here anyway? Why would a man on a Harley drive by my house three times in one morning? He doesn't belong out here, Jeffreaux..." I could not hide the fear and anger in my voice.

Sheriff Jeffreaux Dalton McCane, (JD) gave me a look that made me feel like everything would be OK. He is a man of few words. He sort of Nodded his head (the way men do) toward the road to let me know that the Harley was coming back, now. It was black, and the man driving it was dressed in black, with a black face shield on his black helmet. We could not see any of his facial features. He was going very slowly, and he coasted to a stop as soon as he saw the official vehicle blocking the road. JD took out his little scanning thing and typed in the license plate number. Then he took a picture of the man and his motorcycle. The man took off his helmet and JD Took another picture of him.

"Good afternoon, sir. I am Travis County Sheriff JD McCane. May I see your license, registration, and proof of insurance, please?"

The man appeared to be mid to late thirties, with lots of prematurely gray hair. He was attractive and probably younger than I thought. Since I turned fifty(ish), everyone seemed very young to me. He nodded politely and began to walk our way. Jeffreaux told him to "stand down" and asked him to place his paperwork on the trunk of the car. He had moved the shotgun into the crook of his arm…ready. JD is not a man to be trifled with. The cyclist immediately stopped with his palms up and said that he would have to unzip his leathers to get to his paperwork. When the sheriff asked him if he was armed, the man said, "No sir, I do not have a gun, but I do have a boot knife. I won't touch it unless you want me to place it on the trunk, also…" JD said that would not be necessary, so the biker slowly got his papers and laid them on the car. He took two steps back and waited politely until JD put his documents back where he could reach them.

"Well Mr. Iley, what are you doing out here today? This is a dead-end road in a fairly isolated area. I know all the families living out here, and you just do not seem to belong in this neighborhood."

That was a lot of words for Jeffreaux to speak at one time. He was not asking any questions, just stating facts.

Mr. Iley spoke confidently, "Well Sheriff McCane, I am actually here looking for a family member. I believe that my mother's twin sister lives here."

When he spoke, he Nodded at my house! At this point, he and Jeffreaux both looked pointedly at me.

"Well, don't look at me! I do not have a twin sister! I only have twin brothers. I do not have any sisters at all."

My tone was brusque, almost rude. I wanted this guy to know that he was not going to pull any wool over my eyes. I had lived here all my life. JD and I grew up together. He is as close to me as my own brothers are. Mr. Iley needed to know that he was trying to swindle the wrong old lady.

"Ma'am, my name is Rick Iley, and I have some very good reasons to believe that you are in fact, my Mother's twin, and my aunt."

I snorted derisively and shook my head in a "Can you believe the nerve of this guy" kind of way.

"Look, Rick, I don't know what you're trying to pull here, and I don't care either. I am not some lonely old woman that can be baffled by your bull. You need to get back on your bike and ride on back to whereever you came from." I looked him straight in the eyes as I spoke to him. "You think that I'm going to take you in and make you an heir just because you show up and say the word Twin to me? Anyone can find public birth records. Anyone can find that I have twin brothers and twin daughters. Everyone knows that twin genes are very common in some families." I was almost shaking with indignation as I snarled at him.

Rick Iley was quite calm as he listened to my outraged response. As I finished, he looked at Jeffreaux as if to say, "Mother,/Father, may I?" The sheriff Nodded at him, and both of them turned back to me again.

"Miss Kassie, may I please show you some pictures of my Mama? Please Ma'am, just look at these pictures… You must be interested in your identical twin sister. She is your twin…"

Now, I actually shouted at Rick, "No! I do not want to look at your pictures! I do not have a…"

My voice trailed off as Rick turned to JD, who Nodded at him as he held out his own hand for the pictures of my non-existent twin sister. Was he falling for this fraud?

"Oh, please, come on, Jeffreaux! You, of all people know how ridiculous this story is! You have known me all my life, and our parents knew each other all their lives. I was born and reared here. I do not have any sisters! Why are you even giving this guy the idea that we are going to listen… He is just trying to get his hands on my property… He…" Words failed me as Jeffreaux's eyes met mine. He had been studying the pictures carefully while I yelled about Rick.

Now I literally backed away as JD tried to hand me the offensive photos. I would not be hood winked by this liar.

"Kassie, you gotta look at these."

This was not a question or suggestion; he was giving me an order.

That is his job, and he is very good at it. No one in his right mind would ever think of not doing what Jeffreaux Dalton McCane tells us to do. He stepped close to me and held my eyes with his. Again, I knew that he was telling me that everything was going to be OK. He was Family to me, and I totally trusted him. However, I just could not make my eyes focus on those offensive pieces of paper. I could only stare into his eyes. He put his left arm around me as he forced the pictures into my right hand.

The Man of Few Words, softly says, "Look." So, I looked at the pictures.

My first thought was, "Where did this guy get these pictures of me?" Seriously, I thought it was me, myself, or I, for a second or two. Then, I snapped back into my attack mode and said, "Well, crap… Anyone can photo-shop anything nowadays! This does not prove anything. You could have a thousand pictures of me for all I know. My friends and family are always putting something on that stupid interweb! Even the youngest kids know how to photo-shop and do all other kind of junk. My grandkids are always showing me crazy stuff they have done with family photos. They send me hysterical pictures on my phone all the time. In my front hallway, there's a picture of the queen of England's head on my body, in my yard, with her Corgis! It looks amazingly real… You could have taken some interweb pictures, or…something. Just who do you think you are dealing with here? I was born and reared here. My family has been here for generations. You probably know all about our home place and every intimate detail of our lives here. Nothing is sacred anymore. Anyone can learn anything about anyone else anytime they want to…You cannot just waltz in here and scam me with your identical twin pictures… You should be imprisonated for this. Tell him, JD; tell him that you know the truth as well as I do."

When I slowed down to draw an indignant breath, I expected Jeffreaux to say something like, "Time to move along, Mr. Iley. You have wasted too much of our time today." Instead, Jeffreaux put his hands on my shoulders, and kind of gave me a little squeeze. He searched my face and said, "Hear him out, Kassie." I just shut up.

All three of us just stood there in silence for a period of time. I knew that something needed to be said or done, but who knew what? Rick looked at me, and then JD, and then, back at me...politely waiting for one of us to make a move. I almost busted a gut, keeping quiet. We heard a car coming, so the sheriff said for Rick to move his motorcycle inside the gate, while he pulled the cruiser into the driveway and turned off the light bar. He got out, leaned on the fender, crossed his arms, and looked at me, and then at Rick. He gave him "The Nod" and Rick Nodded back.

When he turned to me, he said, "Miss Kassie, I give you my word that these really are pictures of my Mama, your identical twin sister. I swear, with my hand to God, that I am telling you the truth. I am not lying. These are real photographs. This is my Mama in her back yard. She works outside all the time, just like you do, Miss Kassie. You two are as much alike as two peas in a pod... You two were tragically separated at birth, because..."

"Oh crap, that's just a load of bull...Separated at birth, really? Can't you find a better line than that? I don't want to hear another word..." Words had begun to jump out of my mouth again. I guess they were not good words because Jeffreaux gave me a sort of stink-eye. I shut up...again. Sometimes he is a Man of No Words.

"Miss Kassie, I cannot imagine how upsetting all of this is for you. I am truly sorry for causing you this distress. I do not want to hurt you. Believe me when I tell you that I would never cheat anyone for any reason. I do not need your money or your property. I have a successful law practice, and my parents will leave me a very nice inheritance when they pass. My life is prosperous and successful. This is not about money, land, or anything like that. I promise you that. I am not a liar nor a scam artist. If someone showed up at my house telling me a story like this, I would be angry and scared, too. I know I would, but I would also want to know the truth. I would not rest for one second until I discovered the truth, the whole truth, and nothing but the truth. Will you please give me a chance to prove that truth to you today, Miss Kassie? Please let me show you the documents I have found during the last fourteen months of my research. If you will just allow me to share these facts with you, I promise that I will leave and never bother you again. I give you my word. Please, just give me some time? Please?"

I was so angry and confused and… scared that it took me a while to be able to speak calmly. Jeffreaux had his arm around my shoulders as if he were trying to keep me under control or something. He and Rick were both waiting for me to say something, again. As they were waiting, Rick said, "Sheriff, I am not wanting to get shot today, so will you allow me to take these leathers off and get my papers out for Miss Kassie to look at?" JD gave him the universal Nod, and he quickly produced a stack of documents and a cell phone, which he claime, had "additional evidence" on it. I could not believe that he was still here, still talking to me, and still getting "The Nod" from JD McCane. I expected that he would have been racing for the hills fifteen minutes ago, or maybe even in jail by now. Instead, he was producing evidence! I could not handle this. I needed to sit down.

"Miss Kassie, will you please take a look at these documents from the Coryell County Courthouse? These are certified copies… you…"

"I gotta sit down." The words burst out of my lips before I knew it. JD was holding my elbow in a supportive manner, and he quickly started walking me to the shaded patio as if I were some feeble old woman that was unable to function by herself. Suddenly, I thought of one of my favorite lines from the movie "Steel Magnolias." Dolly Parton said she was "So confused that she didn't know whether to wind her butt or scratch her watch." Thinking about those words always made me smile. Today, that phrase just about summed up exactly how I was feeling.

As Jeffreaux went to get us some tea, Rick knelt by my chair with a concerned look on his face. He kept apologizing for "the shock" he had caused me. It seemed like I needed to answer him, but words just escaped me. That rarely happened to me, but it appeared to be happening now. Instead, I just looked at Rick as he began to ramble about his Mama. Tears came into his eyes as he told me how much she was going to love me and how he just could not believe how "identical" we are. Honestly, I just wanted him to shut up and let me think. Rick Iley needed to know how mistaken he was about my being his Mama's twin sister. Where in the heck was JD McCane? He should be out here reading this lunatic his Miranda Rights. It was way past time for this charade to end.

My back door opened, and Jeffreaux appeared with a tray of iced tea. He put it on the coffee table in front of Rick and me. While handing me a glass, he asked, "You OK?"

I just looked at him as if we were all insane. This whole thing was just madness. I looked into the eyes of Jeffreaux Dalton McCane, my oldest and dearest friend. Mentally, I was begging him to make this all go away. However, no words came out of my mouth. He knelt in front of me and... Nodded slowly. His hands closed around both of mine, which were trembling feebly. I had a strangle hold on that glass of tea, and he gently guided it to my mouth to help me take a sip. After two more swallows, JD stood up, looked over at Rick, and Nodded. Then he sat down on the glider, real close beside me. I finally said, "Tell me why you think I am your Mama's twin."

My unwanted guest started speaking again, much softer than before. "Miss Kassie, my Mama's birth name is Krystalline Elaine Barker Iley. She and her identical twin sister, Kassandra Ilene Barker Stevens, were born on February 14, 1969, in La Fayette, Louisiana, to a scared, seventeen-year-old girl named Francine Barker. There was no Fathers name recorded, but I have found him and confirmed his identity as the biological father of Francine's twin daughters. His name is Leslie Alexander. He readily submitted a DNA Sample and said that he never knew about the pregnancy or the birth of his own children. All he knew was that Francine's parents had shipped her off somewhere to keep her away from him." Rick started to sit down, but he pulled his chair closer to me and leaned forward as if to hold my hands. "He was a nice man, Miss Kassie. He wept when I told him about his twin daughters. He wants to know both of you. He cried as he told me that he was arrogant and selfish at nineteen. He said he knew it was wrong to seduce Francine. He told me that he was Crazy Mad In Love with her and intended to marry her."

"Even at the age of seventy-four, he recalled the despair of not being able to find the True Love of his Life. His determination to find her almost landed him in jail. Francine's parents could have had him arrested for trespass and harassment, but her father, Conrad, felt sorry for him and showed him mercy instead. Young Leslie sat in the back seat of a local cop car while Conrad convinced him to get out of town and make a life for himself somewhere else. Leslie was forced to understand that Francine's Mother, Blanche, would Never allow her daughter to be a part of such a scandalous, sexual affair. She was only seventeen years old and they would not allow him to ruin the rest of her life. Leslie clearly remembered the steely determination behind Conrad's warning to leave his daughter alone.

Leslie was never told that Francine was pregnant. He never knew, Miss Kassie. He never knew about you and Krissie. He said that when Francine disappeared, his hair turned white in just a matter of months. I assured him that prematurely gray hair is a genetic trait that many of his descendants share. He was deeply moved when he told me that he would have moved Heaven and Earth to find her, if he had known the truth. Conrad and Leslie reached a Gentlemen's agreement that day and shook hands when they stepped out of that Police vehicle.

Instead of going to jail that day, Leslie joined the United States Air Force. Your father retired as a Brigadier General and still serves on several committees for Veterans Affairs. He is a man of integrity. That handshake was his Word of Honor to stay away from Francine, forever. Now he cannot wait to meet you both. He wants to know his daughters. He wants to love you. On the day that I met with him to talk about this, he warned me that nothing would keep him from finding you and Krissie now. You can expect him to come here to find you. Eventually, your biological father will come to your door. No matter what you and I decide to do, Leslie Alexander will find his twin daughters. He swore that only death will prevent him from knowing his own children." We all silently considered how that reunion might play out. I was experiencing a hurricane of emotions that I cannot even define.

JD had taken the glass of tea from me and put it on the side table while Rick talked. His right arm was around my shoulders, and his left hand was covering my left hand in my lap. He had been touching me gently in one way or another ever since we walked onto the porch. He was "Grounding Me," keeping me stable while my whole world was crumbling around me. Jeffreaux had always been our Family Stabilizer. He had always kept my crazy twin brothers out of trouble and was the perfect epitome of the phrase, "Bridge Over Troubled Water." He made everything All Right. He had a gift, a gift from God. I suddenly realized how much I had come to depend on him, since my husband had died. Rick and I both looked at Jeffreaux, and he Nodded as if to say, "It's OK Kassie." And, "Go on and talk, Rick."

Rick's voice was soft as he held my eyes. "I want to tell you about Francine, too, Miss Kassie. I want you to know what a Wonderful person she is, now. There is just so much that I want you to know… It would take me days to fill you in on the things I have learned in this past year. There is just too much… too many facts and too little time …I do want you to know that Francine named you girls. She made a small stipulation in the adoption agreement, demanding that her babies were to be called Krissie and Kassie. Whoever adopted her twins had to call them what she had been calling them for nine months. My Mama is Krissie and you are Kassie. You are the identical twin that my Mama has been missing her whole life."

We could hear birds, insects, leaves rustling, and the creek gurgling as he waited for me to reply.

Something deep inside of my heart was screaming "No! No! This is all a lie. I do not have a twin sister. My Mother and Father are Edna and Eli Stevens. I am their only daughter. I know who I am. This is all wrong!" Something deeper within my spirit was saying, "I know this is true. I have been waiting for her to come back to me for my whole life." The confusion was just overwhelming me. What is the truth? Who am I? Why is this happening to me? Has my whole life been a lie?

The County Sheriff started massaging my shoulders a little. He leaned forward to look into my eyes. He did not speak. I didn't either. One reason that Jeffreaux always seems to be so smart is that he doesn't talk a lot. On the other hand, could it be that he doesn't talk a lot Because he is so Smart? Either way, I impressed myself by choosing, (Wisely?) to remain silent, just as he did. God only knows what might have come out of my mouth if I had opened it.

Rick was waiting for "The Nod," and after he got it, he resumed his narrative. "Miss Kassie, my Mama was adopted by a wonderful, loving couple that thought they would never be able to have children of their own. However, as you know, adoption frequently spawns pregnancy, and she became the oldest of three siblings. She also has twin brothers. Mama loves her family completely. She always says how blessed she was as a child and what a perfect childhood she had. Still, she always felt like she was "Missing Someone." She felt guilty for feeling that way because of her Perfect Family. She could not bear to hurt them, so she didn't talk about it much when she was a kid. When she married my Dad, she told him about all those things that she had been hiding her whole life. He assured her that everyone has those feelings and that she was perfectly normal. Dad reminded her about the Déjà Vu phenomenon and other baffling brain anomalies. He was supportive to Mama in every way. He just did not know the Truth.

None of us knew the truth until about two years ago. That's when I learned that Mama was adopted. She had only known for six years herself. My Nonnie, Mama's mother finally told her the truth as she lay dying. Mama never told anyone. She could not bear to think about who or what might be in her past. She did not want to look for her "Birth Mother" because of her love and loyalty to her adopted family. They were completely devoted to my Mama, and to all of us. My Aunts, Uncles, Cousins, everyone in the family loved us and treated us with great affection. Mama and her two brothers inherited equally when Nonnie and G'Paw died. We really do have a near perfect family. If only Nonnie would have told Mama that she was a twin, then…" Rick's voice faded off, and we waited for him to continue.

"For the last six years, she assumed that the "Missing Someone" was her Birth Mother. She did not know that she was a twin. She would have found you immediately if she had. She still does not know about you, Miss Kassie. I could not tell her until I came here first to make sure that you would want to be a part of her life. I had to be sure that you would be…Good(?) to Mama. I know that good is not the right word. I'm sorry; I know that you are a good person. I just need to protect Mama…I can't explain…" His voice had dropped lower as he stopped talking and drew in a long breath.

JD and I sat quietly until Rick resumed his narrative. "We all remember how Mama was constantly saying, 'Someone is Missing.' Every occasion, like dinners, weddings, award banquets, vacations, reunions, I mean all the time, Mama would look all around the room and mumble, "Someone is Missing. She would look kind of confused and ask us kids if Someone was Missing. All my life she was Missing Someone. She was missing you, Miss Kassie." Tears were gathering in his eyes. He looked at me and said, "Mama was always going to the window or the door and looking for Someone. Krissie has been looking for Kassie all her life. She has been Missing you all her life. She was needing you all her life. Did you miss her, too? Like she missed you? Did you know Someone was Missing from your life, too, Miss Kassie?"

I Did. My voice was shaking as I answered him. "I have been waiting for her to come back to me for as long as I can remember." Rick's head dropped into his hands and he wept like a little child. I could not stop my hand from reaching out to stroke his hair as he cried. Tears were cascading down my cheeks, too. At some point, when I could speak, I was surprised to hear myself say that I had always, always been Waiting for Someone to come back to me. Someone had been with me, and then... that Someone had been taken from me. I knew this even when I could not really know anything. Were my memories of her from in vitro? Could we remember each other from the womb? Could an embryo remember that there was another half of itself ... Somewhere? Could my DNA know that it was not Complete? Could my cells be longing for that other half of me? I had grown up with twin brothers, and I had given birth to twin daughters. I knew all about the Twinnish Connections. How in God's name had this truth about my own identical twin sister eluded me for fifty-three years?

Why was that truth hidden from me? Why hadn't my parents told me the truth about who I am? Didn't they know that I felt like half of me was missing? Memories flooded through my brain as I cried and stroked Rick's hair. Jeffreaux was still holding my other hand. Periodically, he had pressed Kleenex into it as the need arose. I told them about lying awake for hours at night Waiting for Someone to come back to me. I talked in my sleep, too. I tossed and turned fitfully. The Twins told me that I was always mumbling, "Is she coming yet? Where is she? Why isn't she coming yet?" We never knew what those words meant. I remember going to the windows and doors looking for her, waiting for her, weeping for her.

At times, I was inconsolable, and I think my Mother was scared for me. I remember holding my hand over my heart as I wept. I even told her that something was broken in my heart. Mom would lay her own hand on my chest to see if she could feel an irregularity there. Many times, she put her ear over my heart to make sure that it was beating properly. Every doctor visit included questions about my Heartache. When I told the doctor that my heart was broken, there were many more tests for a long, long time. Every medical examination confirmed that I was completely healthy. However, the pain did not go away. Many people made remarks about my apparent heart condition. Evidently, I frequently laid my hand there, trying to stop that pain.

My poor Mother was driven to distraction by my grief. She tried so hard to comfort me, to help me be happy. She frequently sent the twins to distract me, to make me laugh, to take me outside and push me on the High Swing, (not my baby swing). As I matured, I learned not to show my pain because it only hurt the family that I loved so much. However, I still cry and mumble in my sleep, to this very day. For thirty years, I had awakened my husband asking if She was coming yet. I started looking for answers about these things in my late thirties. That was the Golden Age of the Inner Child and the Forgotten Memories. Every doctor, counsellor, pastor, and therapist that I ever saw surmised that I needed to help the Younger Me get healed so I could be free from that pain. All of them agreed that I had suffered some psychic wounds. I had no memory of some terrible pain. If only I had known that I was adopted! If I had known that, I could have found peace thinking that I was waiting for my birth mother to come back for me. Why didn't they tell me the truth? Why was I just learning this now?

Most of my life was over now. I had been Waiting to feel like a whole person for fifty-three years. Why? I did not intend to rattle on like that for so long. It felt like a dam had broken inside of me, and all that anger, fear, hurt, and frustration just came pouring out of me, like a flood. As I was winding down, I thought, "Wow, I really need to shut up." Suddenly, it seemed like I was so exhausted that I could barely hold myself upright. I allowed my head to fall back on the glider as I closed my eyes. I literally felt too tired to move.

Rick spoke softly to JD and they exchanged places on the glider beside me. He gently patted my hand and said, "Miss Kassie, I want to thank you for sharing all of that with me. I know it was terribly hard for you. Thank you so much. I want to tell you that I will leave you right now if you want me to. I will leave here and never try to contact you again, if you want me to. I would never want to cause you another second of grief or stress. Never. Nobody in your family will ever know about us if you do not want them to. I do want you to know that you have a bunch of people in Alabama that would love to love you. You can never have too many people that love you. Some people do not have a family that loves them. You could have two! Nobody knows about you but me. Nobody will ever know if you don't want them to. I give you my word of honor. You can trust me, Miss Kassie. But will you let me show you some other things before I go? We... you and I have so much to talk about... I have so much to tell you and show you. There is so much that I want to know about you and your family, too. We have a lifetime of catching up to do... I'm sorry if I'm pushing too hard and fast. I just want you to know how wonderful your twin sister is. I want you to know what an exceptional family we are. I don't want you to be scared to know us..."

Rick looked at JD and then turned back to me. "Should I go on, Miss Kassie? Do you want me to tell you some more stuff about Krissie?" We both looked at JD, and he gave both of us The Nod, so Rick continued. "Mama was reared to think, talk, dress, and act like lady. Her brothers were to be gentlemen at all times. They loved, liked, and respected each other, their parents, and the rest of the family. They were taught words like Integrity, Responsibility, and Forgiveness. Every generation accepts and supports the others. We all work and provide for ourselves as God intended. Don't get me wrong, I am not saying we are perfect... None of us is perfect, but you do not need to be afraid to know us. We are good, God-fearing people who serve our country and communities. Mama raised us the way she was raised. We enjoy life. We work hard. We love each other. We will love you and your family, too. If you will just give us a chance…"

I guess it was my turn to talk, because both of them were looking at me expectantly. Honest to God, I was at a loss for words. I wanted to hear everything, but I also never wanted to hear another word. I had become a total psycho in the last couple of hours. My whole world had been turned upside down and shaken. I was not sure if all of the pieces could ever fit back together again. If I was this confused and discombobulated, how would the rest of my family feel? Dear Lord Jesus. I was making myself Crazy. We are kind, helpful, Christian people. We are friendly, fun loving, and patriotic. In fact, we are exactly like Rick's family. Exactly. I am proud of us. Anyone would be proud to be a member of our family.

Evidently, I had started to cry, again, because JD was pressing Kleenex into my hand again. I bet Rick was beginning to think I was simpleminded or something. "OK. OK, I, um…I am sorry. God, I just cannot seem to put two brain cells together at this moment… If I can be honest, Rick, I do want to know Everything. At the same time, I don't know if I can bear to know Anything else right now. It sounds like we do have a lot in common? You do not need to worry about our family either. We have the same values that you have. Is she really Identical to me? The poor thing. Does she have… um… talents? Skills? What is she like?" I felt stupid. Once again, I looked at JD for help. He gave me the half smile, half wink, half Nod, which made him famous in half the state of Texas. Then he gave Rick the full Nod to continue.

"OH Miss Kassie! She looks just like you. Just like you… hair, eyes, everything is like yours. My Mama, Krissie, even holds her glass like you do. She is very smart and funny. She loves to cook and garden. She is involved in several civic and church activities. She keeps her head in an emergency. Everyone wants to be her friend. All the females envy and emulate her. All the males love and respect her. When we were growing up, all the other kids thought my Mama was the greatest. Everyone wanted to spend time with her, the boys and the girls. She listened to every teenager in the county. Everyone was welcome at our house. Everyone is still welcome at our house. She draws people to herself, like the moon draws the tide. She has friends from when she was a kid. She never loses anyone. People that leave our area stay in touch with her. She is like… like the glue that holds us all together. She would just die if she heard me saying this stuff. She never thinks she's special. But she is Special. She is the most Special person that I have ever known. I am not making this up. Everyone feels this way about her. She is gracious and wise. She is… Blessed. She is a Blessing. "

All I could say was "WOW. I'm nothing like that." Jeffreaux shook his head and gave me the stink eye again.

Rick said, "Yes you are! You are just like her, Miss Kassie. You certainly are! When I started investigating you, I am sorry to say that I was investigating you, Ma'am. That sounds so impersonal… I am sorry if that offends you. However, let me assure you that the people that know you describe you in exactly the same words as I use for my Mama. You are as well loved and respected as she is. I would never have come here if you were not an exceptional person who could appreciate my Mama and the rest of us. Surely you must know how much this community loves you? Your pastor only has good things to say about you. Even the local law enforcement officers are in awe of you." When he said this, Rick looked at JD, and again, got the Nod.

I was embarrassed by his praise, and I felt sure that he was exaggerating. However, he was kind to try to make me feel good about all this. I told him Thanks for saying those sweet things. I was running out of gas. I was running out of things to say. I seemed to be out of energy, dead in the water. I was not angry anymore. I was tired. I was tired of trying to sort this out. I was just tired for now. I did not want to be rude to him, but I needed him to let me think… or not think for a while.

Jeffreaux spoke firmly, "Tomorrow. Eleven o'clock." Man of few words. We both looked at him, and we both got The Nod. Rick patted my hand again, and then he gave it a little squeeze. The Boss had spoken, and we would obey. They shook hands, and once again, the local sheriff was sitting very close to me as he held my hand. Neither one of us said anything for a while. We just sat, glided, and thought our own personal thoughts.

I finally said, "It's all true, isn't it Jeffreaux?" Rick Iley is right about me, isn't he? I am not who I thought I was, am I? I wasn't born and reared here, was I? Everything that I thought was true..." I sobbed uncontrollably as JD held me in his arms and made comforting noises into my neck and hair. When I was finally able to quit crying, I felt a little bit better. I did not feel like letting go of JD, and I certainly did not want him to let go of me.

My stomach gave a huge grumble, which caused both of us to start and chuckle. JD stood up and acted like he was drawing his gun to shoot something in there. I threw up my hands and said something stupid him putting me out of my misery if one of those disgusting alien things tried to jump out of me.

Laughing, he held out both of his hands to me and said, "We are going to go eat a huge steak; then we are going to eat ice cream. Let's go powder our noses?" That was a lot of words for him to say to me at one time. We walked into my house together, just like we had hundreds of times before. We both knew that things had changed today and that we would never be the same again. He had been my closest friend for most of my life. We literally grew up together because our parents and grandparents were neighbors, business partners, and friends. Our families had been intertwined for generations. Together, we had survived the good, the bad, the ugly, and the indifferent. I had never grown tired of him or his family because they had been my family too. We married, buried, graduated, birthed, and travelled together. We loved each other, respected each other, and supported each other...

After our noses were powdered, we got into the sheriff's car and headed to town. I let my head fall back on the seat rest and groaned, "Dear Lord Jesus." I honestly could not think of anything else to say. What could I say? Jeffreaux probably wished that I were at the bottom of the Dead Sea for putting him through this. He had spent the whole day out there with me. I shook my head, considering how much he must have hated that whole tearful "Family Reunion" thing that went on between Rick Iley and me. God knows that I hated it. I would not have been there either if I had not had to… He probably really just wanted to give someone a ticket or shoot someone or something. Maybe doing that would make me feel better, too. I could feel him looking at me, but I just could not face his piercing, ice blue eyes right now.

"Don't think too much."

HUH??? My eyes flew open and I gaped at him in shocked silence. He looked into my face, raised his eyebrows, and Nodded. I hate it when he's right. He is Always Right. I sat quietly and tried Not to think. It was an eleven-mile drive into town. After a couple of minutes, we looked at each other again. I Nodded. He reached over and held my hand the rest of the way.

When we got to the Diner, he opened the Cruiser door and held my hand as I stepped out of it. He gently pulled me into his arms, and I stepped right into his embrace. There we were, in the middle of town, in the middle of the afternoon, hugging right out in front of God and everybody! He kept holding my hand as we walked toward the Diner. It seemed natural to hold onto him. I suspected that everyone who saw our Public Display of Affection would be talking about it within three minutes. "Listen, JD, Thank you for helping me through this. Thank you for staying with me All Day. What a miserable ordeal for you. I am so sorry to have dragged you into this. I did not expect any of this to happen. Dear Lord. Who could have known? What a mess. You must want to shoot me."

I blathered on for a minute before he gently put his thumb on my lips and said, "Kassie, I'm glad for any excuse to spend the day with the prettiest girl in Texas. I will always want to help you, and I will always stay with you any time you want me to, for as long as you want me to."

I have to say something now. I love Jeffreaux, and he loves me. We have always Loved each other. We are family. We have never been together in a romantic way. I am not sure why. Maybe I was afraid that he was too familiar or too perfect, or too... everything for me. Maybe I was afraid that I was not enough...for him. You just do not know how Great this man is. He is truly larger than life. He always has been. Even when he was a kid, he was the undisputed Ruler of our Universe. I cannot even begin to understand how intelligent he is. Once, when I was a smart mouth teen, I asked him how he could carry that huge brain around all the time. At some Academic Award Ceremony, I had hugged him and whispered that he should have been called JB, instead of JD. He gave me a quizzical stare, until I spread my hands wide in front of his head and said JI-NORMOUS BRAIN. He blushed and looked straight into my eyes and said, "Thanks, Sassie." We never spoke those secret names to anyone else. At odd times in the years to come, at the appropriate moments, I would whisper "JB" to him; he always came right back at me with "Sassie."

Let me give you a little background on Jeffreaux Dalton McCane. He is one of the most intelligent men in the Known Universe. He can think rings around any six people that you want to name. Of course, he was the Valedictorian of his high school graduating class. He Graduated Cum Laude and all those other Latin words, from Texas A & M University in three years, not four, or five. He got his Master's degree from Rice University for some Astronomical Think Tank Project. He also went to some Astrophysicist Something up in Pennsylvania. He could have been a doctor, or lawyer, or professor, or Anything that he wanted to be. I have heard people say that he has a Brilliant Legal Mind.

He has some kind of Agronomy degree, also. I believe it's a doctorate... He developed a super duper grazing grass seed that delivers more nutrients with less water than other seeds. He has a patent and sells it all over the world. The main reason that he developed it was to help the poor people across the Border in Mexico. Our church youth group went down there every year for a Mission Trip and he always felt so sorry for them. He wanted them to have grass, so they could have food to feed their goats and chickens. He donates tons of his grass to our Mexican neighbors every year.

Every time there is a natural disaster, or plague, or fire, or any kind of need, JD sends tons of his grass seed to help whoever needs it. He still makes a lot of money from it. However, he does not need to make money. Both of his parents had been wealthy, single children from wealthy families. He had money, looks, smarts, and land. Jeffreaux Dalton McCane is the Whole Package. I am not the whole package; I am not even half a package.

A few more things about JD--he decided to get a Criminal Justice degree, and went to Law School as well. He serves on several Congressional Committees about child abuse, children's rights, and battered women. He is always drafting Bills about something and inventing something else. He is a stickler about Illegal Aliens. He feels sorry for them, but he expects them to get LEGAL or Get Out. He will help them get their citizenship and find jobs. However, they are not welcome to come into his county and live on welfare. He is some kind of Advocate about that. The governor is always calling him and sending him around the whole country to Teach about ICE and stuff like that. He has been offered every job you can imagine in Homeland Security. He refuses to serve because he cannot abide the double-dealing, self-seeking blow-hards and criminals that run this country.

I told you that he is a Great Man. We all assumed that he would end up in Washington. Lots of us thought he could be the President one day. However, after several years, JD came home to Texas. He married Charlotta Brady, a Beautiful, Smart, Wealthy woman from Round Rock. They had two amazing sons who want to come back home in a few years to be near him. Charlotta was my Dearest Friend, and I still grieve for her. She developed cancer six years ago. She was dead within eighteen months. I sat with her and Jeffreaux until the end. I love her, still and I miss her still.

JD also stood by me and helped me through the death of my husband, Clay. He was killed in a private plane crash a little over three years ago. I will never forget that day. I opened the door and JD stood there with tears in his eyes. You know, I didn't even have to ask if it was Clay. I knew that he was gone. JD stayed with me until the girls, (my twin daughters), and the boys, (my twin brothers), could get home. He was there to help us with everything we needed. He held the boys and the girls as they wept. He is our Rock. He IS The Bridge Over Troubled Water.

It has always been JD with me. We have stood together through every birth, graduation, wedding, and funeral since we were kids. We have been a part of each other's lives forever. It seemed natural and right for him to share this day of confusion and heartache with me. I felt truly thankful and blessed that he was with me now. "Listen, JD, I want to thank you again for being here. I do not think that I could have handled this alone. I just do not have words… I love it that you always come and always stay. You always know how to make things come out right. I love it that you always support my family and me. I love it that I don't have to explain everything to you. I love you always just Knowing everything. I love you being here. I love you… I just love you…"

"Kassie, I love you, too. I always have loved you, Kassie. I always will." He did not hesitate for a split second. He did not hem and haw the way I did. He just said it right out. I knew that we were stepping into a different dimension now. We were saying I Love You in a new way today.

Jeffreaux ordered for both of us; which was fine with me. I

could not make a decision right now if my life depended on it. Everybody in the Diner spoke to us, and a couple of folks came to the table to "visit." After all, we do live in Small Town South Texas. In addition to that, we are both "Naturals," meaning we were both born and reared here. Oh, Crap. Tears almost shot out of my eyes when I realized that I Was Not Born and Reared Here. I had been saying that for fifty years, and, now, all of a sudden, it was not true, anymore. I no longer knew where I was born, or how old I was when I got here.

When I used my napkin to wipe my eyes, Jeffreaux gently patted my arm and said, "Steady, Kassie. Don't think right now." His thumb made a gentle circling motion on the back of my hand before he gave it a little squeeze for encouragement. I Nodded. He almost smiled as he Nodded back. Damn, if I'm not getting the hang of this Nodding Thing, too.

We managed to finish dinner with no more weeping. At least I do not remember if there were any more tears. I just tried not to think. Guess it worked out because none of our fellow citizens seemed to notice anything peculiar about my behavior. We drove out to Dairy Queen for Butterfinger Blizzards before heading back to my place. Even though I had tried Not to Think, some realization hit me like a ton of bricks, and I had to speak. "You believed him, Jeffreaux. You knew he was telling the truth. You Knew. You Knew??? Dear Jesus, you knew all along? How long? Have you always known? Always? JD, Please talk to me. Please tell me the truth. Please."

His voice was firm when spoke. "At home, Kassie. When we get home, I'll tell you what I know." In the darkness, I Nodded.

As soon as we sat down in my living room, I started asking him questions as if someone had pushed Fast Forward on the $2,000,000.00 Lightning Round. It's a good thing that he wasn't much of a talker because he couldn't get a word in edgewise. I kept asking him questions… but then I asked another one before either one of us could breathe. What a Nutcase I had become. This whole

Adoption Thing was making me a blithering Idiot. You would think that I had just seen my own face on a Milk Carton or something.

I do not know how JD picked which question he was going to answer first, but when I was winding down a little, he said, "I don't think that you should call the Boys (my twin brothers) or the Girls (my twin daughters) right now. Let's hear what Rick has to say tomorrow, OK? Then we can get everyone together and tell them all at once. OK?" Perfect.

Jeffreaux leaned forward with his hands on his knees for a second or two. Then he turned to look into my eyes and said, "Tell me what you remember about my Mom and Dad." HUH??? His Mom and Dad? I'm sure that shock and surprise was written all over my face. "Just tell me what you remember The Most about my parents."

"The Most? What do I most remember about your parents? I… well, I most remember how much they loved you. How much they loved us. How good they were to all of us. I most remember how your parents were so loving and thoughtful to everyone they knew. They were the Best." It seemed like I was running out of words. What was this about? Why was JD asking me to remember his parents? Wasn't all of this about me? Wasn't this all about my parents? What in the world?

"Why are you asking me about your parents? What difference does it make what I remember about your parents? What do they have to do with any of this?" Panic began to fill my brain as I considered that question. There was no way that Jeffreaux was going to sit here and tell me that his parents were involved in my adoption. His Mom, Emily, would never give up her twins for adoption. She had always told me how much she loved me and would have loved to have a daughter like me. She often sang my praises at family gatherings. I thought that she was afraid that the Boys were upstaging me. Twins are a hard act to follow. Most of the time, I was in the background. However, my Mom and Dad were always careful to give me my own space. After all, I was The Baby. I was the only girl. I held my own.

Being almost four years younger than the twins worked in my favor. We never had to compete in the same arenas.

JD's Dad, Anthony, was a Federal Judge who served in Washington only when it was absolutely necessary. He spent most of his time here, in Texas, at home with his family. Everyone says that he could have been a Supreme Court Justice anytime he wanted to. He did not want to. He wanted to be right here. He served on many Judiciary Committees. He was instrumental in drafting many important Human Rights laws. He was always looking out for the best interests of Texas and her people. Anthony McCane was one of the most sought-after litigators in the country. He knew everything anyone needed to know to be successful. He knew everyone that was anyone in the Federal Government. He knew all the Nobodies too.

JD's Mother, Emily, was a beautiful, tiny, Godly woman that was content to stay in her husband's shadow. When she was younger, Emily worked tirelessly for her church and for the local children's home. She influenced my Mom to get involved with the kids, also. I think that she wanted to have other babies, herself. However, she was always a little bit "Sickly." I was speaking aloud now as I thought about some of the things that had happened so long ago. "I think your Mom was hospitalized several times when we were kids, but I guess I didn't know why. Even though she always went to our games, award banquets, rodeos, camping trips, and everything else, she seemed 'Fragile' to us. Now, I realize that your Mom was ill. Wasn't she, Jeffreaux? She was sick for a long time. That's why she died young, isn't it?"

Tears were flowing again as I remembered Emily and her love for us. She was so precious to my family and me. I had grieved her death as a child, but now I wept for her as an adult child. Now, I am aware of what a tremendous loss she was to me. I lost a family member, a friend, and a precious mentor. She was always in my corner. She made it a point to stay connected to me. "She loved me so much. I loved her then, and I love her, now, Jeffreaux, I always will. We never really lose the people that we love, if we hold them in our hearts. I want you to know that I hold your Mom and Dad in my heart. I keep them close to me, as I do my own." I hugged him, and we clung to each other for a time. When we finally moved apart, we both Nodded into each other's eyes. It felt good to tell him how much I loved his parents, and how I knew that they loved me, too. We are family, in every way that counts.

Why haven't we ever talked about these things before? Why is Jeffreaux leading me down this particular path on this particular night? My heart was filled with a great fear of what might be revealed here. I was afraid to know the answers to my questions. Curiosity was never one of my strong suits. Talking was certainly not one of his. "Why did you ask me about your parents tonight? Why would you bring them into this conversation about my adoption? What does one have to do with the other? Please, JD, tell me what you know. Please? I cannot bear to go any further without knowing the truth. I have to know who I am. Now. Tonight. Talk to me. But don't you dare tell me that I am your sister. Don't. You. Dare."

While holding my hands and my eyes, Jeffreaux Dalton McCane said, "You are not my sister. You were supposed to be my sister, but, Mom and Dad could not, in good conscience, adopt you when they found out that she was dying. Your parents knew every detail of our lives. They knew that there had been two disastrous adoption attempts many years before. They knew that my Mom had looked for you for over a decade. Your parents loved us. They also loved you. They were waiting for you to come home just as all families wait for the new baby to be born and come home. You were already deeply loved, Kassie. Even before you were born, we All loved you. We All wanted you. There was no way that you were Not going to be a part of this family." JD stopped talking as he searched my face to see how I was taking all of this. Evidently, he thought it was all right for him to continue with his narrative.

"Kassie, my Dad had put all of the legal adoption wheels in motion before Mom knew that she was terminal. You know that he was a top-notch attorney. Well, he made sure that Nothing would go wrong with this adoption. It was iron clad. All of our parents met to talk about how to keep you in the family. Your Mother immediately said that they would adopt you. She did not even have to ask your Dad. They were all in agreement. You would become a Stevens, instead of a McCane. My Mother would see you as often as she wanted to. In addition, she could love you just like she loved the Boys. She could have all the good times and none of the bad.

Everyone agreed that she had to rest and take care of herself, no matter what. Dad contacted Francine and convinced her to allow the adoption to proceed as planned. Up to that point, no one had thought about how to tell us… I mean your brothers and me. They were only three then, but I was almost six. I was old enough to know a little about the "Baby in the tummy thing." Thankfully, they were not interested in details about Anything. You know how they were. A little bit… uh… Wildmen." He paused, and we both reflected on the Wildmen for a minute or two. I could not help but smile, recalling a few scenarios from those devilish little Wildmen. We both shook our heads and smiled at each other.

JD stood up and said that he had to move around a little. We walked out onto the patio for some fresh air. He was right, as usual. We had been sitting all day long. We had never spent so much time sitting in one spot in our whole lives. Both of us are Doers, Movers and Shakers, Not sitters. Neither one of us liked to dwell on the past. Neither one of us liked to talk about deep, personal issues. This had been quite a day for us both. "Let's walk down by Cherokee Creek for a minute or two," I suggested. There was enough twilight for a nice little stroll on a perfect Texas evening. We both knew every square foot of this place by heart. All our memories are stored here. The very earth and sky breathed life into us as we walked. This is the place of our Generations. At least, the only generations that I knew of were here. I did not know these other generations… this Francine and her family were all strangers, aliens to me.

This is my home, my family, my...place in the world.

"Do you want me to continue?" JD asked.

I told him, "Yes, I do. I want to know Everything. But, Dear Lord, this is totally overwhelming for me. How long have you known? Have you always known that I was adopted?" My voice was quivering again, so, JD pulled me into his arms for comfort. I leaned into him for support, as I had been doing all day long. Well, I had been leaning on him for support all my life.

He began to speak again as we continued to walk by the gurgling stream. "One night, right before Dad died, he called me into his office to talk. That is when he told me the things that I'm telling you now. I did not Know these things for a fact when we were kids. However, when I got older, I asked Mom a few questions about your birth. She quickly told me that you were as much a member of our family as the boys and I were. She told me that I would understand more when I got older. She made me promise to Never Ever Speak of those things again. Therefore, I didn't. Did I know? Yes and No. I did not Really Know until a couple of years ago, when Dad told me that this day might come. He told me that Francine had become a wonderful woman with two other children and a loving husband. He said that he had kept up with her all those many years. My Dad never mentioned Krissie. I did not know about her myself, until Rick..." He seemed to be weighing his words carefully, trying not to say anything to upset me any more than necessary. It was difficult for me to keep quiet, but I waited for him to continue.

We sat quietly for a few minutes before he said, "Kassie, I want you to know that Rick called me several months ago. I checked him and his whole family out thoroughly before I called him back. I told him that he could come here to see you. I also told him that he would have to convince you that he was telling the truth. I told him that I would be impartial... to a point. He seemed to be an honest, hard-working family man. You know that I would never let anyone hurt you. You know that I would give my life for you? Do you believe me, Kassie? I knew that this visit would be devastating for you. However, I also knew that it would be one of the greatest blessings in your life. Moreover, Dad had already told me to be ready for a visit like this. I felt like he and Mom would want you to know all the rest of the story, too."

"I questioned Rick more, and he gave me two names. One was the doctor who delivered you, long dead, of course. The other name was that doctor's oldest daughter. When I called her myself, she quickly offered to fax me all her father's medical records. Even though legal and ethical laws of secrecy bound him, he kept tons of personal notes on his patients. She did send them to me that very day. Honey, after reading his entries, there was no doubt in my mind that Rick was telling the truth about you and Krissie. We both have those hand-written documents if you want to read them… We have both confirmed them to be factual and accurate. You were delivered last, which is probably why you have always felt like you were Waiting for Someone to come back to you. Krissie was taken away immediately. You always felt abandoned… She always felt like Someone was Missing. God only knows how Francine felt. Devastated, I would imagine. I am so thankful that Dad stayed in touch with her. She could take comfort knowing what a wonderful life she had given you. I am also sure that she managed to keep tabs on Krissie, too. Francine appears to be way above average in every way."

We had gotten back to the patio, now. As we sat on the glider, Jeffreaux spoke with emotion in his voice. "Kassie, your Birth Mother came from a very wealthy family. After she gave you and Krissie up for adoption, she became a Pediatric Oncologist. Her family funded an orphanage, in Mississippi, which still operates, today. She served on the Board of Directors until just last year. Dad stayed in touch with her until he died. He told me that was the best way to make sure that she never intruded on your life here. The language of your adoption papers is very strong. There was never to be any contact

with Francine or any of her family members. It was quite apparent
that both parties wanted this event to be a well-guarded secret. My
assumption was that Francine's very wealthy family demanded that
the whole incident be covered up and forgotten. Maybe her Mother
feared that someone would use that teenage pregnancy to bring
destruction into their lives. None of us can say for sure what happened back then, but there were to be extremely stringent reprisals
for violating the legal terms of your adoption. I am trying to make
you understand how this was kept so secret for so many years. No
one knew about Dad's relationship with Francine. No telling what
would have happened if her family had known…" Jeffreaux was
really struggling, trying to help me understand things that he could
not even understand himself.

Once again, he leaned forward and put his arms on his knees
while he spoke softly to me. "After Dad passed, I received notifi-
cation of a very large memorial, made in his name, to a Cross the
Bridge Foundation._When I researched it, I learned that Francine
chartered this organization to help Orphaned Mexican Children
find adoptive American families. She started this Foundation when
my Mom died. Francine did this to honor my Mom, but also to
honor you and Krissie. Her whole life has been about taking care
of children. Allowing her twins to be adopted defined Francine. I
know many women allow those things to destroy them. Not her.
She became the best possible person anyone could ever hope to be
because of it.

She never forgot you or Krissie, Honey. She never tried to in-
trude, but she always watched out for you. Dad kept meticulous
records, and I found amazing memorials in your parent's names and
for both Charlotta and Clay, too JD's voice broke when he spoke
our spouses' names. Of course, I had been crying like a baby the
whole time. "I don't know why we were never told about your twin
sister. I am so sorry for you and Krissie. I wish…" He was overcome,
unable to speak the words to define my loss, the heartache from

childhood, the Waiting… I was at a loss, also. Sometime, there just are no words. Despite the pain, I was impressed with the details about Francine's life. I was deeply grateful for her relationship with Anthony McCane.

It became obvious to me that as she matured, Francine became a Godly woman of great integrity. I was very proud of her and the life that she lived. Francine had not wanted to give her babies up; but fifty something years ago, teenagers had to do as their parents told them to do. It was a different world, then. Her parents wanted her to finish school and take her place in the world. They had known families that adopted children, and they had friends that were adopted as well. That seemed to be the best course of action for everyone concerned. All the adults in Francine's life agreed that she needed to give her twins the best life possible. They knew that Chosen Children were Blessed and Greatly loved. My Birth Mother did not give us up because we were not loved. It was because she loved us so much that I came to live here, in this wonderful family. I was Chosen. I was a Gift. It was so hard for Francine to make that decision. She was really too young to understand what would happen and how she would feel. She loved as a child loves. She was just a kid. Nevertheless, she made the right decision. Krissie and I have had great lives with loving families. That is the most important thing to remember. She made the right decision for all of us.

"Kassie, Dad told me to make sure that you know how excited we all were to have you. He made me promise to help you see all the facts when this time came. It broke his heart to think that you might feel unloved or unwanted, especially when the exact opposite is true. You were very much loved and wanted by all of them. That is the truth, Honey. I swear it is. My Dad never told me a lie. It is vital that you believe me."

"I do, JD; I believe you. In my heart, I know and understand more than I can explain. It's as if God is giving me a vision into the past. I am so thankful for your parents and mine… Thank God that they chose me. Thank God that Francine could give us up. I cannot wait to meet her, and Krissie. I cannot wait."

What a day this had been. JD had talked more today than I had ever heard him talk in all the years of his life. He had managed to make me feel good about all of this. I knew his parents, and as he spoke, I knew that he was telling me the truth. I fully believe that Francine had done the very best that she could, considering the circumstances she was in. Adoption is an incredible blessing for people who want children, and for children that need parents. Looking back on my life, I can honestly tell you that my family, friends, and community have loved me. I have had an exceptionally blessed life. I thank God for placing me here. "Thank you for telling me the truth, Jeffreaux. Thank you for helping me through this day. Thank you... for ... everything. Please help me with just one more thing tonight. Your Mother lived until I was almost thirteen... I remember her funeral. Why did she think she was going to die so many years earlier? I'm sorry, I do not mean to sound like I wish she had died. I mean, you know I would never suggest that... I ... I'm confused. She could have been my Mother? Why didn't she adopt me?"

"Kassie, my Mother was literally saved by the drug that is now known as Interferon. It was created and dispensed by a clinic in Mexico. My Father knew someone, who knew someone ... that had been helped there. They were desperate. Many people went to Mexico for medical treatments, back then. This was before The A.M.A. black balled Interferon. It was not called that when Mother was taking it. They called it Esperanza Negro, or The Black Hope. It was a black viscous substance that they injected into the area where the Cancer was located. That Black Hope kept many people alive for many years. If you want to know the truth, people still sneak into Mexico for those injections. Sometimes, it helps; sometimes it does not. It worked for us. By the time they knew that Mom would live, you were settled and happy with your family. God always knows Best, Honey. We cannot question Him, now." He was right, as He always is.

"The Bible says that the Truth will set you free. I believe that. You are now Free to know and love your twin sister and her family. I know that they will love you. Everybody loves you, Kassie. Sometimes, we just have to move forward in faith. I have faith in you, and our families, and in God. We are all where He wants us to be. Everything is going to be OK. I am telling you the truth when I say that I Love You. I cannot keep pretending to be your Big Brother or your friend. I want to be Free, also. I want to be Free to love you and be a part of your life as I should have been all along. I was a fool to play this game for this long. I refuse to play anymore. We belong together. We both know it's true." He leaned over and kissed me. I kissed him back. Then, I laid my head on his chest and listened to his heartbeat for a minute or two.

I could not think of what to say. Imagine that! I was speechless for the umpteenth time that day. "You are going to bed, now, and tomorrow Rick will help us take the next step…together." He knelt on one knee in front of me, held my face in his hands for a minute, and Nodded. There was nothing for me to do but Nod Back. I am a quick study.

I slept like a dead man. It must have been total exhaustion, because I am a terrible sleeper. I did not wake up until sunlight was flooding into my bedroom. Usually, I'm awake from four o'clock on; but it was after seven AM when my eyes flew open. God knows that I needed the rest. It was wonderful to have a break from the confusion and uncertainty of the night before. Of course, it all rushed back; trying to overwhelm me before I could even get my slippers on. Thinking about Jeffreaux's last words to me was a big help. I decided to wait until Rick got here to take the next step.

The livestock were letting me know that it was time to get moving. I milked, gathered eggs, fed, and watered everyone as needed. I love doing these chores. I love my simple farm life. Never, in a million years, would I have ever dreamed that anything would change in my little world. Now, I know that Everything will be Different.

Today…Now. I am different. Jeffreaux is different. I have a twin sister. In addition, I have a whole new family to get to know and love. I am shocked to realize that I want this new life. I want to hug my twin sister and hold her to my heart, the heart where she has always been Waiting. She was hurting for me, as I was hurting for her. My hand had unconsciously slid up to cover my heart as I thought of her. I had been holding her in my heart forever. Soon, I will hold her in my arms as well. I cannot wait. What a miraculous event!

At nine thirty-five, JD turned into my driveway. My heart skipped a beat when he stepped out of the cruiser. What do I do now? How am I supposed to act? I was suddenly nervous. I am Not the prettiest girl in Texas. However, he is definitely in The Top Ten of everything good. What if he's sorry that he said all that stuff to me last night? When our eyes met, we were already moving into each other's arms. He squeezed me and kissed the top of my head. I leaned back to look up into those ice blue eyes; we were smiling as we kissed. It was a real kiss, the kind of kiss every woman dreams about. This is the Kiss that I have been needing and wanting from him ever since Clay died. I absolutely cannot stop smiling. I believe he is happy, too because he smiled as he picked me up and we whirled around like kids. God, I love this New World! Both of my hands were clenched in his thick, curly, dark hair as I held his forehead to mine. Our eyes were locked together as he slowly lowered me to the ground.

We heard the motorcycle coming as we joined hands and began walking toward the patio. Rick slowly turned into the gate with an extremely large pot of Shasta Daisies balanced on the seat in front of him. How in the heck had he managed to get out here holding those flowers? Goodness me! That could not have been safe at all. I felt the need to start chiding him for being so reckless; but he was grinning so BIG that all I could do was grin right back! "Honey, I love Shastas! They are my absolute favorite flowers. These are too beautiful! How sweet of you to risk your life to bring them out here to me, Rick. Lord, you could have been killed wrestling these…

Thank you so much." He was still sitting on the motorcycle while I was hugging his neck and fussing over him.

"I hoped that you would love them as much as my Mama does, Miss Kassie. I didn't see any in your yard yesterday. But Mama has several beds at home, so I took a chance on your liking them, too… The Twinnish thing, you know…" JD was now holding the huge pot of Daisies for us. He shifted them to his left arm and reached his right hand out to welcome Rick and Nodded approvingly. They shook hands like old friends.

"You are one hundred percent right about the Shastas, Rick. They are my very favorite flowers. My beds are in the back yard, where they can get the afternoon sun. You can't see them from here." What an amazing difference a day makes! Just twenty- four hours ago, I hated Rick Iley and wanted Jeffreaux to arrest him. Now, we were hugging and grinning like fools. What a miracle.

He got off the bike and we started walking toward the shaded patio. We settled into comfortable chairs before I spoke. "Rick, I want to say that I'm sorry for the way I acted yesterday. I am truly sorry for being so rude to you. I did not even give you a chance to explain anything. Can you please forgive me and give me another chance?" I was holding both of his hands in mine as I spoke.

He squeezed them gently and said, "Well, of course I forgive you, Miss Kassie. You have nothing to be sorry for. I cannot imagine how difficult this is for you. I know it must be stressful and frighten-ing. I could not expect you to just grab your purse and say, *"I knew it! What took you so long? Take me to her!"* We all chuckled a little at the improbability of that ever happening… with anyone.

Rick glanced at JD a little sheepishly and said, "I'm just thankful that I wasn't shot or "Imprisonated" yesterday." Jeffreaux cleared his throat,shook his head a little, and shrugged, as if to say, "Who? Me? Sweet little old me? I would never do anything like that…" He would not ever do anything like that. He is a kind, peaceable man. He just does not tolerate any kind of injustice. He does not "Suffer Fools" gladly. Rick was no fool. He was very thoughtful and smart. He had tried to handle this situation as carefully as he possibly could without causing anyone too much pain. I admired him for that.

"Rick, JD told me a lot of Stuff last night. I know the facts that he considers the most important. But, what else can you tell me? Duh...that was a stupid question. You can tell me everything. You know all about Krissie and her whole life. You even know about my whole life. What do you think is the most important thing for me to know? Can we please move forward to when I get to meet my twin sister? If Krissie does not know about me yet, when do you plan to tell her? What are your plans for us to meet?" I hoped that I was not sounding too "Pushy." For some reason, I was starting to feel a sort of "Urgency" to get to Krissie as quickly as I could. I had been Waiting for her for to come back to me for fifty something years. Now, I cannot wait to get back to her.

Rick had been looking at JD and his own hands as I was speaking. JD was looking at his hands, also. I am not the brightest bulb in the box, but I knew that something was "Wrong." Neither one of my companions wanted to say the wrong thing; which really made me nervous. "What's going on, guys? What's wrong? Rick, I am getting the feeling that I just asked you the wrong question... Is there some reason why you do not want me to meet Krissie right away? Please, just tell me the truth. We have come too far to shy away from the truth, now. Rick, there has been a miraculous change in my heart since yesterday morning. I already love you and Krissie, and I cannot wait to meet her. What's wrong with that? Isn't this what you want from me?"

"Yes, Ma'am, this is exactly what I have been hoping and praying for. You have no idea how thankful I am that you just said that you love both of us. This is so much more than I dreamed could ever happen so quickly. You certainly have not done or said anything wrong, Miss Kassie. I am sorry if I have made you feel uncomfortable. There is just so much to tell you before we go to see Mama...I want to explain a little more...history to you so you will know...

everything. OK? I promise you that I will tell you as much of the truth as I have been able to uncover. Ok? Let me go one step at a time, so it will be less confusing for you."

"About two years ago, I was visiting with Mama's oldest living relative, Myra, about some legal issues. She started reminiscing, the way old folks often do. She thought we knew about the adoption, and I did not want her to stop talking, so I played like I did. She told me that Mama was probably ten days old when Nonnie and G' Paw brought her home. Oh, I should tell you that my Mama's mother was Kathryn Lucille Dickenson. My Grand Papa's name was Kyle Jacob Iley. Myra said that they were just giddy with happiness. She said Mama was a real small baby; some folks thought there might be something wrong with her. However, she soon started thriving and everything was OK. The family wanted them to tell little Krissie the truth as soon as she was big enough, but Kyle and Emily absolutely forbade any discussion about it. They threatened to leave the state and never see the cousins again if anyone even thought about revealing anything to anyone…Ever. They told about the wealthy family and the strong legal demands in the adoption agreement. They warned that Krissie could be found and taken from them if anyone disclosed her whereabouts. Emily almost became hysterical and literally swore them to secrecy.

Emily and Kyle did leave Georgia within a year or two. Myra said that she was sure they moved to keep the family from breaking the Oath of Silence. I was just stunned when Myra said how relieved she was when Emily assured her that Krissie and her Twin brothers knew the truth. Mama did not know the truth until six years ago! Her twin brothers still do not know the truth. Nonnie was clever enough to keep everyone in the dark about everything until she died. At that time, Mama simply did not know how to deal with it; so, she didn't." Rick seemed to be very stressed about this history lesson that he had insisted on giving me. He was much more uncomfortable now than he had been yesterday. Why was that?

I reached over and patted his hand as I smiled encouragement to him. "Honey, what's got you so tense this morning? Yesterday you were so brave when you came and told me your news. I didn't shoot you and Jeffreaux didn't imprisonate you, then; so why are you so flustered now? I am surely more open to knowing you and Krissie now…Do not get tongue-tied here, at the most important part of the story, Rick. If you do not want to tell me anything else at all, that is just fine. OK? You have done a wonderful job, so far. Do not worry about trying to explain every little detail to me. I think I'm ready to meet my twin as soon as she is ready to meet me."

When I finished speaking, I Nodded at Rick and looked to JD for support. He also Nodded his agreement with what I had said. Then, we both waited for Rick to continue. "Yes, ma'am, I am worried this morning. There has been a whole lifetime of secrets and deceit surrounding your birth and your birth family. I want to be so careful not to create any more problems for Anyone, now." Rick stopped speaking again, as he looked intently into my eyes. There was a strong connection between us, now. He was looking into my heart, just as I was looking into his. His eyes widened for a split second and he projected some deep sorrow and fear from his spirit into mine.

My right hand was suddenly covering my heart as it had been doing all of my life. My heart was hurting! I gasped while reaching out to clutch Rick's hands with my left. "Dear Lord God! There's something wrong, isn't there? Is she ill, Rick? Is Krissie sick? I feel like there's something wrong with her." Jeffreaux had quickly come to my side and placed one arm around my shoulders. He gently placed his other hand on Rick's shoulder, too. Rick's heart was breaking as he Nodded and began to weep.

After a minute, JD handed both of us some Kleenex and said, "Rick, it's OK, Buddy. We want to help. Please explain what's wrong with Krissie." After wiping his face, Rick spoke with trembling lips. "Miss Kassie, you are familiar with Victoria's Syndrome, aren't you? It is a liver problem found in multiple birth babies. Until about thirty years ago, only one of the many newborn twins survived their delivery. Some twins died in vitro. Others only lived a couple of hours or days. Usually, one twin was healthy, while the other was extremely underdeveloped. I am sure you know all about it. As the mother of twins, you had to consent to a couple of blood tests before your girls were born. One of those tests helps doctors diagnose the Syndrome earlier, with the hope of correcting that liver problem. Thankfully, there has been great progress in this area. Early detection has proven to be the key to almost eradicating this heartbreak. That was not the case fifty-three years ago." Rick stopped speaking for a moment as he struggled to find the right words for us.

I wanted to urge him to hurry and let me know about my twin sister, but I knew how hard this would be for anyone to go through, so I just held my tongue. In my mind, I was screaming "NO! NO! Please God, Please! Don't let me lose this One that I have been Waiting for all my life. God, Please bring her back to me. Please God, let me get to her. Please do not take her from me again. PLEASE." I tried not to show how terrified I was, but when I looked at Jeffreaux, his face told me that he knew how desperate I felt.

He knelt by my chair, and said, "Hold steady, Kassie. We are not done yet. God is not going to give us more than we can handle. You know this is true, Honey. Rick, we are going to get through this together. We are Family, now. Tell us about your Mama and what we need to do now." His words were so true, so confident, so sensible.

I pulled myself together and reached out to cradle Rick's face in both of my hands. "He's right, Rick. We are going to get through this. Together. As a Family. Don't be scared to tell us everything, Honey. You have been so alone through all of this. We are here for you now. You are not alone, anymore. Let us help."

He could not speak for a minute. Then words just came rushing out. "Miss Kassie, I need for you to come and give Mama half of your liver. Please. She will die without it. I cannot let her die. I cannot let her leave this world without knowing you. She has to know who she has been Missing all her life. I had to come get you. I am sorry... But, Please...You are the only one that can save her. The Victoria Syndrome has been dormant in her liver for most of her life. However, fourteen months ago, it struck her like a bolt of lightning. No one could find out what was killing her liver. The Specialists say that there is some kind of weird anti-body in her blood... It is very rare. None of them can find a single donor that is compatible. One doctor said that it is almost as if she has had this liver damage before. Like, maybe she was able to fight it off before? He told us something about pre-natal Mitochondria and stuff that I cannot remember or understand. God finally led us to the one doctor that identified her condition as what he had seen in twins who were born with Victoria's Syndrome. That is why I started looking for someone in her birth family. I knew that Mama had to have a twin out here somewhere. I know this is selfish to ask you, and I really am sorry, but... Please, please come and save her." He almost collapsed under the grief and fear that he had been carrying.

It took me a half of a second to say,
"I knew it!
What took you so long?
Take me to her."

EPILOGUE

Three Months later

Well, that was the Beginning. I won't try to tell you everything that happened next... But, I do want you to know some of those things.

I especially want you to know that we are All Living Happily Ever After.

Let us go back to that day when I said, "Take me to her." As soon as I spoke those words, Jeffreaux jumped up and exclaimed, "Yes!" He raised both of his hands above his head, like Rocky Balboa, and nearly leaped over my chair with joy. That was the most ecstatic behavior that I had ever seen him display! That sure broke our solemn mood. Rick and I had been broken and grief-stricken until JD jumped up and started grinning like a schoolboy. At that very moment, he infected us with joy and hope. I do not remember how it happened, but in a minute, we were all three holding hands and dancing around as if we had won the lottery or something. Thank God that Jeffreaux was there! After we danced, hugged, laughed, and cried, he grabbed both of Rick's arms and said, "Call her! Call her right now."

Rick said that he wanted to go home and break the news to her, gently, and then bring us all together. "No!" We both interrupted him and began speaking at the same time.

"There is Absolutely No Way that you are leaving me here!" I said. Jeffreaux told him to get her on the phone and give her the hope that she needed to recover and heal. Again, Rick said that she had been sick for fourteen months, and he did not want to shock her.

The Sheriff smiled as he put his arm around him and said, "Son, if you call her and tell her about Kassie, she will be better in fourteen seconds." Jeffreaux looked him straight in the eyes and Nodded.

Rick looked imploringly at me for help, so I Nodded too. "He's right, Honey. He is always right. JD will never steer you wrong."

Rick's hands were trembling as he waited for Krissie to answer. "Hey, Mama. How you feelin' today? Good? Oh, that is great, just great to hear. Yes, Ma'am, I did have a good meeting. Yes, it turned out even better than I hoped it would, Mama. Actually, this was the best meeting that I have ever had in my whole life! In fact, this is the best meeting in the history of the whole world!" He listened to her talk for a minute before he said, "Well, I'll tell you why this is the worlds' best meeting, Mama. It's because yesterday I met your identical twin sister, Kassie." I held my breath while we waited to hear what Krissie's response would be. My right hand was covering my heart, and Jeffreaux was holding my left. Rick spoke urgently. "Mama, are you OK? Did you understand what I just told you? Yes, I did say identical twin sister. Yes, ma'am, it is possible. I am sitting right here looking at her. She looks exactly like you, Mama." His face broke into a radiant smile, as he exclaimed, "That is exactly what Kassie said! Yes, she said 'Oh, the poor thing', just like you did! Yes, Ma'am, her name is Kassie. She is just as beautiful as you are, and she lives in Texas. I know this is hard to believe, Mama, but I promise you it is true. It would take too long for me to tell you the whole story right now, Mama. We are flying home to you this evening, and you will see her yourself. She is a wonderful person, Mama. She says she has been Waiting for you all her life… She cannot wait another day to meet you. She already loves you…" Rick's voice broke as tears filled his eyes. JD put his arm around me and pushed Kleenex into my hand. Of course, I was crying like a baby, again.

Rick was saying comforting things into the phone as he pulled himself together. I stepped closer to him and put my hand on his arm. "Can I please talk to her?" Rick looked at me, as if he wasn't sure that was such a good idea.

Jeffreaux quietly said, "Honey, are you sure you're ready for this?"

I Nodded to both of them. "Please, let me hear her voice."

Rick gently said, "Mama, are you up to talking to Kassie right now? Yes, she wants to hear your voice, now. OK. Here she is…"

I held the phone to my ear, took a deep breath, and said, "Hello, Krissie?" All I heard was muffled sniffling. My hand clutched at my aching heart.

"Are you OK? Krissie?

She cleared her throat and said, "Kassie, oh Kassie, I have missed you so much.

Please get here as quickly as you can."

MY HEART FILLED WITH JOY, HOPE, AND PEACE.

Maluma's Garden

STRONG WOMEN BUILD EACH OTHER UP.
THEY DON'T TEAR EACH OTHER DOWN...

March 12

I had been driving past that graveyard for over thirty years. I did not have any family or friends buried there, so I rarely paid any attention to it. In fact, many times the whole place appeared to be padlocked as well as deserted and unkempt. I assumed that it was "full?" with no more spaces available for burial plots. It just seemed really inaccessible to the rest of the world. There were never any cars or family members around anywhere, either. As graveyards or cemeteries go, it was always desolate and somewhat sad.

On that day, I felt sad and desolate myself. I was a fifty-ish woman with grown children and grandchildren. Today was my oldest daughter's birthday, but she lived a good distance from me, and we could not celebrate together this year. You know how things happen when we get older. Often, we are left out of family plans because of time, distance, money, health, and many other issues. My husband had gone on to be with the Lord, and the kids were all busy with their own lives. Sometimes I felt useless, lonely, or angry. Sometimes it was just that I felt hurt and empty. Boy, I really needed a hobby or something.

That particular morning, something drew my eyes over to the cemetery. The gates were open, and I quickly pulled over and stopped the car. There was a hooded figure hurrying toward the back fence line. It seemed to be a woman, but it was early morning and the spring mist was too heavy to see clearly. Before I could get the window down, the figure was gone. There must have been a rear entrance/exit that was not visible from the road. However, let me tell you what was visible to me immediately…Someone was cleaning and decorating those burial plots!

There were several graves right there on the front row that had been "swept" free of all leaves, trash, and debris. The headstones had been wiped or polished so that you could read the names and dates. Whoever was working on them had arranged some wild and artificial flowers on each plot. Someone, I guess the "Secret Gardener," was planting wild flowers all along the borders of the neglected graves! There were even some "arrangements" of broken glass, pottery, and pretty rocks. Whoever was doing this was using whatever was lying around to beautify the whole area. There were plants growing everywhere. It was still early spring, but things were growing and getting ready to put on buds! I was totally shocked by this transformation.

Had they hired a new groundskeeper? This was not a perpetual care cemetery. Families were supposed to care for their own loved ones' graves. I do not have to tell you that those were very few and very far between. However, someone was spending a lot of time out here taking care of this place. It had to be the "Secret Gardener" that I had seen rushing away earlier. In a heartbeat, I knew in my spirit that this poor woman was actually living out here among the dead. Somehow, I knew it; I just knew it in a way that I cannot explain.

So many questions were racing around in my head that I was getting dizzy. Who is she? Why was she here? Was she safe out here by herself? Where was she sleeping? Eating? Batheing? I was getting scared for her, now. This place was so isolated…how had she found her way out here? Boy, I did not know anything about the homeless problem. Did our little town have "programs" or "assistance" for those people? I made a silent vow that I would help this "Secret Gardener." But how? Where did I even start?

I decided that the first thing I would do was ask her some questions. I started walking through the cemetery calling out to her in a friendly tone of voice.

"Hello? Hello? Are you there? Your gardens are so beautiful. My name is Janice. I want to be your friend. Hello. Come on out. I won't hurt you. I want to be your friend. I want to talk to you about your lovely gardens. Hello?" It was so quiet and peaceful out there that I could hear birds and grasshoppers and the wind sighing in the trees. No wonder she stayed out here by herself. I hung around for a while calling to her and hoping she would come and talk to me. Walking around that cemetery, I became even more impressed with her creative gardening abilities. She had made displays with all the old, broken figurines and crosses that people left on graves. Everything just looked so pretty.

After a half hour of yelling and waiting, it was time for me to get on my way. I had racked my brain for a plan to get help for the "Secret Gardener." I knew she must be scared, so I decided to write her a note.

That was step one.

HELLO. MY NAME IS JANICE.

DON'T BE AFRAID.

I WANT TO BE YOUR FRIEND.

I WANT TO HELP YOU.

PLEASE CALL ME @ 880-776-6565

I put the note on one of the headstones and weighted it down with a big rock. I called to her several more times and told her I would be back later that afternoon. Still not seeing her or hearing one little sound from her, I got into my car and left.

Now for step two.

Driving into town, I stopped at our largest Thrift Shop, which was run by volunteers for the Hospice program. I love Hospice. They are wonderful people that help dying patients and their families. All the proceeds from the Thrift Shop go to help the Hospice organization. I bought all the artificial flowers they had. They also had lots of figurines and decorations that looked sturdy and weather-proof, so I bought a ton of things like that, too. Everything was so cheap that I got several baskets and containers for the "Secret Gardener" to use in her displays.

Next, I went to The Salvation Army Thrift Shop. I love their work, too. They know all about taking care of the poor, homeless, hungry people in the world. So, as I shopped for my "Secret Gardener," I started asking questions about the homeless in our area. Sadly, I learned many things that I wished I had not. Many of them are institutionalized, imprisoned, or worse. No wonder my friend was so afraid to show herself. She probably had some bad experiences, too. I promised myself that I would not expose her to any kind of danger or mistreatment.

Still shopping for things she might need, I grabbed a weather-proof looking trunk to put some of her stuff in. There was a good chaise lounge with nice padding which would make a passable sleeping cot. She most likely needed a blanket and pillow also. How about a couple of metal plates and some silverware? They also had a couple of live plants that I knew she would love. When the trunk and back seat of my car were almost full, I headed for the grocery store.

By this time, I was learning to prioritize my friend's needs. I bought bottled water and some pre-packaged meals that did not have to be refrigerated or cooked. Would she like crackers and chips? I tried to think what would be safe and easy to keep. Next, I got baby wipes, hand sanitizer, and various other personal items that we all need all the time. My last stop was the garden center. I bought lots of flower seeds and some vegetable seeds, too. Maybe she would like to grow some food as well as flowers? My guess is that she can grow anything.

Now, my car was totally loaded with Stuff that anyone could use. If I am wrong about my "Secret Gardener," I can easily pass all these things along to someone else in need. The best part about my whole shopping trip was that this carload of stuff cost me very little money. However, it can make a huge difference for a person who had nothing.

Now, it's time for step three.

When I got back to the cemetery, there was no sign of life. Sorry, no pun intended. At first, I thought that no one had been there since I left, but then I noticed that my note had been moved. YAY! That was all the confirmation I needed. I called out to her for several minutes without any success. All I heard was birds, grasshoppers, and wind. Very peaceful. As I unloaded the supplies, it occurred to me that maybe there was an old caretaker's cottage where she could stay... Next time I will park several blocks away and walk through the woods toward the back fenceline.

Again, I examined the newly decorated plots. They did not appear to have anything in common. Not the same names, dates, or anything. I wondered if she had found some family member here and was trying to honor their memories by beautifying their graves. No sign of that. It looked like she just started on the first row and worked her way along. No clues there. This whole thing was as much a mystery now as it had been this morning. Nevertheless, I was feeling very encouraged this afternoon. I turned the note over and wrote:

"HELLO. DON'T BE AFRAID.

I WANT TO HELP YOU.

I WANT TO BE YOUR FRIEND.

I HOPE YOU CAN USE THIS STUFF.

I'LL BE BACK

YOUR FRIEND, JANICE"

As I drove away, I felt good about my day. Surely, she would trust me enough to come out and talk to me? Next time, I was going to try to find her by walking in the back way. Maybe she was staying somewhere else entirely? No amount of speculation would help. Only time would tell.

For the next three days, I was extremely busy and could not get back over to the cemetery. Early on the fourth morning, I parked and walked as quietly as I could toward the back fenceline where I had seen the "Secret Gardener" disappear. It was very early, and it was quiet and still out there. In the distance, I could hear someone humming. The tune was vaguely familiar to me, but I just could not quite recall the words or the title. The voice was strangely hoarse and discordant.

Even though I was sneaking up on someone, I did not want to scare her. I just wanted to find her and help her. If things did not turn out right, she would never trust me. Doubts were plaguing me, but I kept moving forward. I was not surprised when I came upon a small cabin. It was really more like a shed…Apparently, this is where she was staying. The whole area had been "Swept" like the graves. It was neat and clean and there was no trash or junk anywhere. In fact, two of the pots I had left her were sitting on each side of the door. She had planted something in them, and several others were sitting in a circle around a tree nearby. When I snuck a peek inside, I was thrilled to see that she was using all the things I had left for her. To my surprise, there was a working faucet, too!

Silently, I thanked God that she was doing so well. I would be shopping for her again today. I could still hear her humming, but the tune was unrecognizable to me. Still, I felt like I should have known it. I was moving quietly toward her voice when I finally caught sight of her. She was working with a "Broom" made of leaves and twigs! I knew that she had made it herself. Now I knew why I thought everything looked "swept." She was literally sweeping the graves clean. Wow. I squatted down to get a better look at her.

She was a small, thin woman that could have been anywhere from thirty to eighty years old. I could not see her face because her back was to me, and she wore some kind of a cape that covered her from her head to her feet. She held her head at a weird angle as she worked and hummed. Occasionally, a few garbled words mingled with the tune she hummed. I could not understand those words at all. Maybe she was… retarded? Handicapped? She had probably been cast out or abandoned because of that? I did not want to scare her away. More and more, I wanted to help her. Finally, after watching her for a few minutes, I decided to bite the bullet and make my move.

I slowly stood and held my hands up where she could see them. I smiled as friendly as I could and made my voice as calm and firm as I could. I tried to remember everything I had ever seen or heard about soothing wounded animals and children. "Hello? Miss? Don't be afraid Miss. I'm Janice. Hello?" She did not turn toward me or act startled. Suddenly, I realized that she was deaf. She could not hear me. Now what? I stomped on the ground a couple of times, and she suddenly jumped and whirled toward me.

I kept me hands up and my smile bright as I spoke loud and clear. "Hello. Don't be afraid. I won't hurt you. Please don't run away. I won't hurt you. I want to help you. I'm Janice. I want to be your friend. Janice...friend...See?" I pointed toward my chest, and said Janice and friend several more times. She wanted to run away badly, but I was between her and the back fence, and I knew she would never run out the front gate toward the road where others might see her. Smiling and speaking slowly and clearly, I told her how beautiful her gardens were. I repeated Beautiful several times and made a sweeping motion toward her work zone. I smiled and nodded like a bobble head in a windstorm.

She still looked fearful, but not as completely panicked as she had been at first. I continued to say Janice, friend, and beautiful in a soothing tone of voice. She was watching my lips, and I silently prayed that she could read them and the intention of my heart. She was desperately worried about me being there and I knew that this could be my one and only chance to communicate with her. I sort of sat down on the nearest headstone and just smiled at her in a friendly, encouraging way. "You have made some beautiful gardens here. Everything is so lovely. Very nice work here." I am sure that I was babbling, but finally, she sort of looked down at her feet and made the smallest little bit of a self- deprecating smile. YAY. I was getting through to her.

When she looked back to my face, I put both hands on my ears and made a shrugging, questioning motion like... gone? She made a very sad nod and looked down again. Poor thing. God help me to help her. I smiled some more and said, "OK. It's OK." I held out my hand toward her and said, "I'm Janice," and pointed toward myself again. Then I pointed to her and said, "Your name? Can you say your name?" Most deaf people cannot speak, sing, hum, or whistle, if they were born deaf. However, if they became deaf after they learned those things, many times, they can re-learn them. Often, they never forget how to say their names. I felt that she had once heard, spoken, and sang. Maybe she would try to say her name, and we could begin to be friends. "Please say your name. My name is Janice. Will you say your name for me, please? I won't hurt you. I want to be your friend." I pointed to myself again and said Janice again. I pointed to her smiling and waiting. She struggled for a few minutes with her own mouth and voice. At last, she said "MaLuMa" and touched her own chest.

MaLuMa??? I asked her if that was right…MaLuMa? She seemed to be a person of mixed race. Maybe MaLuMa was some foreign, exotic name? She also appeared to be young, maybe mid-twenties or so. Again, she looked down at her feet. I smiled as big as I could and said MaLuMa several times. At last, she looked at my face again, and I held out my hand and said "Janice, MaLuMa, Friend." I nodded at my own hand as if to say, "Take it, please." I was again nodding like a fool, but at last, she reached out and lightly touched my hand. I held very still, and she let her fingers touch mine for a second or two. It was long enough for me to feel her own fingers trembling. Her fear just broke my heart. Tears immediately sprang to my eyes, and I could not stop them from slipping down my face.

In spite of those tears, I still smiled as if we had done something amazing. Maybe she understood more than I thought she did. I didn't even know what was happening here. How could I expect her or anyone else to know? MaLuMa was struggling with fear and worry about me being there. I knew that I had to reassure her that she was safe. Once again, I started telling her that her gardens were beautiful and lovely. I told her how pretty everything looked. I was shocked when she tried to speak again. I leaned closer and held my hand to my own ear, waiting for her to try once more. Finally, she garbled, "Pretty garden." YAY!

"Yes Ma'am. Pretty, pretty garden, MaLuMa. Very pretty garden." She smiled and nodded shyly. Thank you, Jesus. We were going to be friends. If only I could learn more about her, I could help her more. Was her hearing loss from illness or injury? Could she be treated? Would hearing aids help? Speech therapy has often produced some miraculous results for deaf people. A very protective feeling was flooding my heart. It would be of paramount importance to keep her presence here to myself. Some well-meaning idiot could cause as much destruction as a malicious fool does. How and where did I start? MaLuMa was nervously shuffling around and acting as if she wished I would leave her alone so she could get back to her gardening. Amazing. All she wanted to do was work, and I was in her way.

I stood and spoke to her about food and supplies. I asked her about different kinds of things to eat, but she was too embarrassed to answer. Once again, I smiled and did my bobble head act as I made soothing OK sounds. Speaking slowly, I told her that I would be back in a while with some supplies. I asked her to please come and talk to me again. Please come and be my friend? Suddenly I had an idea…" MaLuMa, can Janice work with you? Janice work in garden? Janice help MaLuMa?" She looked at my clothes as if to say, "Seriously, Janice?" I was definitely over-dressed for this job. These were certainly not work shoes. Smiling the whole time, I told her I would put on "work clothes" next time. When she nodded and smiled back, I knew that she was reading my lips and starting to feel better about me being there. Thank you, Jesus. Still, she could not wait for me to leave so she could get busy again.

Telling her that I would be back later, I made good-bye sounds and motions. She barely acknowledged my departure, and I was not sure if I would see her again. Nevertheless, I was going to make the thrift shop runs again before I went to get her some more food. Dear Lord, I was both terrified and thrilled with this new relationship. I was so thankful for this great spring weather. At least she was able to be comfortable without boiling or freezing. Hopefully, she would be in a nice home (?) before cold weather? Maybe even my home? She needed someone, and I needed someone to need me.

Now for step four.

Before the shopping started, I stopped at my lawyer's office. His name is Joel Lindsey. He was pretty good and had helped me a lot after my husband died. He gave me some financial advice as well as legal help with wills and all that stuff. Several friends had told me that he was big guns in Seattle. Guess he was trying to lay low here. However, I wanted to make an appointment to ask how to proceed with MaLuMa. I decided to just pull into his parking lot as I passed his office. When his assistant buzzed him to say that I was there, he said that he would be right out! In five seconds, he opened the door and welcomed me into his office. Guess he was not too busy today. After the obligatory greetings, he offered me coffee, tea, or water and told me to make myself comfortable. He was a comfortable kind of guy, and within a very short time, I was telling him everything. I do mean everything. You know, he did not scold me, caution me, or make me feel like an idiot. He listened intently and encouraged me to give even more details about the last four days. He did not write anything down, so he must have a photographic memory or something close to it.

When I ran out of steam, he looked at me closely and thought for a minute before he spoke. "Janice, I am going to ask you several questions rather quickly. Do not try to answer them right away. I have had some success with this form of interrogation. It stimulates your memory. OK? Could you tell anything about her ethnic origins? Did she have any specific characteristics or mode of dress that suggested any country besides the U.S.A.? For instance, did she wear dreadlocks or any other distinctive hairstyle? What about this cape? Did it appear to be African, Caribbean, or even South American? Some European countries still wear capes. When she spoke, did she have any accent? Did she sound like a black woman? What kind of string or knots did she use on her broom? Did she have a mouth full of teeth? How about her hands? She obviously works hard, but are her nails healthy? Did her eyes appear to be clear or cloudy?" He stopped and waited for me to respond.

Holy smokes! He was right about stimulating my memory! Just how smart is this guy anyway? Boy, am I glad he's on my side! After a lengthy discussion, he smiled and told me that I had done very well. He still had not written anything down, but I was sure that he knew even more about all of this than I did. He asked me again if I wanted something to drink. On the other hand, would I like to go and have an early lunch with him? He was such a gentleman. I declined his offers but thanked him for his kindness. He assured me that it would be a pleasure for him to spend more time with me. Nice guy. I asked questions about how much this investigation was going to cost me. He knew pretty much everything about my finances, so I was relieved when he said not much at all. A few phone calls, some internet searches, and he would have plenty of information in five to seven days. Wow. What a genius. Thanking him profusely, I told him that I would call to make another appointment in six days. He told me that he was going to arrange to have Utilities supplied out there ASAP. Excellent. He said that he would have everything put in his name to keep people from speculating about my involvement. "Outstanding. I'll pay you back the next time I come in, Joel. I can't thank you enough." He walked me to the door, opened it, and said that this was a wonderful act of brotherly love and that he admired me tremendously for it. Wow. I felt proud and humbled at the same time. He inspired confidence in me without even trying.

After some very successful shopping, I had another carload of things that I knew MaLuMa would enjoy. She was getting brooms, rakes, hoes, nippers, and many other gardening tools. There were a couple of sign language books with lots of helpful hints for me, as a beginner. They had plenty of pictures too. I asked the thrift shop ladies if I could have their broken knick- knacks, instead of trashing them. I bought her a lot more food this time. When I unloaded all her stuff, I was tired, but happy. I called her for several minutes, but she never appeared. Not wanting to put too much stress on her, I decided to leave her alone. I left her a note saying "Enjoy. Your friend, Janice." I still did not even know if she could read!

When I went for my 4:30 appointment with Jacob six days later, he had more information than I had imagined could be possible. Let me start with the good news first. He had electricity connected at the cabin! I asked him if those people had scared MaLuMa out of her wits. He assured me that nobody saw her. He had a small travel trailer and a handy man on hot stand-by…just waiting for me to say, "Hook it up." He was talking to the property owners about me buying the whole kit and caboodle, which included the cemetery and eighteen additional acres! Huh? Hold the phone…Are things moving too fast here? Suddenly, He stood up and said, "Janice, get your purse…we are going for a drive."

You know, we drove straight out to the cemetery. It took a while, but MaLuMa finally came out to meet him. She was so petrified that I literally felt like I needed to hold her up to keep her from fainting. I kept saying, "Friend, MaLuMa, Friend. Joel Friend. Janice Friend. Friends Help MaLuMa. It's OK. OK. Don't be afraid." I went into my babbling, smiling, and bobble-heading act again. Joel was very cool. After a few minutes, he began signing to her! She was still trembling but managed to respond to him quickly. You could have knocked me over with a feather. Joel was making a simple hand motion that looked like the baseball umpire declaring the runner "Safe." MaLuMa was starting to calm down a little. Thank God. She and Joel were not "spelling" each letter; they were using the more expressive hand signals that I had seen in those books. I tell you, he is a gifted man. They "talked" to each other for several more minutes when Joel turned to me and asked me if I remembered the "Cross my Heart Pledge" from when we were kids. Of course, I did. He told me to make it to MaLuMa, along with the real sign of the cross that

Catholics make. Now, I am not Catholic, but I know for a fact that God always sees and appreciates that cross sign. So, I made both to MaLuMa, knowing that she needed to see them, too.

Now, they really talked for a while. He walked around the building, pointing and gesturing. I could tell that he was describing the little trailer and where it could sit. No telling what all he told her. One thing for sure, I was learning that sign language ASAP. Several times, they both looked at me, and I knew they were "talking" about me, too. On more than one occasion, he shook his head sternly, like fathers do, and seemed to be correcting her. She was probably arguing with him, but he was adamant and would not take no for an answer. After all, wasn't he Top Gun in Seattle? You Betcha. He is probably Top Gun in many places. Especially right here. Eventually, MaLuMa was happy. Joel was happy. I was definitely happy, too. We were all exhausted, and she was thrilled when we finally got ready to leave. Joel made her shake his hand. Then, he made her shake mine, too. I cried again. She did, too. I think he wanted to cry, himself. Walking to his truck, he told me that his baby sister was deaf and that he did a lot of pro bono work for deaf people. I could not talk at all for a while. I was starting to love her.

Driving back into town, he told me some more good news. The owners had just inherited this place last year and were horrified by the fact that there was a cemetery on it. They could not wait to get rid of it. They were sending an appraiser from Ohio that week. We (?) were going to get it all for a song. Too bad they had not come before MaLuMa had made some of it look so pretty. He said not to worry about anything because he could "awful-ize" this situation to our (?) advantage. He had already convinced the appraiser that it was a legal nightmare to "own so many dead bodies… Especially in Texas…" As a lawyer, he could mitigate many problems by deeding a portion back to the state for more dead bodies…Wow. He said not to worry, because he knew exactly how to work this all out. We

(?) would actually make money on this deal. Lots of money. We (?) could discuss all the details later.

Joel stopped at the best steak house in town and told me that we were celebrating here tonight. First, the bad news. He turned on the dome light and looked at me solemnly. "Janice, never ask me or MaLuMa about her family again. Never. They are…gone. We (?) are her family now. We will take care of her. Trust me. This is not my first rodeo. OK? Now, for our celebration dinner."

Again, I cried.

APRIL 15- ONE MONTH LATER

I had been coming to work with MaLuMa every third day for a month now. You would not believe how beautiful this cemetery is. Everything is blooming, green, and fabulous. We were becoming semi-famous gardeners. The first time someone stopped to praise us, I thought she was going to run out the back gate again. However, I put my arm around her while I recited Joel's "cover story." It was basically all true.

I am the new owner.

She is my deaf gardener.

She can read lips and sign, so please look at her, and speak slowly.

We are opening a new section for pet burial plots.

She will personalize each plot, if asked.

She is also available for private garden design or consultation.

Joel and I were both teaching her to look at people and say a few easy words. I squeezed her a little as if to say, "It's OK. Don't be afraid. Say Hello to these nice people. I'm right here, and I won't let anyone hurt you." She lifted her head a little, smiled a little, and said "LO." Oh My Gosh! I almost burst with pride. She was learning to trust herself, others, and me. Thank you, Jesus. She also said, "Tank u," and "Bye." When the car was out of sight, I grabbed her and whirled her around and around as I whooped and hollered like a wild Indian. We both laughed like kids. She was starting to love me.

She wanted to get back to work immediately, but I wanted to have some lunch. I signed eat and food to her. Did I mention that we are all three working on my signing skills? There was plenty of food in her cute little trailer, and I asked her permission to go in and fix lunch. She nodded and said, "Yes, Jan." I love it that she wants to please me by using her voice. I love it that she calls me Jan. Then she says, "Where Joe? Work?" I love it that she calls him Joe. Jan and Joe. Isn't she clever? You Betcha. Very clever.

When I was ready for her to come and eat, I opened the door and listened to her hum for a minute or so. She just sounded so happy. She was once again mumbling some unintelligible words. It drove me crazy that I could not get this song. Listening intently this time, I really watched her. She had closed her eyes and turned her face up to the sun. I studied her lips and listened with my whole heart. She threw her arms around herself and sang, "…If you MaLuMa dollin…Lu, Lu, if you MaLuMa dollin."

Skip to my Lou my darling! I finally got it! Her name was Lou. She was remembering someone singing to her, and hugging her, and loving her. I cried. I cried for the little child MaLuMa. I cried for her lost family, her lost hearing, and her lost speech. I cried for the MaLuMa singing here today. She was radiant as she hugged herself with tears running down her cheeks.

THREE MONTHS LATER- JULY 27

You would not believe how well everything had worked out for all of us. We have opened our new five-acre pet cemetery. We require the owners to cremate their little companions before interment here. Of course, this is a perpetual care facility. I have an excellent gardener that works for a song. Most owners have things that they want MaLuMa to decorate with. If not, we design whatever they like. This whole hillside is one big garden now. Many people have asked us to design and landscape their properties, too. We are making a great deal of money, which is fine by me. Most of it is going into accounts for my retirement and MaLuMa's future. Five percent goes into a fund to help the hearing impaired in our area. Joel has developed several business plans for us. He thinks we will be rich soon. He loves both of us.

After more research, Joel learned about a child from rural South Carolina that fit MaLuMa's description. If she is this child, her last name is probably Duncan. One school district said that she had gotten some elementary education, before losing her hearing. After several months, they have no record of her going to school there anymore. If this is her, she is most likely in her mid to late twenties. We will not ask her about any of this for some time. Joel says that she will tell us more when she is ready. She might not even remember most of her past. Sometimes, trauma causes black holes in our memories. In God's time, we will know more.

I have more good news! My home sold for three times what I expected it to. The new owners will let me stay for six months. Now, I am getting ready to build a new home on five of my remaining ten acres. There will be a very large green house with a nice apartment attached. My hope is that MaLuMa will want to live there. Whatever happens, she will never be alone or homeless again. She knows all about all kinds of plants. She even dries the seeds and saves them to replant. Joel has hired a tutor to come out and help MaLuMa get her high school diploma. She will also be taking speech therapy. We are waiting until January because she is still afraid much of the time. Joel has finally convinced her that the only way to protect herself is to learn how to function in this world. He keeps telling her to speak and listen when others speak to her. She cannot be crippled by fear any longer.

It appears that Joel may be living out here also. He keeps insisting that we get married. Seriously, I am too old for that. He seems to be an extremely patient man. We will see. He and MaLuMa are best buds. I love both of them. His little sister will be coming for the holidays. She is deaf, also and cannot wait to "Talk" with MaLuMa. Both of us expect our children and grandkids to be here for several days, too. I just pray that MaLuMa does not run away from all of us. We are both telling her about our families, now. Maybe she will not be totally overwhelmed when they get here. Joel and I both always tell her how smart, cute, and sweet she is. We tell her that we love her and that we are her family now. We tell her that everybody else will love her, too. We tell her that it is normal to be nervous about meeting new people. We speak confidently to her.

She is getting better all the time. In a couple of weeks, I am taking her to an audiologist and a regular G.P. She seems to be as healthy as a horse. Praise God. We both just want to know how to help her. She does not know about the doctor's appointments, yet. However, when we ask her questions about what happened when she became deaf, she does not remember a doctor. I know that she will be terrified, but the doctors are going to examine me at the same time. Joel will be with us to confirm his support. We seem to be a real family. Maybe we should get married after our family members get to know each other?

One more thing I want you to know. Now, when MaLuMa starts humming, I sing the words with her. When we get to the part about "Skip to my Lou my darling," I grab her and hug her close to my heart.

She knows somebody loves her again.

How Great is that?

CPSIA information can be obtained
at www.ICGtesting.com
Printed in the USA
BVHW03*1457300818
526054BV00001B/6/P